THE
GUEST

THE
GUEST

B. A. PARIS

ST. MARTIN'S PRESS
NEW YORK

First published in the United States by St. Martin's Press, an imprint of St. Martin's Publishing Group

THE GUEST. Copyright © 2024 by Bernadette MacDougall. All rights reserved. Printed in the United States of America. For information, address St. Martin's Publishing Group, 120 Broadway, New York, NY 10271.

www.stmartins.com

Designed by Omar Chapa

Library of Congress Cataloging-in-Publication Data

Names: Paris, B. A., author.
Title: The guest / B. A. Paris.
Description: First U.S. edition. | New York : St. Martin's Press, 2024. |
Identifiers: LCCN 2023036260 | ISBN 9781250289421 (hardcover) |
    ISBN 9781250322661 (international, sold outside the U.S., subject
    to rights availability) | ISBN 9781250289438 (ebook)
Subjects: LCGFT: Thrillers (Fiction). | Novels.
Classification: LCC PR9105.9.P34 G84 2024 | DDC 823/.92—dc23/
    eng/20230822
LC record available at https://lccn.loc.gov/2023036260

Our books may be purchased in bulk for promotional, educational, or business use. Please contact your local bookseller or the Macmillan Corporate and Premium Sales Department at 1-800-221-7945, extension 5442, or by email at MacmillanSpecialMarkets@macmillan.com.

First U.S. Edition: 2024

First International Edition: 2024

10 9 8 7 6 5 4 3 2 1

For Sophie

Thank you for our precious "Silent Witness"
moments together in The Hague.
I will always treasure them.

THE
GUEST

PROLOGUE

Gabriel handed Iris a glass of champagne, and then gave one to Esme, his fingers shaking slightly on the stem.

"I didn't drink at all at the christening, so I'm allowed this," Esme said. She looked over at Iris. "Thank you for inviting us back here. It's lovely to be able to relax now that it's finally over."

Iris smiled. "You deserve it."

"It was a great day, though." Hugh raised his glass. "Here's to Hamish. And his mum, of course."

"And to you," Gabriel said. "The proud father."

The four of them drank, and Esme gave a contented sigh. "Gosh, I've missed this so much."

Hugh raised his glass again. "Iris, Gabriel, it's been one hell of a summer. Here's to happier times."

A silence fell on the group. Gabriel cleared his throat. "Thank you, Hugh. As you said—"

An almighty explosion, followed by the panicked rustling of birds taking flight from the trees drowned out the rest of his words. Iris's heart thudded, echoing the *boom* still reverberating in the air. And then, deathly silence.

For a few seconds, they were a tableau frozen in time. Gabriel and Hugh standing, their champagne glasses in their hands, their heads turned toward the sound of the explosion; Iris, the alarm in her eyes mirrored in Esme's. Even baby Hamish paused in his nuzzling, and Esme, the instinct to protect her child automatically taking over, tightened her arms around him. Reassured, he went back to drinking, his tiny legs kicking under his blanket, the only movement in the stillness.

"I hope that wasn't the house," Esme joked, breaking the spell the explosion had cast over them. "Not after all our hard work."

"Maybe I should—" Hugh stopped mid-sentence, his attention caught by something. Iris followed his line of vision and saw black smoke billowing into the sky.

In the distance a siren wailed, then became louder.

Gabriel turned to Hugh. "Shall we go and take a look?"

"Good idea. It looks a bit too close to home for comfort," Hugh added, his voice low. He looked over at Esme. "We won't be long."

Esme waited until they'd left. "As long as Joseph hasn't blown himself up," Esme said, detaching Hamish from her breast and shifting him to the other side. "I'm so disappointed in him." Hamish settled, she stretched out her free hand and laid it on Iris's arm. "Thank you for taking him home before he became completely out of control."

"I only suggested taking him home because I didn't want everyone to see him in that state." Iris paused. "Do you think he fell off the wagon before today and managed to hide it from everyone?"

"I don't know, but I'm furious, and disappointed and everything else in between. I'm beginning to regret asking him to be Hamish's godfather." She looked suddenly nervous. "He didn't say anything, did he, when you and Hugh took him home? He tends to shout his mouth off when he's drunk."

"No," Iris said. "Don't worry."

"I should have been upfront with Hugh in the first place," Esme fretted.

"It doesn't matter now. Joseph is leaving tomorrow, isn't he?"

"If he's sober enough." She moved Hamish to her shoulder and began to pat his back and, as Iris listened to her chattering about the christening, and how lovely it had been, an extraordinary sense of well-being flowed through her body. For the first time in months, she felt at peace.

"Oh, they're back!" Esme exclaimed.

Iris turned her head toward the terrace, but before she could register that anything was wrong, Esme had thrust Hamish into her arms and was hurrying across the lawn toward Hugh. Alarmed, Iris caught Gabriel's eye, and her heart dropped at the desolation on his face. Moving Hamish to her shoulder, she took comfort from the warm, sleepy weight of him and, as she began rubbing his back, her eyes fixed worriedly on Hugh and Esme, he obligingly expelled little pockets of milky air. And then a wail started, and at first she thought it was coming from Hamish.

But it wasn't Hamish, it was Esme, weeping brokenly in Hugh's arms.

FOUR MONTHS BEFORE

1

Iris thought they'd never get home. Oban to Markham, five hundred and twenty miles, journey time nine hours without stops. They'd left at ten this morning, and it was now ten in the evening. No wonder they were both shattered.

It wasn't meant to be this way. They were meant to have broken their journey with an overnight stop in York, and only arrive home tomorrow. Iris had booked a beautiful hotel and if everything had gone to plan, they would have finished dinner by now and would be heading up to bed. Instead, they were heading down the hill into Markham.

Iris laid her head against the seat rest and closed her eyes, shutting out the bright lights of the town. Normally she would have welcomed them, this sign that she was almost home. But tonight, their garishness, so at odds with the dark velvet nights of the Scottish Isles, jarred.

She shifted restlessly, peeling her bare legs from where they'd stuck to the cream leather seats. She was desperate to get out of the car, feel blood circulating in her ankles again. Sensing her discomfort, Gabriel threw her a guilty glance.

"I'm sorry," he murmured. "Maybe we should have stopped in York after all."

Iris gave him a smile, hiding her disappointment. "It's better this way. We'll have tomorrow to relax."

Her disappointment wasn't because she'd been denied dinner in a Michelin-starred restaurant followed by a night in a luxurious hotel, but because, during the two weeks they'd been away, she hadn't been able to get Gabriel to open up to her. Despite the idyllic sea-view cottages, the beautiful scenery, the long, lazy walks along deserted white beaches, she hadn't been able to get him to talk about Charlie Ingram.

Charlie had only just been reported missing by his mother when Gabriel, out for an early morning run, had spotted him lying at the bottom of the old limestone quarry, surrounded by the tangled metal of his bike.

"He must have taken the path around the top, gone too fast, skidded through the trees and down over the edge," Gabriel had said, his face ashen. "Or hit a stone that sent him off-course. What a tragic waste."

Charlie had been alive when Gabriel found him, but he'd died before help arrived. And during those few minutes, when he'd been hovering between life and death, Charlie had entrusted Gabriel with a message: *Tell Mum I love her.*

"It was as if he was waiting to be able to give that last message," Iris had said, wanting to comfort him.

But her words had distressed him more, and for the last two months, Charlie Ingram—eighteen years old, popular, good-looking, a place guaranteed at university and a year younger than their daughter Beth—had continued to haunt him. Maybe if Gabriel hadn't known Charlie, it might not have hit him so hard. They hadn't seen each other since Charlie's childhood, but they had recognized each other immediately.

Iris's stomach fluttered with guilt. She should have given Gabriel time to wind down, to acclimatize to being at home before rushing him to Scotland. It couldn't be easy to be told, however gently, by your partners, that they were putting you on compassionate leave, especially if you were a doctor in the local, understaffed medical practice. Gabriel had refused at first, unable to accept what Iris and his colleagues had been able see, that he was suffering from burnout. Already depleted by the death of his beloved father four months earlier, plus an increasingly unmanageable workload, Charlie's death was the straw that broke him. It had devastated Gabriel to the point where he was unable to talk about what had happened. Despite Iris's efforts, and those of his colleagues, the few minutes that Gabriel had spent in the quarry with Charlie Ingram before he'd died, before help had arrived, remained locked deep inside him.

Night was chasing dusk into its shadows as Gabriel pulled into the drive. Unable to stay in the car a moment longer, Iris snapped off her seat belt and opened the door. A blast of warm air wrapped itself around her as she climbed out of the air-conditioned car. Her legs, stiff from sitting, gave slightly and she put a hand on the roof to steady herself, then pulled it back quickly. Like the air around her, the sun-scorched metal had retained its heat.

"How is it possible for it to be so hot at this time of night?" she asked, transferring the grime from the car to her face as she swiped damp hair from her forehead.

Gabriel eased himself from the driver's seat and stretched his arms high above his head, loosening the muscles in his lower back. "They had a mini heatwave here while we were in Scotland, remember? And it is the beginning of June."

He lowered his arms, moved toward the trunk.

"Leave the bags," Iris said, stifling a yawn. "We'll unpack tomorrow."

"Good idea." Gabriel glanced toward their home, an old stone farmhouse, in the small village of West Markham, its interior tastefully brought into the twenty-first century by its previous architect owner. "Do you know what the best thing is about going on holiday?"

Iris smiled. "Coming home?"

"Exactly." He came around the car to where Iris was standing and kissed the top of her head. "Thank you for a wonderful holiday."

She reached a hand to his cheek, relishing these few moments when he wasn't preoccupied by that other, darker thing. "Do you have your keys?"

He took them from his pocket. "Come on, let's get to bed."

"A long bath for me first."

Hand in hand, they walked to the front door. Gabriel unlocked it and, impatient to be inside, Iris was about to step over the threshold when he shot out an arm, barring her way.

"There's no mail," he hissed.

Iris frowned, then realized what he meant. Usually, after two weeks away, there'd be a build-up of mail on the doormat. But there was nothing.

"Put the light on," she whispered.

Gabriel reached inside and found the switch.

"My cardigan." Iris pointed toward the bottom of the stairs where a blue cardigan lay draped over the newel post. "I didn't leave it there. Nor those," she added, pointing to a pair of espadrilles lying haphazardly on the floor.

"Beth isn't here, is she?" Gabriel asked, his voice low, even though he knew their daughter was volunteering at a dog shelter in Greece.

"No, she's not back for another three months. And anyway, she wouldn't be seen dead in my cardigan."

Gabriel moved past her, stepped into the hall and pushed open the door to the sitting room.

"Well, somebody's been here," he said, nodding toward a pile of magazines strewn on the low table.

Iris peered around him, then pointed to the indents in the sofa. "And is maybe still here." She looked at Gabriel in alarm. "Squatters?"

Instinctively, he moved in front of her, then bellowed down the hallway.

"Is anyone there?"

From somewhere upstairs, there was an exclamation of surprise, followed by the sound of footsteps running along the corridor.

"Gabriel?" A woman's voice, breathy, hesitant. "Is that you?"

Iris stared at the figure standing at the top of the stairs, her dark hair tumbling around her shoulders, the legs of her pale blue pajamas pooling around her feet. "Laure?"

Laure placed a hand on her heart. "Iris! You gave me a fright! What are you doing here?"

"Apart from the fact that we live here, you mean?" Gabriel said, sounding amused rather than offended.

Embarrassed, Laure laughed. "Yes, yes, of course, it's just that I wasn't expecting you." Hitching up her pajama bottoms, she ran down the stairs, hugged Iris fiercely, then moved back, reproach in her liquid-brown eyes. "You said in your email that you wouldn't be back until tomorrow."

"We decided not to stop off in York," Iris found herself explaining, aware that she was practically apologizing for coming back earlier than expected to her own house.

While Gabriel swept Laure into a hug, Iris looked up the stairs, waiting for Pierre to appear. It would do Gabriel a world of good to see his best friend. Pierre must have had a meeting in London, and he and Laure had come to surprise them. "Where's Pierre?" she asked. "Don't tell me he's already asleep?"

Laure shook her head, then sank onto the stairs, her pretty face etched with misery. A chill crept down Iris's spine.

"Laure, what's happened?"

"It's Pierre."

"Is he all right?" Gabriel's voice was rough with urgency and, turning toward him, Iris saw that his face had drained of color. She reached for his hand and gave it a reassuring squeeze. *Please don't let anything have happened to Pierre, not on top of Charlie Ingram and Gabriel's dad.*

Laure nodded quickly. "Yes, he is fine, he is very fine," she said, her normally impeccable English deserting her, a sign of her distress. "He has a child, why wouldn't he be fine?"

There was a stunned silence.

"Pierre has a child?" Gabriel stuttered.

Laure nodded. "It is what he says."

"But—When? How? I mean, it's not possible."

"It seems he had an affair."

"He couldn't have," Iris protested. "He loves you."

And Laure burst into noisy sobs.

2

Leaving Laure and Gabriel talking in the kitchen, Iris headed upstairs for a shower.

Yawning with tiredness, she pushed open the door to their bedroom, then stopped. The bed was a tangle of rumpled bed sheets. There was a mug on her bedside table, a magazine on Gabriel's pillow, and a mound of used tissues strewn over the floor. While one part of Iris's brain was telling her that Laure wouldn't have moved into their room when there were two perfectly good guest rooms, another part was reminding her that she'd stripped the bed before leaving for Scotland.

"Laure!" she called.

Laure came running up the stairs and burst into the bedroom.

"I'm so sorry! I was going to move out before you came back tomorrow! I felt so alone when I arrived, I couldn't stop crying and all I wanted was to hide myself away. I was afraid that if I was in the guest room at the front of the house, one of your neighbors would see the light on and I didn't want to have to explain why I was here. The room next to yours had stuff on the bed, and I didn't want to use Beth's room. And I know it's stupid but I felt closer to you in here." Hurrying past Iris, she began pulling the pillows from their slips. "I'll change everything, it won't take me long. I'll move to one of the guest rooms."

A wave of exhaustion took hold and Iris sank onto the bed. "It's fine. It doesn't matter for tonight, we'll sort it out tomorrow."

She was about to add that she would have her shower in the en suite anyway—she'd mentally swapped the long bath she'd planned to have for a quick wash long ago, what did a luxurious soak matter when weighed against the devastating news of Pierre's infidelity?—when she caught a glimpse, through the open door, of towels piled on the floor and clothes slung over the edge of the bath. There was something familiar about the clothes and they reminded Iris of something that had distracted her when she'd first seen Laure at the top of the stairs, and which had continued to be a distraction even while she'd been listening, open-mouthed, to the story of Pierre's betrayal.

"Are those my pajamas you're wearing?"

Laure's eyes welled with fresh tears. "I didn't bring any clothes with me. I didn't think about packing a case, I just took my bag and passport, and left."

Iris pushed to her feet and enveloped her in a hug. "It's fine."

Releasing Laure, Iris dug a pair of pajamas from a drawer. When she turned back, she saw Laure by the window, looking into the night.

"How's Gabriel?" Laure asked.

"Still devastated. Charlie Ingram will be with him forever, I think."

"Was that his name, Charlie Ingram?"

"Yes."

"It's a nice name." She turned to Iris. "Can you turn off the light? Then we'll be able to see the quarry and we can say a prayer for him."

Iris turned off the light and moved to Laure's side. Together, they stood looking out at the quarry, its walls gleaming white in the moonlight, and each in their own way, said a silent prayer for Charlie.

"Tell me again why we're sleeping in our guest room," Gabriel said.

Fresh from his shower, he had a towel wrapped around his waist and smelled of mint, a mix of shower gel and toothpaste. Before, Iris would have taken the towel off him and pulled him onto the bed. But not anymore.

"Exhaustion. I was too tired to help Laure change the sheets."

He came to sit beside her and bounced up and down, testing the mattress.

"It seems quite comfortable," he remarked. "I don't think I've ever slept in here before."

"Once, when you had that awful bout of flu."

"Oh yes, I remember."

Iris reached over and flipped back the covers on his side of the bed. "Come on, let's get some sleep."

He climbed in and turned off the bedside light. In the dark, they lapsed into silence.

"What are you thinking?" Iris asked.

"That this bed isn't as comfortable as ours." Sensing Iris's smile, he sighed. "I'm thinking about Pierre, about him having a child, a daughter. I'm thinking—when? How old is she? Did Laure tell you?"

"Not exactly. She thought that maybe Pierre had some sort of mid-life crisis and that the birth was recent. But apparently, the daughter is older. He said it was a one-night stand. I can't work out if that's better or worse."

"Better for Laure maybe, but not for the child." Gabriel's voice was grim. "Has Pierre had any contact with his child, or the mother, since?"

"Not since he discovered he was the father—at least that's what he told Laure."

"Then why say something now? Why not let sleeping dogs lie?"

"Maybe he had a crisis of conscience."

"Or regrets. He and Laure never wanted children, did they?"

"No. Well, Pierre didn't and Laure went along with it because she loved him. If he'd wanted ten kids, she'd have accepted it."

"Really?" Iris sensed Gabriel frown. "Did she tell you that?"

"Yes, last year, when she hit forty."

She shifted closer to him, hoping he would put his arms around her and draw her close. But he moved too, rolling from his back onto his side, and lay facing the wall. It was new, this turning away from her. Before, they would start their sleep with him curled around her, his chin resting on the top of her head, his arm across her body, anchoring her to him. Now, she was the one to curl around him. Not only that, he'd taken to wearing a T-shirt in bed, whereas before, he would sleep bare-chested. It was as if he hoped this thin material barrier would dampen any desire she might have for him.

Soon, his breathing deepened and to stop herself from worrying about him, about them, Iris turned her thoughts to Laure and Pierre. She and Gabriel had met them in the Bahamas twenty years before, where she and Gabriel had gone to celebrate their first wedding anniversary. Laure and Pierre had been on their honeymoon, and the two couples had hit it off immediately. Iris had been enchanted by Laure; petite in build, with straight brown hair that fell midway down her back in a glossy sheet and inky eyes framed by long lashes that almost touched her fringe, Laure was the epitome of a chic Parisienne. She had a neat nose that turned up ever so slightly at the end, and her lips were so naturally red it seemed she was permanently wearing lipstick. Once Iris got to know her, she'd been surprised to learn that Laure never wore makeup and realized it would be the equivalent of someone scribbling over a beautiful painting.

Their friendship had strengthened over the years, with a weekend visit every couple of months, and a holiday together once a year. They had keys for each other's homes. Pierre sometimes traveled for his job, and if Laure was joining him for the weekend, Iris would get a cheery email: *The flat will be free for the last weekend in the month, if you want a break in Paris.* Likewise, if Iris and Gabriel were going away, they would let Laure and Pierre know that their house was free. It was why Laure had felt able to move in while they were in Scotland; Iris had messaged to tell them they'd be away. It was the first time they hadn't had any advance warning—*Yes, wonderful, thank you, we'd love to use the house for a few days!*—but Laure understandably had had other things on her mind.

Restless, Iris latched onto the rhythm of Gabriel's breathing, hoping it would draw her into sleep. But before it could, he moved quietly from her arms, slid silently from the bed and left the room, closing the door softly behind him. She listened to where his footsteps took him; along the landing, past their bedroom where Laure was sleeping, and down the stairs.

She fought the instinct to go after him. If he'd wanted to talk, he would have woken her.

3

In the quiet of the house, in the dark of the night, Gabriel paced the sitting-room floor, softly treading a path from wall to window and back again, acknowledging how he had taken for granted the ease at which he used to fall asleep. Tired in both mind and body at the end of a crushingly busy day at the surgery, he would be out like a light as soon as his head touched the pillow. But for the past two months, since finding Charlie in the quarry, sleep had evaded him. And now there was more grief to keep him awake.

He couldn't get his head around Pierre having a child. He'd wanted to phone Pierre, to offer his support, act as a buffer between his two friends, but Laure had persuaded him not to. She'd said to wait until tomorrow, and he had respected that, mainly because by then it was past midnight in France. There'd been something else stopping him. Laure had apparently walked out of their flat in Paris last Sunday, which meant Pierre had had six days to phone him, had he wanted to talk. But he hadn't called. Perhaps he was afraid that Gabriel would judge him. He wouldn't, of course—although when he thought back to the conversations they'd had when Pierre heard of yet another friend who'd been having an affair, Pierre had always been outraged. Maybe he didn't class a one-night stand as an affair. But in Gabriel's book, a betrayal was a betrayal, whether it lasted a few hours, a few months or a few years.

Gabriel paused in his pacing and gave a sigh so heartfelt it was almost a groan. The word "betrayal" brought back the guilt he'd felt earlier when he'd told Iris he preferred to come home instead of stopping overnight in York. He'd known what Iris had planned, and had enough self-awareness to know that he wouldn't be able to go through with the romantic evening, and night, that she would have been expecting. For some reason, since finding Charlie, he hadn't been able to make love to his wife.

He continued his restless pacing, another worry presenting itself to him. How was he going to be able to cope with being at home for the next however many months until his colleagues deemed him fit to resume his duties?

"Take your time," they'd said. "We have a locum to cover for you, we can cope. Don't come back before you're ready."

"Two months," he'd said grudgingly. "I'll take two months off but no more."

He hadn't seen it coming. Burnout had crept up on him slowly, insidiously, suffusing him with a mounting dread, first the dread of trying to keep on top of his workload, then the dread of the ever-increasing demands of his patients and not being able to do his best for them, then the dread of actually going into the surgery. It had come to a head one Wednesday when he hadn't been able to get out of bed, when the thought of the day in front of him had overwhelmed him to the point of terror. He knew he needed a break; he hadn't taken any holiday for almost a year. When the other partners in the practice told him they didn't want to see him back at work for months, he'd been shocked. But he wasn't the first of them to have suffered from burnout, and he suspected he wouldn't be the last.

They'd talked to him about doing something for himself, finding a new hobby. He used to enjoy running and would often go for a run before work, when dawn was just breaking, and the world silent and still. That was how he'd found Charlie in the quarry. He hadn't been running since.

Gabriel understood that if he was to get better, he would need to keep himself busy both mentally and physically, but he couldn't think how. He was also worried about getting under Iris's feet. She was an interior designer, and was used to spending a large part of the day working in the office they'd created for her in one of the outbuildings. He didn't want her to feel that she should be spending time with him.

He and Iris had been lucky in their twenty plus years of marriage. They'd met when she joined the squash club where he played a couple of times a week. She was twenty at the time and still at university, and Gabriel twenty-six, and three years later, they had married. Two years after that, they'd been blessed with the birth of Beth. Gabriel would have liked to have more children but it had been a difficult pregnancy. Iris had had terrible sickness, not just in the morning but throughout the day, which had left her clinically depressed. She hadn't wanted to go through it again and Gabriel couldn't blame her.

When Beth had been born, and the midwife had handed her to Gabriel, he'd been overwhelmed by a flood of emotions.

"Happy?" Iris had asked him, noticing his tears, and Gabriel had told her that yes, he was, because after those difficult nine months, the baby was finally there. But there had been more to his tears, because at the very moment he'd held Beth, so tiny and fragile, in his arms, he couldn't understand why they had decided to have her, when one day she would die. He had never shared this darkness with anyone and, eventually, it had gone away. Until Charlie Ingram.

Maybe if he hadn't known Charlie, his death wouldn't have affected him so much. But he had instantly recognized, in the bruised and battered almost-adult face, traces of the boy he used to coach at football, back in the days when he was a volunteer at Beth's primary school on Saturday mornings. He'd sometimes chatted to Charlie's mum, Maggie. Like Beth, Charlie was an only child, and when Gabriel had seen the light leaving Charlie's eyes, the terrible darkness he had felt at Beth's birth had come back. Would Maggie have gone ahead and given birth to Charlie if she'd known she'd have to go through the pain of losing him eighteen years later? The answer had to be yes, because of the joy Charlie would have brought Maggie during those eighteen years. But if it were Beth—well, Gabriel didn't know. Somehow, the immense joy she had brought him over the last nineteen years made it harder for him to accept that one day, she would die.

He stopped his pacing and shook his head vigorously, wanting to rid his mind of thoughts of Beth dying. Weary, he slumped in a chair. He would have liked to go back to bed but he was afraid to, afraid that if Iris woke, and reached for him, he would have to hurt her feelings by turning his back on her. There were other bedrooms; he could sleep in one of those instead.

4

Iris tiptoed down the stairs to the kitchen, careful not to wake either Gabriel or Laure. Gabriel hadn't come back to bed last night; she presumed he'd slept in the other guest room.

Yawning, she reached for the kettle, filled it with water and switched it on. The hiss of air bubbles joined the hum of the fridge, the sounds too loud in the early morning silence.

The door opened, making her jump.

"Hello." Laure was standing there, wearing one of Iris's navy T-shirts tucked into a pair of her white tennis shorts, tightened at the waist with a belt to stop them from slipping down. The too-big clothes only enhanced Laure's vulnerability; even in the misery of her situation, she managed to look beautiful, her dark eyes bright with unshed tears. "I thought I heard you down here."

Iris pushed all thoughts of a quiet cup of tea from her mind and gave Laure a hug, conscious that her friend was showered and dressed while she was still in her dressing gown. "I couldn't sleep."

"Me neither."

"Tea?"

Laure gathered her hair into her hands, pulled it over her right shoulder and twisted it nervously. "Please."

They made their tea the way each of them wanted—Laure's without milk—and carried it through to the sitting room where they would be more comfortable for the heart-to-heart chat Iris knew they were going to have.

"Is this okay?" she asked, pulling the low table nearer to the sofa so that their tea and phones were within easy reach.

"Perfect."

Laure settled at one end of the sofa, Iris at the other, their legs drawn up onto the cushions so that their feet met in the middle. As Laure reached for her mug, the early morning sun streaming through the window burnished her hair a rich mahogany.

"How are you?" Iris asked.

Laure took a careful sip of her too-hot tea. "Hurt. Confused. He said he never wanted children. Maybe if we'd had some, I wouldn't be feeling so betrayed."

"How did you find out that he has a child?" Iris asked, because Laure had been so tearful last night it had been hard to follow the actual sequence of events.

Laure cupped her hands around her mug. "I first knew something was wrong after the holiday we spent with his family at Easter. It was to celebrate his mother's seventieth birthday so all Pierre's cousins were there with their children, and his sister with her four children. It was lovely, but always after these holidays, Pierre and I joke about the lucky escape we had, because we are exhausted from playing with his nieces and nephews. I like that we joke about it, I need to hear Pierre say it, because sometimes when I see all the families together, I've wished that we'd had children. But when I see how relieved he is that we didn't go down that road, the sadness I feel goes away because I know we did the right thing in deciding not to have any. At least, for him," she added, gulping back tears. "But then, after those holidays, he became very quiet and I thought it was something to do with his work. I kept asking him what the matter was but he said he was fine. It got to the point where he was no longer talking to me and last week, I said that I wished we'd had some children because at least I'd have someone to talk to. I was trying to make a joke, because I needed to see him smile; I was trying to get him back to how he used to be. And that's when he told me."

"What did he say?" Iris asked, struck that for the last couple of months, both their husbands had been in crisis.

Laure put her mug down on the low table, took a tissue from her sleeve and blew her nose delicately.

"He just turned and looked at me and asked me how I would feel if he told me that he had a child. My first reaction was that he was joking. Then I saw something on his face and it made me so scared. It was like—desperation. And I thought, this is real, this is not a joke, and I knew we'd reached a defining moment in our marriage and that I needed to stay calm and say the right thing."

"And did you?" Iris asked, trying to think of what the right thing would have been. "Stay calm?"

Laure gave a little laugh. "No, of course not. I was so upset that I couldn't be nice or reasonable. I thought it was recent, that the baby had been born a few weeks before, it would have explained why Pierre had been withdrawn for the last couple of months. But then he told me that it had happened some years ago."

Iris's mobile buzzed, interrupting Laure. She glanced at the screen and saw a message from Beth: *Hi Mum, free for a chat?* She hesitated, torn between her daughter and her friend, but answering Beth at this point in Laure's story felt rude. Reaching out, she turned off her phone.

"So how did Pierre know about the baby? You said yesterday that it was a one-night stand and that he hadn't kept in contact with the mother."

Laure nodded. "Apparently, a few months ago, he bumped into the woman in Paris. She was with a child and Pierre said that as soon as he looked at her, he felt this connection and immediately knew that

she was his. But when he asked, the woman denied it; she was annoyed that he should think it just because they'd slept together once. Pierre apologized and suggested they had a coffee together for old times' sake. And while they were sitting on the terrace of Les Deux Magots, while the mother wasn't looking, he took a stray hair from the child's head and used it for a DNA test."

"What?" Iris couldn't keep the shock from her voice. "Can he do that? I mean, is it legal? Without the mother knowing or giving her consent?"

"I don't know." Laure gave a Gallic shrug. "I don't think it's against the law."

"So what does Pierre intend to do, now that he knows the child is his?"

"I don't know. He says he wants to be involved in her life, because he has already missed so much of it. But he doesn't want to make trouble for the woman."

"He already has, by telling you."

"I almost wish he hadn't, because then I wouldn't have had to leave. But I couldn't stay, I couldn't bear to look at him." Laure reached for her mug, took another sip. "It was all right me coming here, wasn't it? Now that Mum has moved in with her new man, I didn't feel I could go to her, especially when I don't particularly like him. I didn't want to stay with any of my friends in Paris as I didn't want them to know, and anyway, I wanted to get as far away from Pierre as I could."

"I'm glad you felt you could come here. But what about your job?"

"I called and told them I'd had a personal crisis and asked to take the rest of my holiday allowance. I've been here a week now so I'm due back at work on Monday the twenty-seventh. Is that okay?"

Iris made a quick calculation; three weeks. She gave Laure a smile. "Of course."

"I thought at first it might be Claire."

"Sorry?" Iris said, her mind still on the three weeks.

"I think Claire might be the child's mother."

"Claire?" Iris frowned, thinking of Pierre's childhood friend who, on finding herself on her own at the age of forty and desperate for a child, had conceived her daughter using a sperm donor.

"Yes. Pierre said it wasn't, he was angry when I suggested it, and when I said I would ask Claire myself, he became even angrier. I asked him to tell me who she was, this woman he had slept with and who had borne his child, and he said it was someone he'd met on a business trip, that they had got drunk and had ended up sleeping together."

"So why do you still think it's Claire?"

Laure gave a hollow laugh. "How can I believe anything Pierre tells me when he has lied to me for the past six years?"

"Is that how old his child is?"

"It's how old Claire's daughter is."

Iris nodded. "What did Pierre say when you told him you were leaving?"

"That he understood. And that it would give him time to think. That's what I don't get—think about what? He said he doesn't want to make trouble for the woman, so what does he need to think about? Unless he wants to find someone younger, someone he can start a family with."

"He wouldn't do that," Iris said indignantly. "He can start a family with you, if that's what he wants. It's not too late."

Tears welled in Laure's eyes. "Yes, it is. I'm already into the meno-pause, I started it early, so it would be very difficult for me to conceive now. And why would he want to have a child with me when he could have someone younger?"

"Because he loves you."

"That's the problem." Laure's tears spilled over. "I'm not sure that he does. He hasn't called me once since I arrived. I think he's with her, Claire."

"You don't know that," Iris said, reaching across the expanse of sofa and giving Laure a hug. "Gabriel will call him this morning; we'll know more then."

5

Hearing the murmur of voices in the sitting room, Gabriel crept past the closed door and headed for the kitchen. Desperate for a proper cup of coffee, he was worried that the noise of the beans grinding would bring Iris and Laure through, and settled for already-ground coffee instead.

Reaching for the kettle, he ran the tap at a trickle and filled it through the spout. While the water was heating, he searched the cupboard for the tin of coffee and shook some into the cafetière, ignoring the measuring spoon wedged into the brown powder. He wanted to phone Pierre, but he needed a coffee first. And he wanted to speak to him without any further input from Laure.

He was having a hard time believing Pierre had slept with another woman. On their many holidays together, Gabriel had seen the way women looked at Pierre. Pierre might not be good-looking in the classic way but he had an easy charm and elegance that automatically drew others toward him. He was of average height—he towered over Laure but was no taller than Iris—and slight of build, and had a wide, engaging smile which gave the impression that he was always happy.

Yet Gabriel knew that Pierre sometimes struggled with depression, a legacy of his father's tragic death when Pierre was just eleven years old. They'd been walking home from school, and were crossing over to the boulangerie where they always stopped to buy Pierre an *éclair au choco-lat* when they'd been struck by a lorry. Pierre had not only been physically scarred, but seeing his father trapped beneath the lorry's wheels and hearing his agonizing screams of pain, had left him so mentally and emotionally traumatized that on the anniversary of the accident, Pierre would retreat into himself and disappear for a few days to Brittany, where his family were originally from. Gabriel often wondered if it was why Pierre had never wanted children; he hadn't wanted them to be left without a father in the event of anything happening to him.

The coffee made, Gabriel slid open the patio doors as quietly as possible and carried it onto the terrace. He was about to sit at the gray wrought-iron table when he realized that Iris and Laure could come through at any moment and find him there. And he didn't want to be found, not this early in the morning, not after so little sleep.

As he walked to the end of the garden, his heart was heavy with thoughts of Winston, his beloved Great Dane, who should have been walking by his side. When his partners had spoken to him about taking compassionate leave, citing not just Charlie's death but also his father's four months previously, he had waited for them to mention Winston, who had died two months before his dad. They hadn't, and it had made him irrationally angry, because Winston's death had hit him as hard as his father's, and had left the same-sized hole in his life.

Finding a bench hidden from the house, alongside the old walled garden, Gabriel perched his mug on its wooden arm. The walled garden was another thing to feel guilty about. When he and Iris had first moved into the house fifteen years ago, he had vowed to restore it to its former glory, to plant vegetables and hollyhocks, and salvias and hibiscus, flowers that had abounded in the garden of his childhood. But keeping on top of the rest of the garden, with its wide lawn and flower-bed borders, took up the little free time that he had.

He reached down and when his hand found only air, he cursed the reflex that he hadn't yet managed to overcome, to pat Winston's head as he lay at his feet. Sometimes, he would feel a nudge against his leg and would look down, expecting to see Winston there. Whenever it happened, Gabriel would wonder if Winston was trying to tell him something. He'd felt Winston's presence the day his father died, and had taken comfort from it.

Gabriel shook his head at himself. If Winston were here, and if he could speak, he would be telling Gabriel to get a grip. But he felt so damned useless. His job had defined him; now that it had been taken away from him, he didn't know how he was going to fill his days.

The sun warming the ancient stone of the walled garden drew his eyes to the once-green wooden door, its paint almost entirely flaked off by sun, wind, and rain. Leaving his mug where it was, he walked over and pushed open the door. Warped from being exposed to the elements for so many years, it groaned in retaliation at being scraped along the gravel, then sagged sorrowfully as it came to a stop, its hinges no longer capable of holding it fully upright. As he stood on the threshold, Gabriel felt a little like Mary Lennox in *The Secret Garden*, almost expecting to see a robin on the branch of the gnarled and withered apple tree that stood to the right of the path. It wasn't a big garden, maybe thirty yards by fifteen, and it certainly wasn't beautiful. But maybe it could be.

For the first time in months, he felt a surge of something like excitement.

6

Leaving Laure to move her things into the guest room next to theirs, Iris went to find Gabriel. She'd heard him come downstairs while she and Laure had been talking—the fourth step creaked, no matter where you placed your foot—but she hadn't blamed him for not coming to join them.

Finding the patio door ajar, Iris crossed the terrace and walked down the path, her nose picking up the sweet scent of lily of the valley. There was a lawn to the left of the path, a couple of sheds and her office on the right, and tucked away at the far end, a walled garden—or rather, a walled wilderness. They hardly ever went that far down the garden nowadays, so Iris was surprised to find the faded wooden door pushed open, and Gabriel standing on the threshold.

"Morning!"

He turned at the sound of her voice.

"Morning. How's Laure?"

"Devastated. Draining," Iris added guiltily.

He smiled. "I'm sorry I didn't come and join you."

"You're not really, are you?" she teased.

He laughed, and Iris caught a glimpse of the old Gabriel, the Gabriel before Charlie.

He came over to join her, stooping under the open doorway, and took his mug from the bench.

"She's taken all that was left of her holiday leave," Iris continued.

Gabriel paused, the mug halfway to his mouth. "How much?"

"Three weeks. Do you mind?"

"No, of course not. But I hope, for her and Pierre's sake, that she'll go back before then." He looked at her, concern in his eyes. "They will get over this, won't they?"

"I hope so."

He sat down on the bench and Iris joined him.

"I think you might have missed a call from Beth," she said, guessing that their daughter would have phoned Gabriel first. "She called when I was with Laure and I didn't feel I could answer."

"I must have been in the shower. She told me she'd call this morning but I didn't expect her to phone so early."

Iris heard the disappointment in his voice, and threw him a sympathetic smile. "Why don't you call her?"

"I will. Then I need to phone Pierre. Did Laure tell you anything else?"

"Not really."

"But—did Pierre always know that he had a daughter?"

"Apparently not. He told Laure that he bumped into a woman he knew, and that just from looking at the child who was with her, he knew that she was his."

Gabriel frowned. "So he just thinks he's the father? He has no proof?"

"He does now. Apparently, he was so convinced he was the father that he suggested he and the woman had a coffee together, and while they were in the café, he took a hair from the child and did a DNA test."

Gabriel burst out laughing. "I'm sorry, but that's just not believable.

That might happen in a film, but not in real life. If he was so convinced the child was his, why didn't he ask the woman outright?"

"He did. But she denied he was the father, which is why he took the hair."

"And does this woman have a name?" Gabriel sounded skeptical.

"No. But Laure isn't convinced it's a random woman." She paused. "She thinks it's Claire."

"Claire?"

"Yes. Her daughter was conceived by sperm donor."

"No." Gabriel was adamant. "Pierre wouldn't do that."

"Not even as a favor to a friend?"

A frown furrowed his brow. "Are you suggesting that Claire wanted a child, so Pierre gave her one?"

"It's what Laure is suggesting."

"She's crazy."

"Maybe—but it fits."

Gabriel was scowling now, and Iris cursed herself for the dip in Gabriel's mood. Looking for something to distract his thoughts away from Laure and Pierre, she nodded toward the walled garden. "Are you thinking of making a start on that?"

She'd meant it as a joke, so she was surprised when he nodded.

"Yes, actually."

"Really?" Iris couldn't keep the relief from her voice, not because the garden might finally be restored, but because it would give Gabriel something to focus on. "That's great."

"Not that I've got any idea where to start."

"We can get someone to help."

Gabriel shook his head. "I want to do it myself. I need to do it myself." He pushed to his feet. "I'm going to phone Beth, then I'll call Pierre."

Iris watched him leave, his long denim-clad legs striding up the path toward the house. Would having Pierre to worry about take his focus away from Charlie Ingram? Or would Charlie continue to over-shadow everything, even Gabriel's best friend—even her? She tilted her face toward the sky, barely noticing the warmth of the sun on her face.

She had a lot to think about.

7

Gabriel paced his study, waiting impatiently for Beth to answer his call. It was new this, his inability to sit still, a reflection of his state of mind, which churned restlessly night and day.

"Hey Dad!" His computer screen juddered, then settled, and Beth was there, tanned and smiling, her hands busy plaiting her hair into a long dark snake that hung over her right shoulder.

Finally able to sit, he sank into his desk chair. "It must be your day off," he said, noting her red bikini top. "How are you? All good?"

"All good," Beth confirmed, securing the end of her hair with an elastic and flipping it behind her back. "And yes, it's my day off."

Gabriel caught sight of himself in the tiny rectangle on the screen and wished he'd thought to run a comb through his hair before calling her. "Are you doing anything nice?" he asked, raising a hand and smoothing it down.

"I'm going to the beach with Rosa now, and later we're taking the bus to Thessaloniki with some of the other volunteers to see a bit of nightlife."

Immediately, a whole set of scenarios flew through Gabriel's brain—

the bus crashing on the way to Thessaloniki, Beth's drink being spiked, Beth becoming stranded after an argument with the others, Beth missing the last bus back and being offered a lift by a stranger. He didn't voice any of these worries, but he knew he wouldn't be able to fully relax until he received a reply to the casual message he'd send tomorrow morning, asking Beth if she'd had a good time.

"Sounds good," he said, wondering, not for the first time, if he would be as obsessed with Beth's safety if he and Iris had had more than one child. Or would he just have three, or four, or five times the amount of worry? He searched for the names of some of the dogs in Beth's care. "And how are Loki and Penny and Goldie and Homer?"

While Beth brought him up to date, Gabriel searched her face, listening carefully to the cadence of her voice for any sign that she was anything less than happy and healthy. She talked animatedly, gesticulating with her hands, laughing as she recounted something that one of the volunteers had said. Reassured, his eyes roamed around the screen, taking in the white-painted walls of the tiny room she shared with Rosa, where photos of friends and family made a colorful collage. He picked out the photo of him and Winston, another of him and Iris, saw the messy tangle of duvets on the wooden-framed beds, just visible behind Beth, and felt his body relax. Everything was as it should be.

"And how are you, Dad?" Beth asked. "Were you and Mum still asleep this morning? I couldn't get hold of either of you."

Gabriel shook his head. "Laure is here."

"Cool! I didn't know she was coming to stay. Was it a last-minute thing? How is she? Is Pierre there too?"

Despite himself, Gabriel smiled at her rattled-off questions. "Yes, not bad and no," he said, making Beth laugh.

"Mum must be pleased to have Laure staying for a while. How is she? Mum, I mean?"

"She's fine. She's sorry she missed your call. You can speak to her after."

"It will have to be another time, I'm afraid. Rosa is waiting for me." She paused, looking at him mock-severely. "You didn't answer my question about how *you* are."

"I'm good."

"Hm." Beth didn't seem convinced. "You're going to need to find something to do, Dad, something to keep you busy, especially now that Laure is there," she added, laughing again. "You're going to need to escape."

"I'm actually thinking of restoring the walled garden."

Beth's eyes widened. "No way! That's such a good idea! It could be so beautiful. I used to love playing hide-and-seek there with my friends, do you remember?"

"Yes," Gabriel said, smiling at her enthusiasm. "I do."

"How about you get it ready for when I come back at the end of August?"

Gabriel thought for a moment. "That would give me nearly three months. I could, I suppose."

"So, do we have a pact, Dad? You make the walled garden beautiful for when I come home—"

"And you promise to come back safe and sound." Gabriel couldn't help himself.

"Deal!" Beth looked over the top of her screen and mouthed something silent. "Dad," she said, turning her attention back to him. "I'm sorry, I need to run. Rosa is threatening to leave without me."

"No, I wouldn't do that, Mr. Pelley!" Rosa's lilting Italian accent filled the room.

"It's fine," Gabriel said, smiling. "We'll speak again soon. Have fun."

Beth's hand stretched toward her screen, searching for the off button.

"Thanks, Dad, love you."

"Love you too." But she had already gone.

He sat back, the smile still on his face. Beth was always able to lift his spirits, just by being, and in that moment, he understood why

Pierre wanted to be part of his daughter's life after missing out for so many years. He couldn't imagine what it must have been like for Pierre to come face-to-face with his daughter in the street—if that was what had happened. He was still unconvinced. What were the chances of Pierre bumping into, on a random street in Paris, a woman he had slept with once? And then, deciding that the child with the woman was his, despite the mother telling him that she wasn't? How could Pierre have been so sure, from that one meeting, that the mother was lying, that he'd taken a hair from the child to do a DNA test? And why would the mother agree to go for a coffee with Pierre for old times' sake if she had something to hide? Nothing made sense.

There was a part of Gabriel that wanted to warn Pierre what the next years would be like, if he did become involved in his daughter's life, about the thousand deaths he'd die along the way. It was only when Beth had left for Greece last summer that Gabriel realized how cushioned he'd been from the visceral anguish of parenting while she'd been away at boarding school, safe in the care of her teachers. Remembering that he needed to phone Pierre, he located Pierre's number, then resumed his pacing while he waited for his friend to pick up. But it went straight to voicemail and, caught unaware, Gabriel paused.

"Pierre, it's me, Gabe. Give me a call. I'm here for you."

And with that unsatisfactory message, he hung up.

8

"What would you do, if you were in my position?" Laure asked, not for the first time.

"I don't know," Iris said, also not for the first time.

From the other side of the table, she heard Gabriel supress a sigh. For the last three days, every conversation had been about Pierre.

"I suppose it depends whether Pierre is serious about wanting a relationship with his daughter," Gabriel said, stepping into the silence.

"He said that he did."

"But her mother might not want him to be involved in her daughter's life. Does she know that Pierre knows he's the father? If he is," he added.

Laure frowned. "So you don't believe that he is?"

"As I've already said," Gabriel said gently, reminding Laure that they'd had this conversation the previous night, and the one before that. "I think there's room for doubt."

"But he did a DNA test."

"Did he though? I know he told you that he did, but secretly taking a hair from a child's head doesn't strike me as something that Pierre would do."

Laure reached for her glass. "So does having a one-night stand strike you as something he would do?"

"Well—no."

"Sorry, Gabriel, I'm not having a go at you." Laure took a sip of wine. "It's just that I'm wondering how well we really know Pierre. It's not just that he had a one-night stand, or that he has a child. It's that he doesn't seem to regret any of it, even though it might destroy our marriage."

"I'm sure he does regret it," Gabriel said.

"Why would he, when it has given him something he didn't know he wanted until now?"

Gabriel gave a sigh of frustration. "I wish he'd call me. I've left several voicemails, and all I've had in return is a WhatsApp message saying he doesn't want to talk for the moment."

"It's because he's too embarrassed to talk to you," Laure said. "He knows what you will be thinking of him, after everything he used to say about people who have affairs."

Iris allowed herself to drift out of the conversation. The last three days with Laure had been draining. As well as having to support her friend, she'd also had to put the finishing touches to her sketches and mood boards so that her latest clients—the owners of a surprisingly beautiful five-bed new-build outside Winchester—could approve the fabrics and color schemes. This morning, Laure had sat in the office with her, pulling out folder after folder of swatches, exclaiming over the patterns and materials, questioning Iris's choices—*Wouldn't this one have been better for the sitting room?* or *I think this would be perfect for a child's bedroom.* She'd only been taking an interest, but it had had the unfortunate effect of making Iris question everything she'd already done.

"What will you be working on after this?" Laure had asked, unknowingly adding to Iris's worry about the lack of work on the horizon.

"It's not easy in the current economic climate," she'd explained. "But I have a potential client in the pipeline. She's in the process of buying a six-bed house in London and she wants an estimate, not just for the soft furnishings for each room, but also for furniture. It will be my biggest project to date and would look great on my CV. But I'm up against a couple of others. She was quite frank about that, which I appreciated. If I get the contract, I won't have to look for anything else for a while, which would be great. If it goes to someone else, I don't have anything on the horizon, so I'll have to start looking, something I haven't needed to do since I first started out."

"Wow, a house in London! Can I see your ideas for it?"

Iris had hesitated, then brought up the file on her computer.

"This is amazing, Iris," Laure had said, peering over her shoulder. "Those colors for that second reception room are stunning; who would have thought that blue and green would go together so well? You have a real talent, Iris."

Iris had smiled, please with Laure's reaction. She was hugely proud of the color schemes she'd chosen, glad that the potential client had given her carte blanche, saying she didn't want anything bland.

"What would you do, Iris?" Laure's voice broke into her thoughts and Iris swiftly zoned back into the conversation. "If Gabriel suddenly told you that he had a child by another woman, and that he wanted to have a relationship with that child, would you be able to accept it?"

"It's a tough one," Iris acknowledged. "It would depend on so many things—whether it was a one-night stand or an affair, if he'd only just discovered he had a child or had known about it for years, the age of the child—"

"But would you agree to meet the child yourself, welcome him or her into your home?" Laure interrupted.

Iris shrugged helplessly. "I don't know."

Laure sighed. "I'd love to think I'd be able to. But I know I couldn't do it. Especially if Claire is the mother," she added darkly. "It would be the ultimate betrayal."

"We don't know that she is," Gabriel reminded her. "We don't really know anything."

"By the way, I'm going to London tomorrow," Iris said. "To see Samantha Everett. My potential client with the town house in London."

"Great," Gabriel said. "Was that in your diary or did she suddenly ask to see you?"

"Neither. I was showing Laure my designs earlier and I thought it might be a good idea to hand deliver them rather than send them. So I phoned Samantha and said I'd be in London tomorrow and could I call in and see her. I thought it might give me an advantage if we met in person."

"Good move," Gabriel said approvingly. He pushed his chair back from the table. "Why don't you two find a film for us to watch, while I try Pierre again?"

But Pierre didn't pick up and Gabriel left another increasingly worried voicemail. *Pierre, please, just call me and let me know you're okay. We don't have to talk if you don't want to.*

9

Iris closed the door extra quietly, because to close it any louder might have shown her desperation to be out of the house.

She'd left Laure sunning herself in the garden, her face lathered in cream, and hyper-fine gloves on her hands to protect them from the sun. Her plan was to say, when Laure asked why she hadn't mentioned going for a run, that she'd thought she was asleep. Iris was heartbroken for her, for what Laure was going through, and had spent countless hours consoling her. But she had been with them for ten days now and it seemed to Iris that she never had any respite from Laure and Pierre's crisis, because even when she was asleep, their situation haunted her.

Already feeling guilty for snatching these precious minutes for herself, Iris paused on the doorstop, giving Laure time to come looking for her, as she always did when Iris was out of sight for more than a few minutes. When there was no sound of Laure calling her name, or her footsteps running down the hallway, Iris slipped the black elastic from her wrist and gathered her hair into a ponytail. Laure always insisted on accompanying her on her daily runs, but it was a new sport for her and she hadn't built up her stamina yet, which meant that Iris had had to adapt to a slower pace.

Their house was situated at the end of the village; if you went out of the gate and turned right, there were no more houses, just a stile and then two paths, one leading across the fields and up a slight incline toward East Markham, the other through woods that eventually led to the quarry where Charlie had been found.

Iris was in a mood to run fast and far, but instead of heading for her usual route across the fields, she turned left and ran through the village, intending to go as far as their local pub, then head straight back. The round-trip would only take twenty-five minutes but it wouldn't be kind to leave Laure for longer.

Yesterday, after a day working in the walled garden—Iris was beyond grateful that Gabriel's decision to restore the garden had become his raison d'être—he'd offered to go running with Laure, but she had declined, saying she preferred to stay with Iris. Gabriel had given her a helpless shrug—*sorry, I tried*—and she had loved him for trying to give her some space. She'd wished that Laure had accepted, not just for her sake but also for Gabriel's, as it was the first time he had shown any desire to go for a run since finding Charlie in the quarry. He never went out on his bike either, something he had previously loved to do.

Despite the relentless heat beating down on her, Iris's feet pounded the tarmac. As she followed the road around to the right, she waved to a woman sitting on a bench in her front garden, and further on, said a breathless hello to a neighbor walking his Dalmatian. She no longer socialized with many people in the village. Once Beth had left for boarding school, Iris had gradually lost contact with the other mums. It didn't bother her much. She enjoyed her own company and until now, her work had kept her busy. But now and then, she would have liked to have someone she could drop in on for a chat, or have someone drop in on her.

Close to the village pub stood a house that Iris had always coveted.

Set back from the road, the gray-stoned manor house sat at the end of a driveway bordered by trees and, despite its air of obvious neglect after being empty for years, it had managed to retain something of its original majesty. When it had finally come onto the market six months ago, Iris had tried to persuade Gabriel that they should buy it. She'd badly needed a new project, and restoring the interior would have been a dream. But Gabriel pointed out what Iris had already known, that the house was too big for the two of them, and that they would have had to take out another mortgage to be able to buy it.

Soon after, they'd heard the house had been sold. The removal lorry had been parked in the driveway the day Iris and Gabriel had left for Scotland. Now, Iris slowed her pace to peer through the open gates, and then she came to a stop, sweat trickling down her back, her eye caught by something bright and colorful coming into her line of vision, then disappearing again, then reappearing. It was a child, she realized, swinging backward and forward on a rope strung over the branch of an ancient oak tree, halfway up the drive. Intrigued, she watched as the girl, her arms stretched taut so that her body was almost parallel to the ground, swept to the left, then to the right on her makeshift swing, her flame-colored hair brushing the grass as she spun on each turn until, aware of Iris's eyes on her, she pulled herself upright and slid off the rope, stumbling a little at the sudden loss of movement.

"Do you want to come in?" she called, grabbing the rope to steady herself, and Iris saw that it wasn't a child, but a woman. Embarrassed at having been caught watching, unsure if the woman was being genuine or sarcastic, Iris hesitated. "Please! I need a break," she called again. "And a friend! I don't know anyone here."

Her plea was so heartfelt that Iris found herself walking down the drive toward the woman, who was hurrying barefoot to meet her, her canary yellow dress billowing behind. She came to a stop in front of Iris and held out her hand. She was tiny, bright and beautiful, like an exotic bird.

"I'm Esme, and I'm dying for a cup of tea. Would you like one?"

Iris couldn't help laughing. "I'm Iris and I'd love some tea." Her hand, grasped warmly in Esme's, felt like a giant's.

"Please tell me you live in the village."

"I do. At the far end."

Esme put a hand on her heart. "Thank God. I've hardly met anyone yet." She waved toward the swing. "I was trying it out before the baby comes." Her hand slid down to her stomach and Iris noticed the bump protruding from under the folds of her dress. "Do you have children?"

"One, a daughter. Beth. She's nineteen."

Esme turned to Iris, her aquamarine eyes wide with surprise. "Gosh, you don't look old enough to have a daughter that age. You must have had her when you were very young."

"I was twenty-five," Iris said, realizing that Esme now knew her age. She wondered how old Esme was. It was hard to tell; she could be anything between thirty and forty. "Is it your first?"

"Yes." Esme's eyes danced with amusement. "I'm what they call a geriatric mother." She began walking toward the house. "Does your daughter live with you?"

"No, she took a gap year. She's in Greece at the moment, volunteering at a dog shelter for the summer before she goes to Bristol in September."

"How wonderful! Does she love it? All those dogs to cuddle!"

Iris smiled at her enthusiasm. "She does, although some of the dogs are so traumatized by their past experiences she says it's impossible to even touch them. It's a case of sitting near them for hours at a time so that she can eventually win their trust."

They arrived at the impressively large front door and Esme pushed it open. "There is one little haven of peace amid all this mess, I promise," she chattered as they picked their way down a hallway littered with paint pots and ladders. Darting forward, she opened a polished oak door, at odds with the rest of the house. "Here it is," she said with a flourish. "The only room that is liveable, apart from our bedroom."

"This is lovely." Iris moved farther into the room and turned slowly, trying to take it all in. The room was vast, with a kitchen area at the far end, a long oak table with two cushioned benches in the middle and, in an alcove to the right, two fat sofas separated by a low table the size of a door. Looking more closely, Iris saw that it was a door—or at least, it used to be.

"I'd always wanted a big kitchen and I wasn't bothered about having a separate dining room, so we broke down a couple of walls," Esme explained, filling an old-fashioned red kettle, the water splashing noisily into its tinny interior. "I think it's much nicer to eat in the kitchen, even when we have guests. It means I can keep up with the conversation. And, best of all, there's a fireplace. I love a fire, it makes everything so cozy." She spun around. "Is herbal tea all right?"

"Lovely." Iris smiled at her. "Congratulations, by the way. A new baby and a new house. You're going to be busy. When are you due?"

"The beginning of September, so twelve weeks to go." She laughed. "Believe me, I'm counting!"

Iris walked to the window and looked out at the tangle of a garden. "I wanted to buy this house," she confessed. "I wanted us to renovate it, but Gabriel, my husband, was worried I'd never want to move out and it would be too big for the two of us."

"Are you good at that sort of thing, then—decorating? Because if you ever want to give us a hand, feel free."

Iris smiled, her eyes still on the garden. "Not actual decorating. I'm a home enhancer." She cringed inwardly at the name she'd invented to describe what she did. Although Gabriel called her an interior designer, she never described herself as such because she didn't have any qualifications in interior design, something she was at pains to point out to potential clients. They didn't care; her work spoke for itself. Her career had started fifteen years before, when she'd helped a friend choose furnishings and colors for her new house. The result had been stunning, and more work had quickly come her way.

Esme gasped and clasped her hands together. "I think God must have sent you."

Thankfully for Iris, the need to reply vanished when a man came into view, pushing a wheelbarrow piled high with stones along a narrow path. From where Iris was standing, she could see the tendons in his forearms straining as he tilted the wheelbarrow and tipped the stones out.

"Is that your husband?" Iris asked.

There was a peal of laughter from behind her. "No, that's Joseph. That's Hugh, over there."

Iris turned to look to where Esme was pointing, and moved to the mantelpiece where a photograph stood, of a man with twinkling eyes, a bald head and a bushy white beard. Aware of Esme's eyes on her, Iris hid her surprise. He looked so much older.

"It's all right," Esme said cheerfully, as if she'd been reading her mind. "I've lost count of the number of times I've been asked if Hugh is my father."

Iris smiled. "My husband is older than me too."

"How much older?"

"Six years."

Esme eyes danced. "Hugh is twenty years older than me."

A noise, which started as a low moan before developing into a shrill whistle, had Esme reaching for a fat china teapot sitting on the side.

"That's a sound I haven't heard for a while," Iris remarked.

"I love it." Esme moved the kettle slightly off the hob, reducing the noise to a whimper. "Something as good as a cup of tea should be announced properly, don't you think?"

As if mesmerized by an ancient ritual, Iris watched as Esme heated the teapot with water from the kettle and swirled it around before emptying it into the sink. Stretching to the cupboard above her head, she retrieved an old tin and spooned some of the contents into the pot before adding the still-boiling water.

"There!" she said happily. Grabbing a tea towel, she wrapped it around the handle of the teapot and carried it over to the low table. "Come and sit down while I get some mugs."

Iris waited until Esme had poured the tea. "How did you and Hugh meet?" she asked, unable to hide her interest.

"He lived down the road from my parents, but I only really met him when I moved back home after I split up with my partner, who I'd been living with for three years." Esme reached for her mug and brought it to her lips, holding it there a moment, warming her mouth against the hot china. "It was a painful time for me and I wasn't in a good place. I was thirty years old and the man I'd thought I was going to spend the rest of my life with had suddenly got cold feet, probably because I'd been banging on too much about having babies. It meant I had to give up my job because we both worked for the same company, and it was too hard seeing him every day. So, there I was at Mum and Dad's, trying to get my life back on track, when Mum asked me if I'd help Hugh out. His wife had died a few months before and he needed someone to pick up his son from school and look after him until he came back from work, and as I didn't have anything else to do, I agreed to step in." Esme paused to take a sip of tea. "I'd met Hugh once before but couldn't remember anything about him except that he was old, so I never imagined I'd fall in love with him."

Iris smiled. "But you did."

"Yes. It was a gradual thing. At first, as soon as he arrived home in the evenings, I'd leave him and Marcus to it. But after a while, he began asking me to stay and have dinner with them and before long I was totally in love. When he admitted that he loved me too I was over the moon, although we were a little worried about what my parents would say. Luckily, they were really happy for us, and I found myself with a ready-made son."

"How old is Marcus?"

"Twenty-two. He lives and works in London, where we lived before moving here." Esme lifted her legs onto the sofa and tucked a cushion under her knees. So, your turn now—how did you and your husband meet?"

"Playing squash. We were paired together in the mixed doubles. I was twenty and still at university and Gabriel was twenty-six."

"You've known him a long time, then."

"Yes." Iris's mind slipped back to the man she'd seen in the garden. "So, if Marcus is Hugh's son, who's Joseph?"

"A family friend. He's a landscape gardener by trade, and he's giving us a hand with our garden."

As Iris nodded, her eye caught sight of the time on the huge clock face that adorned one of the walls in the kitchen area.

"Is that the time?" she exclaimed, struggling to get out of the sofa that had seemed to swallow her up. "I need to go. I've been gone nearly an hour."

"You're welcome to stay longer." Esme sounded wistful. "I haven't got anything planned for the rest of the afternoon."

"Thank you, but I can't. We have a friend staying with us, and I need to get back." Sensing Esme's disappointment, Iris hurried to explain. "She's going through a bit of a rough time at the moment, so it wouldn't be fair to leave her on her own for any longer."

"Of course." Esme heaved herself up. She looked at Iris, taking in her shorts, T-shirt and trainers. "Were you really out jogging in this heat?"

"Yes, but I'll be walking back. It really is too hot to run." She turned to Esme. "Thank you for the tea. It was a lovely break."

Esme put a hand on Iris's arm. "Come for supper," she said impulsively. "Saturday, if you're free. That way you can meet Hugh. Bring your friend, if she's still here."

"But you've only just moved in," Iris protested. "Why don't you come to us?"

"No, really, come here."

"Are you sure?"

"Absolutely."

"Then, thank you."

Esme accompanied her to the front door. "Are there any nice walks around here? It's something Hugh and I love to do."

"Yes, there are. If you walk to our end of the village, there's a footpath that leads across a couple of fields, and another into some woods. There's a quarry, but it's out of bounds now."

"Is that where they found that poor boy? We saw it on the news just after we'd bought the house, they mentioned a quarry outside Markham."

"Yes." Iris nodded. "That's where it happened."

She didn't tell Esme that it was Gabriel who found him.

10

Gabriel stuck the spade into the ground and took off his gloves, pleased with the progress he'd made on the walled garden. It had taken him a couple of days to actually get started, but after a week of pulling out weeds, digging over soil and picking out stones, about a quarter of the plot had been transformed into something that looked as if one day, it could be filled with vegetables or flowers.

He was surprised at how good he felt, not just physically but also mentally. He had Beth to thank for that; she had already phoned twice to see if he was keeping to their pact and he was determined to impress her when she came back in August. Not only that, but with each day that passed, he'd found himself worrying less and less about his colleagues at the surgery, and about the patients he'd abandoned. Because that was how it had seemed at the time, that he had abandoned them.

He took out his phone, and moved to the old wooden bench that he'd dragged into the garden so he'd have somewhere to sit. He needed to try Pierre again; he still hadn't been able to speak to him. All he'd received in response to the numerous voicemails he'd left for his friend was a second message—*I appreciate your concern but I have nothing to say for the moment. I'll call in a few days.* That had been three days ago and it had left Gabriel bemused and frustrated, a frustration he'd had to put aside, because when Pierre had asked him about Charlie, he'd said more or less the same thing, that he didn't want to talk about it, and Pierre had respected his wishes. Now, he owed it to Pierre to do the same. But at least he had answered Pierre's calls.

He called Pierre's number, not really expecting him to pick up.

"Gabriel." Pierre's voice came down the line.

"Pierre, thank God." Gabriel took a moment to rid his voice of reproach. "It's good to hear from you. How are you?"

"Not great."

"No, I can imagine." Gabriel paused. "Is there anything I can do to help?"

"Thanks, but it's something I need to sort out for myself. You're already helping by having Laure to stay with you. How is she?"

"Hurt. Confused. You need to talk."

"We will."

"You could come here."

"Maybe. But not yet. I need some time."

"Then call her."

"I will."

"How about I come to Paris?"

"No, please don't. Sorry, but I don't want to see anyone for the moment."

"Okay. But if—"

"I have to go," Pierre interrupted. "I'm at work."

"All right—make sure you keep in touch."

But Pierre had already gone. Gabriel cursed under his breath at the feeling of a missed opportunity. He'd hoped that Pierre might tell him something that he could take back to Laure, but all he'd learned was that Pierre wasn't ready to talk, and that he didn't want to see anyone. On the other hand, having nothing to tell Laure meant that he didn't need to go and find her yet. Beth had been right; the walled garden was proving to be a great refuge.

Perhaps he was being harsh, perhaps it was normal that her every conversation was about Pierre. If he was honest, it wasn't all bad having her around because she was filling the space between him and Iris, a space he himself had created by not opening up to her about what was troubling him. He wanted to, but before he did, he needed to reconcile himself with the decision he'd made that day in the quarry. It had seemed the right thing to do at the time. Sometimes, though, he imagined Charlie turning in his grave and saying *You bastard*.

Gabriel had played that "if only" game a lot afterward. If only he hadn't taken the quarry route that day, if only he'd left half an hour later, because if he had, the chances were that Charlie would have died before he'd come across him. But would he really have wanted Charlie to die alone? Charlie had recognized him, had called him Mr. Pelley. It made Gabriel think that he'd been predestined to find him, predestined to have had to make a difficult choice. Maybe someone up there thought he'd had life too easy and had decided to screw it up a bit by giving him a lose-lose situation, where you're damned if you do and damned if you don't. And now a letter had arrived.

He stuck his hand in his pocket and pulled it out. It had come while he and Iris were in Scotland and the only good thing about it was that its contents had trumped his worry over Pierre. He looked at the earth he'd just turned over, and fought the urge to bury the letter deep into the soil.

He took a breath, then stuffed it back in his pocket.

11

Laure put her head around the bedroom door.

"Iris, could I borrow something to wear, please?"

"Of course." Iris waved a hand toward her wardrobe. "Help yourself."

They were due at Esme and Hugh's for supper in an hour. Wrapped in her bathrobe, Iris carried on putting the finishing touches to her makeup.

"It's kind of Esme to have invited me," Laure said.

"She's lovely, you'll like her. She's very natural, really happy in her skin."

In the mirror, she watched as Laure pulled a yellow-patterned dress from the rail; it was already mid-length on Iris and completely swamped Laure.

"What do you think?" Laure asked.

"Too big," Iris said firmly. "Try one of my shorter dresses. Or a skirt."

Laure took out another dress, shorter this time. It was still a little big, so Iris found a black leather belt to nip in the waist.

"That looks lovely," she said, admiring Laure's slim figure.

Laure grimaced and shook her head. "It doesn't feel right."

"That's because all my clothes are at least a size too big for you. Are you sure you don't want me to take you shopping? I know you said you could manage with borrowing mine until you go back to Paris, but we could at least get you a pair of shorts and a dress that fits."

Laure shook her head. "It's not worth it. I've already got a lot of clothes so I don't really want to add to my wardrobe."

"Okay." Iris ran her eye along the rail and pulled out a denim skirt. "How about this, with a white shirt?"

"Not dressy enough." Laure spotted a black dress. "This looks nice."

"Try it."

But it wasn't right either, and by the time Laure had decided to wear Iris's new white dress, it looked as if the wardrobe had exploded, shedding clothes on every available surface.

"What do think?" she asked, tying a colorful scarf around her waist and looking at herself from different angles in the mirror.

"Stunning," Iris replied with a mixture of relief and exasperation, relief that after forty-five minutes, Laure had finally found something she was happy with, exasperation because she had planned to wear that dress herself.

"We need to leave!" Gabriel called from downstairs.

"Ready!" Laure sang back.

Except that Iris wasn't, and as she hastily pulled on the black dress that Laure had discarded, she already felt exhausted.

Downstairs, she took the beautifully-scented yellow roses she'd cut from the garden, and tied a ribbon around the stems.

"Isn't that the dress that you were going to wear?" Gabriel murmured, nodding toward Laure, waiting by the front door, designer sunglasses adding to her film-star looks.

Iris rolled her eyes. "Don't ask. But just to warn you, the bedroom looks like a battlefield."

They walked to Esme's, the early evening air heavy with the woody smell from fired-up barbeques, and at each sound of laughter coming from a back garden, Iris found herself smiling in anticipation of the evening ahead. She was happy to be going out tonight, relieved to be expanding their circle from three to five, because if she had to have one more meal with Laure, even with Gabriel and Laure, she might have screamed. The conversation was always about Pierre, and she was tired of hearing about Pierre. She was beginning to resent him; he still hadn't called Laure, even though he'd promised Gabriel he would. Nobody was communicating with anybody; even she and Gabriel were no longer talking, no longer exchanging small signs of affection, a kiss here, a caress there. Iris told herself it was because they didn't want to upset Laure. But deep down, she was afraid something fundamental had changed between her and Gabriel.

They arrived, and Esme led them through the house onto a covered terrace heaving with old sofas and armchairs. A huge bear of a man, recognizable as Hugh from the photo Iris had seen, embraced her and Laure in a warm hug.

"Let me get you some drinks," he boomed, clapping Gabriel on the back. "Esme has made one of her cocktails, if you'd like to try it."

"I'd love to," Iris said, immediately drawn to his larger-than-life character.

Esme, resplendent in a turquoise ankle-length skirt, a white embroidered T-shirt and silver gladiator sandals, urged them to sit. In comparison to Esme and Laure, Iris felt drab and uninteresting.

Prompted by Gabriel, Hugh began telling them about their plans for the house, and Iris felt herself beginning to relax. With a glass of Esme's cocktail in her hand—rum-based by the smell of it—she settled into a wicker armchair, wondering again how old Esme was. She looked from Esme to Laure and decided that Esme must be younger, late thirties perhaps. The mild annoyance she felt, that they were both younger than her, because Laure was forty-three, made her smile.

"I never expected to be undertaking such a huge project at sixty-one years of age," Hugh said, and remembering that Hugh was twenty years older than Esme, Iris made a quick calculation; Esme was forty-one. Her rush of pleasure, that she and Esme were on the same side of forty, was quickly replaced by dismay, because she looked so much younger. At least, that was how it seemed. For a mad moment, Iris wanted to ask Gabriel what he thought.

It was living with Laure for the past two weeks that had made Iris more aware of her physical appearance. She'd always been happy with how she looked—yes, it would have been nice to be half a stone lighter, not to have the few gray hairs that had started to thread through her dark bob—but she had never wished to be a few inches shorter than her five foot nine. The truth was, spending so much time in close proximity to Laure had made her feel ungainly.

Hugh raised his glass. "To new friends."

"And a new baby," Gabriel added, raising his. "Iris told me your good news. Congratulations, both of you!"

"I'm not even sure how it happened," Hugh joked. "I was in Switzerland for most of January."

"For three weeks, and I went with you and stayed on for a few days, remember?" Esme looked at Iris in mock exasperation. "He likes to pretend he had nothing to do with it."

"I'm sorry." Laure's voice, although no more than a murmur, closed their laughter down. She pushed unsteadily to her feet. "I'm not feeling too good. I think I should go home."

Hugh and Esme were on their feet too, concern in their eyes.

"Can I get you some water?" Hugh asked.

"Would you like to lie down?" Esme laid a hand on Laure's arm. "You can use our bedroom."

But Laure shook her off, as if she couldn't bear to be touched.

"Thank you, but I'd rather go home."

"I'll come with you," Iris said.

"No, please stay, I'll be fine." Laure turned to Esme. "I'm so sorry."

She disappeared into the house, and they stared in dismay at her departing back.

"Was it something I said?" Esme asked worriedly. "Was it my pregnancy?"

"No." Iris smiled reassuringly, although she knew it probably was. "I'd better go after her, at least take her home. I won't be long, but please, start without me."

Picking up her bag, Iris hurried through the house after Laure, mentally blaming herself, although she was sure she had told Laure that Esme was pregnant. When she reached the front door, she came to an abrupt halt, because Laure was standing on the driveway, talking to a tall, dark-haired man, whom she recognized as Joseph, the landscape gardener. She took a step back and watched from the shadows.

"No, thank you." Laure's voice was shaky with tears. "I'll be fine. It's not far, just along the road."

"Are you sure? It's really no trouble to walk with you."

Laure shook her head, already moving away. "The walk will do me good. But thanks anyway."

Iris watched Joseph checking on Laure as she headed toward the gate. Once she was out of sight, he took a path that Iris guessed led around to the back of the house. Her instinct was to catch up with Laure and make sure she got home safely. But something held her back, the fear that Laure might ask her to stay, and Iris couldn't bear the thought of spending another evening talking about Pierre. To-night, she wanted to enjoy herself, because she couldn't remember the last time she'd had fun. The holiday in Scotland with Gabriel had been nice, but it hadn't been fun, not in the way it might have been, with teasing and laughter and their usual jokes. Gabriel could make her laugh out loud with his dry wit. But that hadn't happened for a long time now.

She walked to the end of the drive and stood on the path, looking down the ribbon of road, shading her eyes against the evening sun. There was no sign of Laure, she had already turned the corner. Iris decided to give her ten minutes to get back to the house, then call her. If Laure didn't answer, she would go and check on her. If she answered and said she was fine, she would stay at Esme and Hugh's for dinner.

Happy with the bargain she'd made with herself, Iris walked back up the drive, her feet warm under the canvas of her espadrilles. She stopped under the oak tree, her eye caught by the rope swing. She moved closer and examined it; the rope had been threaded through the middle of a small rectangle of wood. As far as Iris could make out, the only way to sit on it was to straddle it.

Sliding her bag from her shoulder, she placed it safely out of the way and with both hands, caught hold of the rope. She gave it a sharp tug, testing its ability to take her weight, in case it was only suitable for children, or small adults like Esme. It seemed fine, so Iris began pulling her body upward, the muscles in her arms already straining. It wasn't easy to trap the plank of wood between her legs, given the dress she was wearing. But soon, she was swinging back and forth, using her body to propel her, gaining momentum as she spun on each turn, and then, when she was feeling confident enough, she threw her head back and stretched her arms taut, so that her body was almost parallel to the ground, as she'd seen Esme do. She closed her eyes, exhilarating in the moment, enjoying the breeze that cooled her skin as she spun and turned, carefree and untroubled. She wanted to carry on swinging but her arms began to cramp, so she kept her body still and gradually, the swing slowed and she was able to slide from the plank.

She stood for a moment, clutching the rope, loving the shifting sensation beneath her feet, like sand on the seabed responding to the pull of the waves. She wanted to fetch Gabriel so that he could have a turn; she wanted him to be able to experience the same sense of abandonment as she had when, for a small moment in time, nothing else had mattered. But of course, everything else did matter. Letting go of the swing, she retrieved her bag and dug for her phone.

There was a message from Laure. She was home, she wrote, and was going to have an early night. She was sorry for leaving as she had, and wished them all a lovely evening. Relieved, Iris messaged back, telling her to sleep well, and that she would see her in the morning.

She walked quickly back to the house, aware that she'd been away so long that Esme and the others might think she'd gone home. Instead of going through the house, she followed the path that Joseph had taken.

"Is Laure all right?" Esme asked, when Iris appeared on the terrace.

Iris's eyes were immediately drawn to Joseph, standing by Hugh's chair. Up close, he was startlingly good-looking, with jet-black hair and piercing blue eyes.

"Yes, she's home and having an early night. She apologizes for leaving so abruptly."

Hugh, suddenly remembering that introductions needed to be made, got to his feet. "Iris, this is Joseph. He's a family friend, who's kindly agreed to help us with our garden."

Esme sighed dramatically. "You don't know how hard it was to entice him away from the delights of Winchester to come and live with us for a few months. He only agreed as a favor to my parents, who nearly died when they saw the state of this place."

"It didn't take much to entice me," Joseph said. "I've heard there's some beautiful countryside around here."

"Hopefully it'll make up for living in a shed." Esme pointed to a small stone outbuilding, covered in climbing roses. "Until there's a bedroom ready for him in the house, that's where he's staying."

"I don't know about the inside, but it's certainly very pretty," Iris remarked.

"It's fine inside, despite what Esme says. I have somewhere to eat, somewhere to sleep and somewhere to wash. What more could a man want?"

Iris was saved from answering by Hugh. "Very little," he said, sitting down again. "I was tempted to move into it myself and leave Esme on her own in the house." He craned his head, looking up at Joseph. "Why don't you sit down, have a drink with us?"

Joseph looked down at himself, wiped his hands on his jeans. "I'm hardly in a fit state. Another time, perhaps." He nodded toward Iris and Gabriel. "Enjoy your evening."

Esme waited until he was out of earshot. "That wasn't very diplomatic," she reproached.

Hugh looked at her guiltily. "Sorry, I forgot."

"It's why I didn't invite him to join us for supper," she explained, turning to Iris. "Joseph needs to avoid alcohol for a while and as there'll be plenty of it tonight, I thought it better not to put him in the way of temptation." She glanced at Hugh, who was talking to Gabriel, and lowered her voice. "Joseph and I go back a long way and when I caught up with him at my parents' a couple of months back, I could see he was in a bad place. He's had a couple of close shaves as a result of getting drunk. He's actually lucky to be alive."

Already intrigued by Joseph, Iris's curiosity was piqued. "Why, what happened?" she asked.

Esme hesitated, as if wrestling with her conscience, then plunged in. "A few months ago, while over the limit, he wrapped his car around a tree. How he got away without serious injury is a miracle. The only thing he lost was his license for a year, and his job, when he could just as easily have lost his life. Then, a month ago, while he was working at my parents' house—they'd given him some work while he looked for another job—he nearly gassed himself to death while he was drunk."

"What!"

Esme nodded. "He went to make himself a cup of tea in my dad's shed, filled the kettle, put it on the hob, turned on the gas bottle but forgot to light the ring. Dad found him and managed to get him out of the shed but he was so groggy Dad called the doctor, who told Joseph he would die of liver disease, if he didn't kill himself first."

Iris's mouth dropped open. "Gosh, that's awful."

Esme nodded. "I know. Luckily, my parents, who are very fond of Joseph—they know his mum—managed to persuade him that getting away from Winchester would be a good thing."

"Is that where you're originally from? Winchester?"

"Yes. Anyway, after checking with us, they told Joseph that Hugh and I were in desperate need of a gardener, and after a bit of persuasion he agreed to come here for a while. I think he understood that if he carried on the way he was going, he'd end up a fully-fledged alcoholic."

Esme paused, and in the silence, Iris heard Charlie Ingram's name mentioned. She turned her eyes to where the men were sitting, their heads close together, and felt a rush of relief that Gabriel had felt able to confide in Hugh.

"All he needs to do now is stay on the wagon," Esme continued.

Iris frowned, momentarily confused, and remembered they were talking about Joseph. "Do you think he will?"

"He has every reason to." Esme rested her hands on her stomach for a few seconds, then stood. "Shall we eat?"

12

Gabriel stared at the ceiling, his hands wedged behind his head, thinking about the evening they'd just spent with Esme and Hugh. He'd enjoyed the evening more than he'd thought he would, maybe because without Laure there, they'd been able to speak about something other than Pierre.

He'd felt sorry for Laure, though. It couldn't have been easy for her, seeing Esme pregnant, if it was true that she had always wanted a child.

Iris stirred beside him and he held his breath, willing her not to wake. She rolled toward him but settled back to sleep. Gabriel let his breath out quietly and returned his thoughts to the evening. When Iris had gone after Laure, he'd been worried that she might not come back and he'd be stuck with a couple he didn't know. It wouldn't have mattered, he'd soon realized, because they were great. At one point he'd been surprised to find himself telling Hugh about finding Charlie in the quarry. He wasn't sure how the conversation had started, or what had led him there, but if they hadn't been interrupted by Esme calling them to the table, he might have told Hugh everything. And if he had, he might be feeling better about what he did that day.

If the paramedics hadn't arrived when they had, Gabriel might have been more prepared. But he was still trying to process that Charlie had just died in front of his eyes. They asked if Charlie had been conscious when he'd found him, and if Gabriel had had more time to think things through, he might have said that he hadn't been. It would have been a lie, but it would have been an easier burden to bear than the one he'd carried since, because once he'd said that Charlie had been conscious, it was inevitable that the paramedics would ask if Charlie had said anything. And Gabriel had said yes. It was only when they asked him what Charlie had said that Gabriel recognized his mistake. The huge weight of the message Charlie had asked him to pass on hit him with such force that, for a moment, he'd been unable to speak. But he'd had to tell them something, so he told them that Charlie had said, just before he died, *Tell Mum I love her*, and the two paramedics had had tears in their eyes, and said what a comfort it would be to her. Then the police had arrived and had asked the same questions, and Gabriel had told them the same thing, that Charlie had asked him to tell his mum he loved her.

Except that wasn't what Charlie had said.

13

Iris pulled up in the drive and sat for a moment before going into the house. She needed to gather her thoughts before facing Laure.

There'd been a dip in Laure's mood since the dinner at Esme's on Saturday. When they'd spoken about it the next day, Laure had told Iris what she'd already suspected, that seeing Esme pregnant had been too much for her, because her three weeks off were coming to an end.

"It underlined what I don't have," she'd said, her eyes bright with tears. "And everything I've secretly wanted."

She had also been understandably apprehensive about seeing Pierre again.

"What if he tells me that I'm right, and that Claire is the mother of his child? And that they've agreed that he can see her on a regular basis? He already knows Mathilde; he's her godfather." Her eyes had widened suddenly. "Maybe that's why he's her godfather; maybe it was an agreement between him and Claire that he would be her godfather so he could have a role in her life. Do you think that's what happened?"

Iris had hesitated a moment too long.

"If she is, I think I might kill him." Tears had filled Laure's eyes. "I'm not going to be able to stay at the flat when I go back this weekend. I'll ask Victoire if I can stay with her."

"Does Victoire know?" Iris had asked, recognizing the name of Laure's childhood friend. "About Pierre having a daughter?"

"No, none of our friends do. All they know is that Pierre and I are going through a bad patch, and that I've come here so that each of us can have some space. They don't know the cause of the bad patch."

Mindful that the engine was still running, Iris turned off the ignition and got out of the car. Glancing up at the house, she saw the flash of a face at the sitting-room window and groaned inwardly. Laure was already waiting for her.

"Did you have a good meeting?" Laure asked, as Iris came in through the door.

Iris put her bag down and kicked off her sandals. "Yes, very productive. This time Samantha had the keys to the house so I was able to actually see it. It's beautiful; it really would be a dream project. She still hasn't made a decision, though." She gave Laure a smile. "How about you, what did you do?"

"I went to see Esme."

"Oh. Hold on, I just need to wash my hands."

Laure followed Iris to the kitchen and waited while she lathered soap into her hands, then rinsed them. "I thought I should apologize for dashing off on Saturday," she said, handing Iris a towel.

"I'm sure she understood."

Laure nodded. "She did, once I explained about Pierre. We had a lovely chat and she offered to take me shopping to buy some clothes." She looked down at her shorts and T-shirt. "I've got so used to wearing yours that I barely notice anymore."

"You know I'm happy to take you shopping," Iris said, irritated. "I've offered, but you've never wanted to go, you said it wasn't worth buying anything new as you had plenty of clothes in Paris."

"I know, but I mentioned to Esme that I wouldn't mind a new dress for when I see Pierre at the weekend. I may as well look as glamorous as possible."

Iris smiled. "Laure, you'd look glamorous wearing a bin bag." She paused. "Has Pierre phoned you yet?"

"No, just a message yesterday saying we'll talk when I'm back in Paris. So, can we go shopping then? Tomorrow? Or Thursday if you prefer?"

"Tomorrow is fine."

"Great." She gave Iris a look. "Can you smell something?"

"Yes—is it possible you've made dinner?" Iris teased, because although Laure often said she'd make dinner, she somehow never got around to it.

Laure nodded. "I asked Esme for a recipe and then I walked into Markham and got what I needed. It won't be ready for another hour, though."

"Perfect. It means I have time to go for a run."

"I'll come with you."

Iris turned away, not wanting Laure to see the frustration on her face. "You really don't need to. You've had a busy day, why don't you relax for a while?"

"No, I'm fine." Iris waited for Laure to add, "Unless you'd rather go on your own?" But she didn't and Iris wondered why she had never realized, in the twenty years that they'd known each other, how thick-skinned Laure could be. She reminded herself that Laure was leaving on Saturday and took a breath.

"Come on, then. Let's go and get changed."

"Are we going over the fields again?" Laure asked, following Iris into the hall.

"We can run through the woods if you prefer."

"And then to the quarry?"

Iris frowned. "It's out of bounds."

"We could still go though, couldn't we? You said there was a path around the top that you used to run. It would make a change. And there's nothing really to stop us."

"Only the memory of Charlie."

Laure dropped her head. "Of course. Sorry. I'm being insensitive, aren't I?"

"It's fine." Iris paused at the bottom of the stairs. "I'd better tell Gabriel we're going. Is he still in the garden?"

"I think so. I haven't seen him since lunchtime."

"You go ahead and change. I'll meet you outside in ten minutes."

"Okay."

Iris walked to the walled garden. She could hear the sound of digging long before she saw Gabriel, tucked away in the far corner, his blue T-shirt dark with sweat.

"I can't believe how much better it already looks," she said as she approached. "Your hard work is beginning to show."

At the sound of her voice, he pushed the spade into the dirt and straightened his back. "You think?" he said, turning to face her.

"Yes. You've cleared quite a bit of it already."

"I promised Beth I'd get it finished for when she comes back in August but I think I was a bit optimistic. What about you? How did your meeting with Samantha go?"

"Really well. She had the keys to the house, which was great—and which is why I'm back so late. She's lovely, I really like her. And we seem to get on well, so fingers crossed."

"Do you think you'll get the contract? It must help that you've been to see her personally twice now."

"I hope so. She's narrowed it down to just me and another designer."

"That's great, Iris."

She smiled. "How much longer are you going to be?"

"Why, what's the time?"

"Gone seven."

"Is it? No wonder I'm hungry. I'd better go and shower."

"No rush. Laure and I are going for a quick run. She's made dinner, it will be ready at eight."

Gabriel laughed. "She made dinner? Wow, that's a first." He peeled off his gloves. "Where are you going for your run?"

"Over the fields, I think." She paused. "Laure asked to go to the quarry."

Gabriel frowned. "Why? It's out of bounds."

"I know. I think she's just curious."

"Well, she can be curious about something else."

Iris's heart sank. "Have you heard from Pierre?" she asked, in an attempt to change the subject.

"No. There's been nothing since I spoke to him last week. Do you think I should have gone to see him, even though he told me not to?"

Her heart ached for him, for the guilt he was feeling. If Charlie hadn't been constantly on his mind, Gabriel would have been over to Paris the moment Pierre refused to return his calls.

"No, I don't think so." She laid a calming hand on his arm. "Let's wait and see what happens when Laure is back in Paris. If it doesn't work out, that's when Pierre will really need you."

14

"I feel mean," Iris said, climbing into bed beside Gabriel.

He put down his book and slipped off his black-framed reading glasses.

"Why?"

"Because I'm relieved that Laure is going back to Paris this weekend."

"It's normal. She's been your constant companion with a one-track conversation for nearly three weeks now. It would try the patience of a saint."

"It's just that she seems to have no boundaries, something I never noticed before."

"What do you mean?"

She turned toward him, propping herself on an elbow so that she could see his face. "You know we went for a run earlier? Well, when we came back, we went to have our showers and as I was going downstairs, Laure called to me from her room. So I went in and she was standing there with a towel around her. And then she just dropped it and walked around naked while she spoke to me about Pierre."

Gabriel hid a smile. Iris was quite prudish when it came to naked-
ness, even with him. It had always amused him that she slept in pajamas. She said it came from being sent to a convent school, and being
brought up by elderly parents.

"What did you do?" he asked.

"There was nothing I could do so I just averted my eyes until she
was fully dressed." She flopped onto her back. "Do you want to carry
on reading or shall we turn out the light?"

"I'd like to carry on reading. But I can go downstairs if you want
to sleep."

"No, it's fine, you can read here." The disappointment shadowing
her face made Gabriel hate himself for rejecting her again. But it was
stronger than him, probably because he'd never lied to her before and
subconsciously no longer felt worthy of her. He needed to get over it
before he hurt her even more.

Iris settled herself into her sleeping position and he retrieved his
book. But instead of reading, his thoughts turned to Maggie Ingram,
Charlie's mum, and the letter he'd received. He had worried about
Maggie after Charlie's death. Her husband was in the army, on a tour
of duty somewhere overseas. According to an article in the newspaper,
he'd left soon after Charlie's funeral.

People had asked why Charlie had chosen to cycle all the way to the
quarry in the late evening, as it would have taken him almost an hour
to get there from his school in Winchester. But it seemed that he used to
cycle there with his father whenever he was home on leave, so the general
feeling was that he'd been missing his dad and had gone to the quarry
to feel close to him.

Gabriel hadn't gone to the funeral. Iris had had a hard time ac-
cepting his decision to stay away, given that he'd known Charlie, and
that he'd been there when he died. He'd told her he wouldn't be able to
face reliving Charlie's final moments. The truth was, it was Maggie he
wouldn't have been able to face. At the time of Charlie's death, she'd
been head of pastoral care at the public school where he'd been a day

pupil, and Gabriel could understand that it must have sometimes been hard for Charlie to have his mum around. But something really bad must have happened between them for Charlie to use his dying breath to give her such a damning message. Because what Charlie had actually said wasn't *Tell Mum I love her* but *Tell Mum I'll never forgive her.*

15

Iris paused at the gate to catch her breath and stretch her calf muscles. For the first time, Laure hadn't wanted to go with her on her run and it was amazing how free she'd felt as she'd run through the dappled shade of the woods.

Her first emotion on waking that morning had been one of relief. Laure was leaving on Saturday, which meant there were only two more days to get through before she got her life back. She'd immediately hated herself for being uncharitable. But the truth was, Laure was harder work than she'd thought.

She moved toward the house, bracing herself. But there was no sign of Laure hovering in the hall, or running down the stairs to meet her. Maybe she hadn't heard her come in. Iris kicked off her trainers, peeled off her socks and tiptoed to the kitchen, desperate for a drink. She pulled the drawer to the right of the dishwasher open and reached for a glass. Her hand came to a stop in mid-air. There were no mugs or glasses, just packets of pasta and rice and other foodstuffs.

Frowning, she walked to the other side of the kitchen, to the row of cupboards near the cooker, where those foodstuffs should have been.

She opened the doors one by one and found not just glasses, but mugs, plates, bowls and other small dishes, all removed from the drawers near the dishwasher and rehomed into the cupboards.

"You're back!"

Iris whipped around. Laure was standing in the doorway. "You re-arranged the kitchen," she said, unable to keep the accusing tone from her voice. But Laure seemed oblivious and nodded happily.

"Yes. I thought it was funny that you would keep cups and plates in a drawer. You never did before."

"No, not until I realized that it was more practical to empty the dishwasher straight into the drawers next to it instead of having to cross over to the other side of the kitchen," Iris said curtly. "Same with the food; near the cooker is more logical."

"Oh." Laure looked crestfallen. "Do you want me to put it back to how it was before?"

"Yes, please."

"Okay. It's just that I've made a decision about Paris."

Iris put a smile on her face. That morning, she'd reminded Laure to book her Eurostar ticket.

"Great. Let's go and sit in the garden and you can tell me about it."

The terrace was almost too hot for Iris's bare feet. She hopped over it quickly, jumped onto the grass and headed for the swing seat, Laure following behind.

"So, which train are you getting?" Iris asked, once they were settled.

Laure turned earnestly toward her. "I'm not. I've decided not to go to Paris this weekend. I'm not ready. Pierre hasn't had the decency to phone, he's only ever communicated by message. I asked him this morning if he'd come to a decision about his daughter and he said he hadn't. So what's the point of me going?"

"To talk," Iris said desperately. "The two of you need to talk."

"Not until he comes to a decision," Laure said stubbornly. "He knows where I stand, we've been messaging about it. It's either me or his daughter. If Pierre chooses to be part of his daughter's life, I won't be in his. It's as simple as that."

Iris took a breath. "What about your job? Can you take more time off?"

"No, it's not easy in the advertising industry at the moment. I spoke to my boss and he said they can't carry me indefinitely. I don't have any more holiday to take, and they don't want me to take unpaid leave."

"Then what are you going to do?"

"I've already done it. I resigned."

"Oh, wow. Right." Iris reached up, took the elastic from her hair, then shook it out, trying to find something to say that wouldn't sound like a criticism, because she couldn't believe that Laure had given up the well-paid job which she'd always enjoyed, especially in the current economic climate. But she couldn't find anything.

Laure reached over and placed her hand on her arm. "Don't worry, I have savings, I won't be a burden on you and Gabriel." Iris did a double take, alarm shooting through her body. *Laure intended on staying longer?* "That is all right, isn't it?" Laure continued.

Once again, Iris found herself searching for something to say. "I thought you'd be going to see your mum. She must be worried about you."

"She's not. She said she's sure Pierre and I would work it out and that all couples go through bad patches."

"Did you tell her Pierre has a child?"

"No. I'd only get an 'I told you so' lecture. She's always said I'd regret giving up my chance to have children, pointing out that Pierre could have one anytime if he changed his mind." She gave a bitter laugh. "She was right."

"Have you told Pierre you're not going back this weekend?"

"Yes."

"What did he say?"

"I think he was shocked, which was good. He asked when he would see me and I said I didn't know. It was good to have the upper hand for once."

Iris gave her a quick smile. "Do you mind if I jump in the shower? I feel really sweaty after that run. We can talk again after."

"Of course, go ahead. I'll still be here when you come back."

Iris walked quickly to the house, blinking back sudden tears. *It's okay,* she told herself. *It's going to be okay.*

In the bathroom, she turned on the shower, stripped off her clothes and let the water cascade onto her, needing to obliterate all thought, just for a few seconds. Her emotions were all over the place. Laure needed to go back to Paris. For three weeks now, apart from two days away, she'd barely had more than fifteen minutes to herself. She didn't know if Laure had become needy because of what had happened with Pierre, or if she had always been needy. She thought back to the weekends and holidays they'd spent together, and arrived at the difficult truth, that Laure was her polar opposite. It had never mattered, during those holidays and weekends away, that Laure had always been by her side, because she'd been happy to see her and spend time with her, and it had only been for two days, or a week, so her constant presence had never felt too much. It had never been indefinite. But now, the thought of Laure staying even a week longer was overwhelming.

Reaching blindly for the tub of body scrub, she twisted off the lid, scooped out the grainy mixture and buffed her body vigorously, mentally wanting to rid herself of the film of shame she was sure was on her skin. She couldn't help wondering if the reason Laure hadn't joined her on her run was because she'd wanted to call her office without her being there.

She finished her shower and wrapped herself in a towel. In the bedroom, she dressed quickly in clean shorts and a T-shirt, and opened the bedroom door. Laure was hovering on the landing.

"I was going to make a smoothie," she said. "Would you like one?"

"I'll make it and bring it to you in the garden, if you like," Iris offered.

But Laure was already heading to the kitchen. "What shall we make for dinner tonight?" she called over her shoulder. "We can make a start on it."

Her mood dipping further, Iris followed her downstairs and while Laure made smoothies, she began preparing dinner. By the time she heard Gabriel coming in from the garden, she was more than ready for him to take over. Laure, perched on the countertop while Iris peeled and sliced, hadn't stopped asking what she would do in her situation. But whatever she said, Laure would challenge it, not because she was being argumentative but because she was challenging everything to do with Pierre, even her own thoughts, one minute hating him, the next loving him. She might have felt that she'd taken back some control of her life in resigning from her job, but to Iris, Laure seemed just as lost as ever.

"Gabriel's here," she said, hoping to stop the constant flow of agonizing.

"Oh good." Laure slid elegantly from the countertop. "Maybe he'll be able to tell me what to do. Sometimes I think he knows Pierre better than I do."

Not anymore, Iris wanted to say.

Gabriel came in and looked at Iris over Laure's shoulder—*How has she been?* Too late, Iris realized she should have gone to find him in the garden and warn him that Laure had decided not to go back to Paris. All she could do was give him a quick smile.

"You look better," he said to Laure.

"I have some news," she announced.

Gabriel leaned back against the countertop. "Oh?"

"I've handed in my notice."

Iris, watching Gabriel carefully, saw him smother his surprise. "Right," he said. "Great." There was a pause. "So, what are your plans?"

"I don't really have any for the moment." She looked at him, her eyes wide. "It is all right, isn't it, me staying here a bit longer?"

"Yes, sure. Of course." He ran a hand through his hair. "I need a drink. To celebrate," he added hastily.

Iris threw him a murderous look. "In that case, let's have champagne. I'll get it."

Gabriel caught her eye—*I'm sorry.*

Relieved to get away, Iris went to the fridge in the garage that they used for overspill, and where they kept champagne for impromptu celebrations. She stood for a moment, letting the gentle hum of the fridge soothe her frayed nerves. Maybe this is where she could hide when Laure got too much for her; here, she could pretend that she hadn't heard her calling. The thought that she might be reduced to hiding in the garage, just to get some peace, made her throat swell.

She opened the fridge. Goose bumps flashed on her skin at the blast of cold air. She blinked in the yellow light and took a bottle of champagne from the lower shelf. Returning to the house, she found Gabriel and Laure waiting silently in the sitting room, as if they didn't want to start a conversation without her being there. There were three crystal champagne glasses ready on the low table, and in the late evening sun flooding through the window, they glittered like small towers of diamonds.

"Here." Iris smiled as she handed the bottle to Gabriel. "I'll let you open it."

Gabriel twisted the wire from around the cork and eased it from the bottle. There was an explosive pop, followed by a splintering sound, and three pairs of eyes swivelled to the large silver-edged mirror that hung on the wall above the fireplace.

"Damn," Gabriel said, staring at the huge fissure running down the length of it.

Laure pressed a hand to her heart. "I've never seen that happen before."

Iris stared at their reflections, Gabriel and Laure on one side of the crack, her on the other, like a photo torn down the middle. She gave a nervous laugh. "I hope it doesn't mean we'll have seven years' bad luck."

"I'm sorry."

"Don't be silly, it was an accident. I didn't like that mirror much anyway." Iris swooped to pick up a glass and handed it to Gabriel. "Come on, let's drink."

Except that nobody seemed to know what to drink to. Instead, they clinked their glasses together and smiled bright smiles.

16

"Are you all right with Laure staying here for the unforeseeable future?" Iris asked Gabriel, when he emerged from the shower.

He gave a helpless shrug. "What choice do we have? We can't force her to leave, any more than we can force her to go back to Paris. As long as she doesn't start making any more changes. You are going to make her put the kitchen back to how it was before, aren't you?"

"Yes, of course."

"Why did she do it without asking?"

"Apparently, as she's going to be staying with us longer, she thought she'd arrange it as she would want it."

"That's crazy."

"She thought we'd be pleased. She still thinks that her way is better."

In the mirror, she watched from under her lashes as Gabriel pulled the towel back and forth over his shoulders, sweeping away beads of water. He'd always been in good shape but he had lost weight since Charlie Ingram. Her senses awakened by the smell of clean skin, she let her eyes travel over his broad chest, then followed the line of hair downward from his stomach. But when he quickly brought the towel down and knotted it around his waist, she averted her eyes. Had he seen her watching, seen her desire?

"More importantly," Gabriel said, returning to the beginning of their conversation, "how do *you* feel about her staying longer?"

"Fine. It's just—" Iris stopped.

"Go on."

She turned to face him. "She's quite invasive, and sometimes, I just need to be on my own."

"Then tell her. She'll understand."

Iris reached for her hairbrush. "I can't even go for a run without her. And she's still asking to go to the quarry. It's like she's obsessed with it."

Gabriel frowned. "Really?"

"Yes. Yesterday, she wanted to go and see where Charlie fell."

Incredulity widened Gabriel's eyes. "But she knows it's out of bounds, doesn't she? There's a huge sign that says trespassers will be prosecuted."

"She said that in France nobody would block off such a beautiful place just because someone had an accident there. Her argument was— why should everyone else pay for one person's stupidity?"

Gabriel visibly winced, then took a towel from the rail and rubbed his hair with it, hiding his face from her. "It's always amazed me how some people get a kick out of visiting the site of an accident. I never thought Laure would be like that."

He lapsed into silence and Iris gave an involuntary shiver at how much had changed between them. Before, he might have reached out and she would have pulled him toward her, and he would have dropped his towel, lifted her onto the sink and held her there, his arms tight around her. And she would have wrapped her legs around his waist and drawn him into her. But not tonight. Tonight he didn't reach out to her. Instead, he went through to the bedroom.

She was about to follow him when she found herself hesitating.

Gabriel hadn't given her body as much as a glance. When was the last time he looked at her with desire, had run his finger down her bare back as she stood cleaning her face in the mirror, and laughed as she squirmed and shivered, unable to bear the butterfly touch on her skin? When was the last time he had told her she was beautiful? What if it wasn't him, but her? Or rather, her body.

Slowly, she turned toward the mirror on the back of the door. She couldn't remember the last time she had looked at herself, *really* looked at herself, closely, minutely. She'd been aware of changes in her face as the years passed, the fine creasing around her eyes, the faint track lines across her forehead, not too deep yet, not something that she'd wasted time worrying about. But she had never examined her body, had never looked for sagging and drooping. None of the older women in her family—her mum, her aunts—had been as slim later in life as they'd been in their youth, and Iris hadn't expected to be either. Breasts drooped, waists thickened. That was life.

Raising her hands, she cupped them under her breasts and pushed upward an inch or so. It was where they used to be, Iris thought, looking at them full-on, then twisting her body for a side view. Which means they'd definitely dropped. She lifted her right arm to the side and with her left hand, pinched the flesh between her breast and armpit, and was shocked at how much there was of it. She faced the mirror again and stuck both arms out, checking for loose flesh. There was none, but when she looked closer, she could see the beginnings of it. Leaving her arms outstretched, she let her eyes travel down her body to her waist. She still had one, but it wasn't as well-defined as before, and she remembered that the last time she'd bought a pair of jeans, she'd had to buy a larger size.

Iris lowered her arms and turned from the mirror. She wasn't worried about her legs; long and slim, they were her best feature. She reasoned with herself; she hadn't doubled in size, she'd put on half a stone at the most. Those few extra pounds couldn't be the reason Gabriel no longer desired her. But still, she was glad to put on her pajamas before walking through to the bedroom.

"How's Esme?" Gabriel asked as she climbed into bed. "Have you heard anything from her?"

"Not since dinner last Saturday. I might go around tomorrow." Iris hesitated, because she didn't want to go back to talking about Laure. But there was something bothering her. "When Laure told me she'd resigned, she said she wouldn't be a financial burden on us because she has savings. But we wouldn't expect her to pay for anything anyway, and even if we did, a few groceries wouldn't break the bank. Why would she think she might be a financial burden on us, unless she intended to stay for a very long time?"

"Try not to get ahead of yourself," Gabriel said. "Let's just take it one day at a time. If it becomes too much, we'll sort something out."

17

Another tug and the withered roots of a small pear tree that Gabriel was sure had never borne fruit emerged from the earth. A final heave and out it came.

Puffing from his exertions, Gabriel stopped to catch his breath. It had taken a huge amount of digging to release those woody tentacles. The crater in front of him must have been six feet wide by four feet deep and the tree had been tiny. It seemed to Gabriel that roots, like lies, were insidious.

In hindsight, he should have told the paramedics—and the police when they'd asked—the true message Charlie had burdened him with. That way, it would have been their decision whether or not to tell his mum, and Gabriel was pretty sure they wouldn't have. Instead, they would have pretended to her that he had never regained consciousness. Now, Gabriel had the burden of knowing he'd betrayed Charlie.

His death had been recorded as an accident, but sometimes, in the dark of the night, another fear haunted Gabriel, that maybe it hadn't been an accident. Because *Tell Mum I'll never forgive her* wasn't all that Charlie had said. In the silence that had followed, as Gabriel sat with Charlie's hand clasped in his, cursing that despite all his medical training, he was unable to alleviate Charlie's suffering, Charlie had whispered the final part of his brutal message—*This is her fault. She shouldn't have done what she did.* And then—*He shouldn't have told me.*

The wooden door scraped open. Looking up, Gabriel saw Iris approaching with two steaming mugs of coffee balanced on a small tray. He smiled gratefully, glad that his mind wouldn't return to the eternal question—what could Maggie Ingram possibly have done to cause her son so much distress?

"You couldn't have come at a better time," he said, peeling off his green gardening gloves and wiping his brow with the back of his hand. He noted Iris's black running shorts and T-shirt. "Good run?"

"Yes, great," she said, handing him a mug.

"Thanks." He looked behind her. "Where's your shadow?"

"In the shower. I've got it down to a fine art. Now, when we come back from a run, I don't jump straight in the shower, I wait until she's had hers, then I have mine. That way, I get half an hour's peace. And I don't get to see her naked," she added.

Gabriel smiled. "Clever."

She nodded toward the fallen tree. "It must have taken quite a lot of work to get that out."

"It did. But I enjoyed the challenge." He paused. "I've decided to go and see Pierre."

"Did he reply to the message you left?" Iris asked, because as soon as Laure had told them she wasn't returning to Paris, Gabriel had called Pierre. As usual, he hadn't picked up, so Gabriel had left a voicemail offering to go over.

"No, which is why I'm going. This whole situation between him and Laure is driving me crazy. I don't understand Laure's decision not to go back. Doesn't she want to see Pierre?"

"I think she's worried about what Pierre might tell her. When will you go?"

"Friday, so that I can spend the weekend with him. I should have gone before, right at the beginning." He moved to the bench, put his mug down, and sat with his arms resting on his knees, staring at the ground. "This business with Charlie—it's made me take my eye off the ball."

"Stop beating yourself up. Pierre told you not to go and you respected his wishes."

"I know, but now I'm kicking myself. Pierre's my best friend, I should have been there for him."

"You were," Iris protested. "Look at the number of times you called, the number of messages and voicemails you left him. He only had the decency to call you once, and he's barely replied to your messages."

"Which is so unlike him, it should have been a warning."

"Stop. You'll be seeing him soon enough. Have you booked your ticket?" Gabriel nodded. "Great." She opened her mouth to say something else, then hesitated.

"What?" he asked.

Iris flushed. "There was something I wanted to run by you."

"Go on."

"You know I popped in to see Esme yesterday? Well, she mentioned that there wasn't enough for Joseph to do, and—"

"Joseph?" Gabriel interrupted. "Oh yes, their gardener. I thought you meant Hugh for a moment."

"No, Joseph. Anyway, Esme was saying that they didn't really have enough for him to do, so I said he could come here three days a week and give you a hand."

"What?" Gabriel stared at her. "But I don't need help. More to the point, I don't want help. I like being out here on my own."

"He wouldn't be here all the time."

An unexpected rage took hold of him. How had she not understood that the walled garden was his refuge, his sanctuary? "I don't want him here at all!"

He waited for Iris to back down, to say that she would tell Esme they didn't need Joseph after all.

"Well, I'm sorry," she said stiffly. "It's done now. He starts tomorrow."

"No." He shook his head stubbornly. "There are plenty of people in the village who need a gardener. Joseph can go and work for them."

"I thought you'd be pleased. I thought you could do with a bit of male company."

"Or maybe you just wanted me to be stuck with someone because you're stuck with Laure," he hit back.

"Now you're being ridiculous."

Knowing that she was right, he pulled her toward him. "Sorry, sorry. That was a stupid thing to say." She remained rigid in his arms and he knew that he would have to give way, not just because going back to Esme would put Iris in a difficult position, but also because he owed her. He owed her for everything he'd put her through since he'd found Charlie in the quarry. "All right," he said, trying not to sound too grudging. "Joseph can come."

18

Joseph peered over Iris's shoulder at her designs for the walled garden, spread out on the kitchen table.

"These are really good, Iris," he said.

Her cheeks flushed at the warmth in his voice. "Thank you."

He moved to the table and leaned on his forearms, burnished a deep copper by his outdoor work, to take a closer look.

"I love what you've done here," he said, pointing to the area she'd earmarked for a lily pond. "It's a really unusual feature."

Iris had worked on her ideas for the garden all day yesterday, most of the time with Laure looking over her shoulder. If she hadn't decided to go for a walk, she'd be peering over her shoulder now.

"What do you think about the stream running through it?" Iris asked Joseph. "Would it be possible?"

He tipped his head to one side. "I don't see why not, as long as we can use the water from the underground well Gabriel mentioned. It's a great idea, much better than the fountain we originally spoke about."

"I'm glad you approve."

Joseph straightened up. "I do, very much. I can't tell you how much

I'm looking forward to working here." He nodded toward her designs. "Can I take these with me? I'd like to study them more closely."

"Sure."

"Thanks. See you later, Iris."

Iris watched him walk down the path, the guilt she felt for bringing him here still with her. It had come from a good place; she'd honestly thought Gabriel would appreciate the help, given that he wanted the garden finished by the time Beth came back in August. It was why she'd made some sketches of how she thought the garden could look. She was glad that Joseph had seemed to like them, but maybe she should have run them by Gabriel first. She sighed. Another thing to feel guilty about.

"I'm back!" Laure's voice was followed by the slam of the front door. Iris automatically reached for a bottle of water and poured herself a glass, mentally preparing herself for what Laure was about to tell her. She knew Laure's moods so well now she could tell from her voice that she was excited about something.

Laure appeared in the doorway wearing the pretty blue dress she'd bought when they'd gone shopping. Iris stared at her; Laure had her hair cut into a shoulder-length bob identical to hers.

"You've cut your hair," she said.

"Yes." Laure gave her a twirl. "Do you like it?"

Iris tried to smile. "Given that it's the same style as mine, yes I do."

"I felt I needed a change. And guess what—I just got a message from Pierre. He said he doesn't want to lose me and has asked me to meet him at the apartment on Saturday." She flung herself into a chair. "I knew I did the right thing not going back to Paris last weekend."

"That's really great, Laure!" Iris said, giving her a hug.

Laure nodded happily. "He said he can't live a lie anymore and he's going to tell me everything."

Iris straightened up. "But—are you sure, Laure? I thought you wanted time to think things through?"

"I did. But I've realized that I'll only be able to do that once Pierre's told me the truth, the whole truth." She moved from the doorway. "I need to book my ticket."

Iris held the bottle up to her, offering her water, but Laure shook her head, in too much of a hurry for a drink. "I'm meeting Pierre at one o'clock at the flat, so I'll have to get an early Eurostar. Will you be able to run me to the station?"

"Of course."

Momentarily distracted by something that had caught her eye, Laure moved to the window. "Is that Joseph?"

"Yes."

"Has he started working here, then?"

"Today's his first day. He'll be here Tuesdays, Thursdays, and Saturdays."

"Does Gabriel mind?"

Iris frowned. "Why, has he said something?"

"No, it's just that I got the impression he liked being out there on his own, that he found it therapeutic."

Iris felt a flash of annoyance that Laure had understood something about Gabriel that she hadn't. "He'll still have plenty of opportunity to be there on his own."

Her mobile buzzed. She glanced at the screen and held up her phone. "It's Beth. Sorry."

But Laure grabbed the phone from her and accepted the call. "Beth! How are you?"

"Laure! I thought you'd be back in Paris by now." Beth's voice echoed around the kitchen, and Iris remembered that her daughter didn't know that Laure had temporarily left Pierre. "Why are you still there?"

Knowing that she wouldn't be able to speak to Beth for at least five minutes, she went into the garden, desperate for some air. At that moment, Joseph emerged from the shed, looking down at his hands, which seemed to be covered in something black.

"There's a tap behind the shed!" she called.

"Great, thanks." He held up his hands. "Oil."

"Good luck!" she said, laughing.

She wandered over to the glass-topped table and sank into a wicker chair. The sound of running water reached her and a couple of minutes later, Joseph reappeared from behind the shed. He held up his hands to show her they were clean and, smiling, she gave him a thumbs-up.

"I'll pass you to your mum now," she heard Laure say. "Bye, Beth." Laure appeared on the terrace and handed Iris her phone.

"Hi Mum. I haven't spoken to you for a while and I wanted to see how you were."

Her words gave Iris a rush of pleasure. Beth and Gabriel were so close that she often felt like an outsider when the three of them were together. Gabriel had been the one Beth would turn to as a child, the one she still turned to as a young adult. When she FaceTimed, it was usually Gabriel's number she called, not Iris's. It hurt sometimes, but Iris only had herself to blame. The trauma of her pregnancy meant that she'd found it difficult to bond with Beth when she was born, and she never seemed able to bridge the distance it had created.

"I'm good," she told Beth. "It's nice of you to worry about me," she added with a smile.

Beth lowered her voice. "I'm going to worry about you even more now that I know Laure is still with you. I love her, but she can be a bit full-on."

"That might just be an understatement," Iris murmured, checking that Laure wasn't in earshot. But she was farther down the garden talking to Joseph, the Eurostar ticket she needed to buy so urgently apparently forgotten.

"Laure told me about Pierre," Beth went on. "They will get over it, won't they? They won't get divorced, or anything like that?"

"I don't know," Iris said. "It depends on so many things. But she's going to see him on Saturday, so hopefully they'll make some headway."

"What about Dad? How's he doing?"

"He's doing okay. He seems to have found a passion for gardening."

"He's keeping to his promise, then. And hopefully, it's taking his mind off Charlie. Even I can't stop thinking about him, and I hadn't seen him for years."

"I'm not really sure why it's affected him so much," Iris admitted. "I know it must have been a terrible experience, but I thought he'd have been able to put it behind him by now. I don't mean he should forget Charlie," she added hastily. "Just not let it affect all areas of his life."

"He needs another dog," Beth said.

"I know. I've talked to him about it, but he says he doesn't have the headspace to cope with one now."

Beth pulled a sympathetic face. "Poor you, having to cope with that *and* Laure." She gathered her long brown hair in her hands and twisted it on top of her head. Holding it there with one hand, she reached for a tortoiseshell clip lying to the side and pinned it into place.

"You've had a fringe cut," Iris said. "It suits you."

"Thanks." Beth turned her head so that Iris could see it from all sides. "I felt like a change. Laure did too, apparently. The bob suits her. How's your work coming along? Have you heard back about the town house?"

"Not yet. I thought I might have by now so it's not looking very hopeful."

"You should chase," Beth said. "Give her a nudge."

"Maybe I will. Anyway, how are you? And how is Loki? Have you managed to win him around yet?"

"I'm getting there. He doesn't shrink away when I go near him, like he did before."

As Beth chattered about her work, Iris couldn't help noticing how animated she looked, how *fulfilled*, and a sense of loss hit her at the realization that she had never felt as passionate about anything. She enjoyed her work, but she didn't glow like Beth when she talked about it.

"I'm glad you're having such an amazing time," she said, when Beth stopped to draw breath.

"I am. Me and some of the other girls have met a group around our own age from Thessaloniki. We hang out with them on our days off and we're picking up some Greek."

"Sounds fun."

Beth glanced to the upper right-hand corner of her screen. "We're going to meet them soon, so I'd better go. Love you, Mum, speak soon."

"Love you too."

Beth cut the call and Iris sat for a moment, thinking about Laure going to see Pierre. And that was when she realized that if Laure was going to see Pierre on Saturday, there wasn't any point in Gabriel going to see him on Friday.

19

Gabriel peeled off his gloves, moved to the bench and picked up a couple of bottles of water. He needed to make an effort; Joseph had been working alongside him for most of the day and he'd hardly said a word to him.

Joseph's presence in the garden wasn't the only thing irritating Gabriel. Now that Laure was going to Paris on Saturday, he had canceled his trip on Friday. He couldn't help feeling disappointed; he'd been looking forward to seeing Pierre, and to having his conscience salved for not having gone before. It was almost as if Pierre had caught wind of his surprise visit and had decided he'd better talk to Laure before Gabriel pulled the truth out of him. What it actually came down to, Gabriel supposed, was that Laure resigning from her job and telling Pierre she was staying on in England had given him the kick he needed.

And then there was Iris.

"You know you were going to see Pierre on Friday?" she'd said last night. "Well, I'd arranged to meet Jade for lunch near St. Pancras so that I could travel up with you. I thought you might have liked some company. I also thought that if Pierre refused to see you, or hadn't wanted you to stay over, I could have waited in London for you and we could have stayed overnight there and had lunch the next day. Just to get away from Laure for a while," she'd added in a whisper.

"I could still come up and meet you after your lunch with Jade, and we could still stay overnight," he'd offered, feeling he had let her down.

"Don't worry. We'll have all Saturday to ourselves. Maybe longer, if Laure decides to stay in Paris for the weekend."

"If it goes well, she might decide not to come back at all," Gabriel had said, and they'd both crossed their fingers jokingly.

Gabriel carried the bottles to where Joseph was working and held one out. "Water?"

"Thanks." Joseph put down his spade, took the bottle, flipped the lid and took a long drink. Wiping his mouth on the back of his hand, he nodded at the border they'd just cleared. "We're making good progress."

"We are." Gabriel hated to admit it, but Joseph was going to be more of a help than he'd thought. The fifteen or so years between them—Joseph had to be in his mid-thirties—made a difference when it came to the backbreaking, limb-wrenching task of gardening.

"Iris has some great ideas for the garden," Joseph said.

"Yes, I never thought interior design would translate to garden design, but I suppose it's all about an eye for color and place." Gabriel shaded his eyes with his free hand so that he could see Joseph's face. "Where was your last job, before coming to Hugh and Esme's?" he asked, before remembering too late that Joseph had lost his job after getting drunk. "I mean, was it a landscaping job or just general gardening?"

"Landscaping."

"Right. In Winchester?"

"Yes, thereabouts."

Gabriel waited for Joseph to expand, and when he didn't, he found mutual territory for their conversation by returning to the plans for the walled garden.

They were interrupted by a buzz on Gabriel's phone, indicating that he'd received a message. He dug it from his pocket; it was Iris, asking if she could talk to him for a minute. He frowned; she must have something to say to him that she didn't want Joseph to hear.

"Sorry, Iris needs me for something. I won't be long."

He made his way to the house. Iris was waiting for him in the kitchen.

"Close the door, please."

Her tone was so serious that Gabriel wondered what Laure had done to upset her.

He leaned back against the countertop, his arms folded across his chest. "What's up?" He'd never seen her look so nervous before. A sudden fear gripped him. Was it Beth?

"I was putting the washing on," she said, "and I found this in the pocket of your shorts."

He was so relieved that it wasn't about Beth that it took him a while to recognize the screwed up letter in her hand. He stared hard at it, as if just by looking at it he could make it disappear. He felt himself go hot, then cold. Iris was waiting for him to say something.

"Oh that," he said, recovering. "It can go in the bin. It's just advertising for a pension plan."

Iris was wearing a red T-shirt, and it seemed to Gabriel that he could see the color reflected in her eyes, indicating her anger at behind lied to. He caught himself; she wouldn't have read the letter; it was addressed to him and they never read each other's mail.

"The thing is," Iris said, her voice unnaturally calm. "I read it."

He resorted to anger to hide his fear. "Why?" he exploded. "It was addressed to me, which means that it's private!"

"I know, and I'm sorry. It's just that I saw the letter in the kitchen weeks ago, where Laure had put the mail that had come in while we were in Scotland. If it had been advertising, you wouldn't have carried it around with you for all that time. I read it because I thought it might be from a doctor. I was worried you were ill and hadn't wanted to tell me."

"You still shouldn't have read it. Why didn't you just ask me?"

"If I had, would you have told me the truth?"

Gabriel ran a hand through his hair. No, he wouldn't have, because she wouldn't have understood his reluctance to meet Charlie's mum. The letter was from Maggie's grief counselor, who had explained that as part of the grieving process, Maggie wished to meet the person who had been with Charlie in his final moments.

"I'm not going to meet her, if that's what you're wondering. It wouldn't do any good."

Iris looked at him, concern in her eyes. "But Gabriel, wouldn't it give you both some kind of closure, allow you to move on?"

"Absolutely not. I would only have to re-live the whole thing, which is something I'm not willing to do."

"I know it would be painful. But what about Maggie?"

"What about her?"

"Doesn't she deserve closure?"

"I don't see how hearing about the final agonizing minutes of Charlie's life would bring her closure."

"No, but I'm sure she'd like to hear what he said."

"She knows what he said! I told the paramedics and the police and they'd have told her. Even if they didn't, it was in the newspapers," he added bitterly, still upset that someone had had the insensitivity to leak *Tell Mum I love her* to the press.

"Well, maybe she needs to hear it from you." Iris paused, unable to understand his reluctance to meet Maggie. "Maybe she just wants to thank you."

"I don't want her thanks," Gabriel growled. "I did what anyone else would have done, stayed with him until help arrived."

Iris folded her arms across her chest. "Why are you being like this?"

For the first time in their marriage, Gabriel wanted to yell at her, tell her that any meeting between him and Charlie's mum would only bring him endless grief and sorrow. It was one thing to lie to the paramedics and police, but a very different thing to lie to a mother's face about the last moments of her son's life.

"It's not as if you don't know her," Iris continued when he didn't reply.

"Last time I saw her, her son was alive and kicking a football around."

"Okay," Iris said. "You've obviously made up your mind. But have you ever wondered how you'd feel if you were in Maggie's place?"

She left the kitchen, and not for the first time, Gabriel wished he could come clean and tell Iris the truth about Charlie's last words. He knew that for some people it might not be a big deal, that doctors, nurses, paramedics probably told what people call an honest lie, to spare loved ones more anguish. But Iris wasn't big on lies, not even when they were told with the best intentions.

20

Iris left the house, happy to be going to see Esme.

It was cooler today. She put her hands in the pocket of the cardigan she was wearing and grimacing, pulled out a used tissue and a hair clip, both belonging to Laure. Laure was still borrowing her clothes, even her sandals, which were a size too big.

She arrived at Esme's. The front door was open but she knocked anyway. There was no reply so she went tentatively into the hall. Esme was expecting her, she had told her she'd call by.

Aware that Esme might be having a nap, Iris walked down the hall and looked through the open door into the vast kitchen rather than call out. Immediately, her eyes were drawn to the right-hand side of the room and she stopped abruptly. Esme was stretched out on the sofa, her red hair fanned on a cushion behind her, and Joseph, perched on the low table, had his hand on the mound of her stomach. As Iris stared, flustered by their intimacy, Esme murmured something to Joseph and he leaned forward and lay his head where his hand had been just seconds before.

Her heart thudding, Iris turned and walked quickly to the front door, intending to leave. She would call Esme once she got back to the house and tell her she'd been delayed. But there was a part of her that wanted to interrupt whatever it was she had just witnessed.

Making a decision, she took a breath and turned around. "Are you there, Esme? It's me, Iris!"

"In the kitchen!" Esme called back.

Iris expected to hear the sound of Joseph hurrying away. But there was nothing and as she moved toward the kitchen, she was half afraid to go in, in case he was still there with his head on Esme's stomach. To her relief, Esme was on her own, pushing herself up from the sofa.

"I'm sorry, were you having a rest?" Iris asked.

"Just putting my feet up for five minutes," Esme said, smiling.

"Can I get you some water?"

"I'd love a tea. But I can do it."

"Please, let me."

Iris loved that Esme didn't insist. She might not have known Esme very long, but she felt comfortable with her, and as she made the tea, Iris pushed what she'd seen to the back of her mind. Hadn't Esme said that she and Joseph went back a long way? It would be wrong to read anything into something perfectly innocent.

"Joseph said that you have some great ideas for the layout of the kitchen garden," Esme said, over the noise of the kettle whistling.

"Yes, he seemed to like them." Iris moved the kettle from the hob and made the tea as she'd seen Esme do, the first time she'd met her. "It's an interesting project to work on. And Laure has said that she'll help in the garden, which will give her something to focus on. Unless she decides to stay on in Paris." She turned to Esme. "Pierre has asked to see her. She's going on Saturday."

"Yes, I know."

Iris frowned. "Laure told you?"

"Yes, she came by this morning."

"Oh, I didn't realize. She didn't mention it." Iris carried the teapot over to the table and went back for the mugs. "She said she was going for a walk, but she didn't say she was coming to see you."

"Apparently, she wanted to talk to someone on the outside, someone who doesn't know her and Pierre."

"It's lovely of you to give her advice."

"I didn't, not really. I was more a sounding board than anything else. She went to find Joseph after, maybe he was more help than me." Esme nodded toward the teapot. "Thank you for taking over. It's nice to be looked after for a change."

"How are you feeling?"

Esme pulled a face. "The nausea is terrible." She gave Iris a sympathetic smile. "Laure told me you were so ill when you were pregnant that you couldn't face having any more children."

"Yes, I was," Iris said, feeling a real annoyance toward Laure, not just because she'd told Esme about her crippling sickness, but also because she hadn't told her she'd come to see her. Why hide it? Had Laure thought she would mind?

A silver bracelet with a beautiful knotted clasp slid down Esme's arm as she reached for her mug. "Was it tokophobia, do you think?"

"I think it was, in some form or other. But nobody really knew about it, as if a fear of giving birth, or of disgust at being pregnant, couldn't exist. But that was twenty years ago. Things have moved on, I hope."

But the conversation brought the bad memories back and, feeling suddenly panicky, she looked for something to distract Esme. "That's a pretty bracelet. Is it new?"

Esme flushed. "Yes, I saw it online and decided to order it."

There was an awkward silence which Iris didn't fully understand.

"How's Joseph getting on? Is he settling in well?"

"Really well." Esme lifted her arm and gave it a little shake. Iris couldn't help wondering if it was a tell, if the mention of Joseph had linked subconsciously to the bracelet in Esme's mind. It would explain Esme's flushed cheeks when she had mentioned it. "The thing I was most worried about was our close proximity to The Watershed," Esme continued. "If we were at the other end of the village like you, the pub might not be such a temptation. But he seems to have resisted so far."

"That's good."

"How's Gabriel? Is he adapting to being at home?"

"He seems much better in himself since he decided to work on the walled garden. It's taken his mind off things."

"Hugh told me that Gabriel was the one who found the young boy in the quarry."

"It's"—Iris searched to explain—"changed him. Which is understandable. But you think he'd feel—I don't know—valorized for having been with Charlie at the end, happy that Charlie didn't die alone. But he has no positive feelings about it at all. There's just this guilt."

"Because he's a doctor and couldn't save Charlie?"

"That's certainly part of it, although he was reassured by the paramedics there was nothing he could have done. But there's something else, something he won't talk to me about. He used to confide in Pierre, which is another reason I'm annoyed with him, not just for what he's done to Laure, but for what he's doing to Gabriel." She paused. "I'm glad he feels able to talk to Hugh."

"Hugh was saying that they should go for a drink together. I'll get him to call Gabriel."

"He'd like that." Iris glanced at her mobile. "I should go."

Esme stood and pushed her feet into a pair of fuchsia sandals. "Are you doing anything nice this weekend?"

"I'm going to meet a friend in London on Friday, for lunch and shopping. Then Laure leaves on Saturday." She turned to Esme. "Why don't you come to lunch on Sunday? If her meeting with Pierre doesn't go well, and she comes back, I might need some help."

Esme smiled. "That would be lovely. Thanks, Iris."

Iris walked home, her mind on what she had seen, Joseph with his head on Esme's stomach. Hugh had said, the night of the supper, that he'd been away for most of January, when Esme's baby would have been conceived. Esme had reminded him that she'd gone with him and had stayed a few days, and, of course, he had been joking. But . . . Iris gave herself a mental shake. But nothing.

21

Gabriel walked to the village pub, glad that Iris had gone to London for the day. He was still angry with her for reading the letter from Maggie Ingram's grief counselor. He'd tried to justify his anger by making it about his privacy being invaded. But deep down, his anger was directed at himself, for being careless. Now that Iris knew about the letter, he wouldn't be able to get out of seeing Maggie, not unless he wanted to go down in Iris's estimation.

Her words about him being in Maggie's place had struck a chord. If Beth had died in the same circumstances, of course he would want to meet the person who had been with her when she'd died. And hear Beth's last words from the person who had actually heard them. And hope perhaps that there'd been other words, which had only been remembered after.

Gabriel's biggest fear was that Maggie wanted to see him, not because she wanted to thank him in person, but because she knew Charlie would never have said that he loved her. Maybe they hadn't had that kind of relationship. In Gabriel's mind—because of Charlie's distress over whatever it was that Maggie had done—there'd been some sort of argument before he left on his bike. If Maggie asked him what Charlie's real message was, how could he tell her the truth? How could he let her carry the burden of it for the rest of her life? But equally, how could he maintain the lie if she were standing right in front of him?

His phone rang. He knew it was Beth, his phone had a special ringtone for her.

"Hi Dad, I'm just phoning to check you're not slacking on our pact," she said, smiling at him from the screen.

Gabriel laughed. "Guilty as charged. I'm on my way to meet Hugh for a drink."

"I thought I recognized the village in the background. Is Mum with you?"

"No, she's gone to London for lunch with Jade."

"That's nice, she'll enjoy the break. I hope I still have my childhood friends in thirty years' time." She paused. "What's happening on the Laure and Pierre front?"

"Hopefully they'll resolve their differences tomorrow and Laure will only come back to pack her bag." He pulled a rueful face. "She's not that bad; I'll probably miss her when she's gone. But it's been four weeks. Just saying."

Beth smiled. "You and Mum should come to Greece once Laure has left. I know you couldn't before because of your work, but you have time now. I haven't seen you or Mum for nearly a year. I miss you."

"Probably not as much as your mum and I miss you. We'll definitely come, it would be good to get away. I'll speak to Mum about it. Sorry, Beth, I'm at The Watershed. I need to go." He flipped his camera so that she could see the pub. "Hugh will be waiting for me."

"You like him, don't you?"

"Yes, he and Esme are great. Esme is just what your mum needs, a friend in the village."

"I'll let you go, Dad. Have fun, don't get drunk."

"I won't. Love you."

"Love you too."

He found Hugh at the bar. They ordered beers and carried them out to the garden.

"Are you missing the surgery?" Hugh asked, after he and Gabriel had established that they were both fine and glad to be away from their respective houses for a while.

It surprised Gabriel that he needed to think about his answer.

"Not as much as I thought I would," he admitted. "The first few days were the worst because I felt guilty for not being there. I kept wondering how they were coping, how my regular patients were. But to be honest, there are days when I forget I used to be a doctor. It's the garden; they say that gardening is good for the soul and, in my case, that's certainly true. If I didn't have that to focus on, I'd be itching to get back to work. Which wouldn't necessarily be a good thing."

Hugh nodded. "How's Joseph getting on?"

"Fine. He's a good worker," Gabriel added, trying to sound generous rather than grudging.

"Yes, he's a great help to me." Hugh clinked his beer glass against Gabriel's. "Here's to youth."

Gabriel laughed and took a long drink of beer. "Iris told me that he got into some sort of trouble a couple of months back. It was kind of you to take him on."

"Yes. He was fired from Jarmans for drunk driving, and worried he would go completely off the rails, Esme's dad asked us to take him in."

"Jarmans?" Gabriel recognized the name of a prestigious landscaping firm. "I was wondering who he'd worked for. So, how are you enjoying village life?"

"It's a huge change from life in the city, but a good one. And the beauty of it is that we're near enough to London if we want to go up for the day."

They stayed a couple of hours putting the world to rights, and as Gabriel walked home, he felt he had a true friend in Hugh. He thought back to what Hugh had told him about Joseph.

He couldn't help feeling there was something cagey about him.

He might only have worked with him for two days, but any attempt he'd made at conversation hadn't got very far. He was so intrigued that when he got back to the house, he googled Jarmans, mentally shaking his head at himself. Joseph was hardly going to feature on their website, not if he'd been sacked. They probably employed hundreds of landscapers anyway. He looked instead at their projects, wondering which of them Joseph had been working on when he'd wrapped his car around a tree. There was a golf club, and a city park, and the grounds of a public school, St. Cuthbert's, just outside Winchester.

Gabriel stared at his screen. St. Cuthbert's was the school that Charlie Ingram had gone to.

22

Iris carried a bowl of beautifully ripe tomatoes and a fresh-from-the-oven onion tart out to the terrace, put them on the table, and walked down the path toward the walled garden. Red flowers—lobelias, geums, and salvias—spilt onto the path, their colors so bright that Iris felt momentarily dizzy.

She stopped for a moment, took a few deep breaths, then continued on her way. At the entrance to the walled garden, she stopped and watched Joseph as he wheeled a barrow of huge stones to the corner they'd earmarked for a rockery, then lifted them out one by one, the muscles in his arms straining as he laid them alongside others already there. She waited until he'd placed the last one.

"Lunch is ready!" she called.

Joseph straightened up and gave her a smile tinged with relief. "Thanks, Iris, I could do with a break."

"It's looking great."

"Only another fifty barrowloads of rocks to go. Shame Laure's in Paris today, she could have helped," he added, laughing. "Have you heard from her?"

"Not yet. She'll only just have arrived at their apartment."

They walked to the terrace and Joseph went to the tap to wash his hands.

"Isn't Gabriel joining us?" he asked, when he caught up with Iris, nodding at the table set for two.

"He went into town for some shopping, so I'm not expecting him back anytime soon."

Joseph pulled out a chair and sat down. "This looks amazing, Iris. I was only expecting a sandwich. You've gone to a lot of trouble. Even I know how many onions you need to prepare for an onion tart."

Iris reached for a tomato and began to slice it. Without warning, blood rushed to her head. Blinded by a bout of heart-stopping dizziness, she dropped the knife to the ground.

"Are you all right?" Joseph's voice, deep with concern, came from a long way off.

Iris nodded, her eyes closed. "Too much sun. It was stifling in London yesterday, and now again today."

"Have some water." He pushed a glass into her hand. "And let me do that." Reaching across the table, he took the tomato from her.

Iris's hand shook as she lifted the glass to her lips. She took small sips until she felt calm again.

"Sorry about that," she said, embarrassed. "I should really wear a hat when the sun's as fierce as it has been."

"No need to apologize. But a hat is probably a good idea."

Iris let him serve the onion tart. They'd barely begun eating when Gabriel appeared.

"Sorry," he said. "You'll have to wait for your shopping. There's so much traffic I turned back. I'll go this evening when it's quieter."

Iris pushed back from the table, her appetite gone. "Here, have my place. I'm not hungry anyway."

She barely heard his protests as she went into the house and upstairs to the bedroom. She lay down on the bed, and the murmur of their voices lulled her to sleep.

* * *

She was woken by the sound of her mobile ringing. She squinted grog-gily at the screen. It was Laure. She snatched up her phone.

"Laure. How did it go?"

"I'm at Gare du Nord." Laure's voice was heavy with tears. "I man-aged to change my ticket for an earlier train. It's leaving now so I'll be at St. Pancras at around five thirty. I've looked up the trains from Waterloo and I should be in Markham at seven. Can you pick me up?"

Iris checked the time. It was three o'clock. "Of course. But Laure, what happened? Why are you already on your way back?"

"He wasn't there. Pierre wasn't there."

"What do you mean? You were meeting him at the apartment, weren't you?"

"Yes, at one o'clock. But he didn't turn up." Laure burst into noisy tears.

"Don't worry, Laure, we'll sort it out," Iris soothed. "Let me know when you're on the train from Waterloo and I'll meet you at the sta-tion."

"All right. Thanks, Iris."

Iris closed her eyes a moment. The need to calm herself was overpow-ering. She took some deep breaths, then made her way to the bathroom and splashed water on her face. As she patted it dry with a towel, she caught sight of herself in the mirror above the sink. It seemed as though she was looking at a stranger. She felt a weird sense of displacement. Who was she, this woman staring back at her?

The thought that she needed to tell Gabriel this latest news drove her downstairs. Lunch had been cleared away and there was no sign of either Gabriel or Joseph. Stifling a sigh, she made her way to the walled garden. Gabriel had been avoiding her since she confronted him about the letter she'd found, but he wasn't going to be able to avoid her now.

He was sitting on the bench, his elbows on his knees, staring into space. She felt a sudden irritation; yes, Charlie's death had been a tragedy, but surely he should be able to take comfort from the fact that if it hadn't been for him, Charlie would have died alone?

"It suits you," she said, looking for a gentle way in before she hit him with the news that Laure hadn't seen Pierre.

For a moment, he looked confused, then remembered he was wearing the bottle green polo shirt she'd bought for him in London the previous day.

"Thanks," he said, giving her a smile, and for a moment, he looked like his old, pre-Charlie self. "It was nice of you to buy me and Laure presents."

"It made me feel less guilty about buying so much for myself," she joked, because she'd come back laden with bags. "Talking of Laure, she just called."

He shifted along the bench to make room for her. "How did it go? Did she tell you?"

"Pierre wasn't at the flat."

He turned to her, a frown furrowing his brow. "What do you mean? She was meeting him there, wasn't she?"

"Yes, at one o'clock."

"And he wasn't there?"

"That's what Laure said. She was crying so much she couldn't really tell me anything. She's on her way back."

Gabriel rubbed his chin. "But if she's already on her way back, how long did she wait? Maybe Pierre went out and was held up or something."

"If he was, he would have phoned to let her know. And it didn't sound as if he had. I hate to say it, but I think he got cold feet about telling her the truth. I'm just so angry with him. Laure doesn't deserve this."

Gabriel cursed under his breath, then stood up. "Right, I'm going to phone him. And I'm going to keep on phoning him until he picks up."

"Good luck with that," Iris said. But he'd already gone.

Iris sat, mentally preparing herself for the fallout from Pierre's no-show. She felt sorry for Laure; she had thought to have the upper hand by turning up with no luggage, a sign to Pierre that she wasn't going to forgive him easily. But there had been no audience for her small act of defiance. She would come back empty-handed, and more broken-hearted than before.

"Are you okay?" Joseph's voice broke into her thoughts.

She looked up, shading her eyes against the sun.

"Yes, fine, I'm just worried about Laure. Pierre didn't turn up, so she's on her way back."

"You mean she went all the way to Paris for nothing? Why didn't he turn up? Did she say?" He raised his hands, palms toward her. "Sorry, it's none of my business."

She hid her surprise at how much he knew. Laure had obviously been confiding in him. "I don't think she heard from him at all. No explanation, no apology, nothing."

"That's harsh. Poor Laure. She must be pretty upset."

But when Iris collected her later at the station, Laure was not as down as she'd expected.

"I got chatting to someone on the train," she explained, pushing her sunglasses onto the top of her head. "The man sitting opposite me saw I was upset and I found myself pouring out my heart to him. He said that for Pierre to make me go all the way to Paris, then not do me the courtesy of turning up means that he's not serious about getting our relationship back on track. I think he's right."

"So where do you think Pierre was?" Iris asked, grateful to the stranger for getting Laure to a better place.

"I have no idea. I thought he might be at Claire's so I tried calling her, but she didn't pick up. I thought of going around to her apartment, but Pierre has humiliated me enough. I need to move on, accept that my marriage is over." She turned her eyes on Iris. "How did I get him so wrong, Iris? How did I get Pierre so wrong? I never thought he would do anything like this in a million years."

"Gabriel's trying to phone him," Iris said, switching on the ignition.

"He shouldn't bother. Pierre has made his choice and now I need to make mine. And I choose to make a new life for myself."

In France or in England? Iris wanted to ask.

23

It was one of those times when Gabriel regretted the old phones you could slam down hard to show your annoyance with someone.

On Pierre's side, it didn't really matter; he would know from Gabriel's voice how angry he was. It was Gabriel who needed a physical manifestation for the frustration he felt. He settled for throwing his phone onto the armchair.

Pierre was acting so out of character that Gabriel feared his friend was having a total breakdown. He wouldn't have thought him capable of such hurtful behavior, especially toward Laure. He had always idolized her. Gabriel could only suppose, in the same way that he felt guilty toward Iris for having lied to her, Pierre felt such guilt toward Laure that he wasn't able to face her. Gabriel sighed. The only thing he could do, in the face of Pierre's refusal to engage with him, was revert to his original plan and go to Paris. He would go on Monday; there wasn't any point going tomorrow because Pierre might have left Paris for the weekend. Besides, Hugh and Esme were coming for lunch.

At least the need to contact Pierre had given him an excuse to leave the garden and get away from Joseph. Earlier, when Iris had left the lunch table so suddenly—he thought it was because he'd come back without the shopping until Joseph mentioned a dizzy spell—he'd seized the opportunity to find out if Joseph had worked on the St. Cuthbert's contract before he'd left Jarmans.

"Hugh mentioned that you worked for Jarmans before coming here," he'd said, helping himself to a slice of the onion tart that Iris had made.

Joseph had reached for his glass and taken a drink, a giveaway delaying tactic, Gabriel decided.

"That's right."

"Were you with them a long time?"

"About three years."

"You must have worked on some interesting projects."

"I did."

It had been like drawing blood from a stone. But it hadn't deterred him from pushing further.

"When I first decided to do something with the walled garden, I looked at Jarmans's website," he'd said, aware of the lie he was telling. "But when I saw that one of their current contracts was landscaping the gardens of a public school, I guessed that my project was probably too small for them to consider."

"You'd be surprised. Some of our contracts were for quite small projects."

"You're from the Winchester area." Gabriel had made it sound as if it was something he'd only just realized. "The public school mentioned on their website—I think it was called St. Cuthbert's—is in Winchester. Was that one of the projects you worked on?"

"No. My last job with them was for a private individual."

"Right." He'd had to swallow his disappointment. If Joseph had worked at St. Cuthbert's, Gabriel might have mentioned Charlie. But even if he had, the chances of Joseph knowing him would have been slim. There must be hundreds of students at a place like St. Cuthbert's and as a landscape gardener working in the grounds, Joseph would have had little contact with them.

Pushing thoughts of Joseph aside, he retrieved his phone from the armchair and called Pierre one last time. It went through to voicemail and with a sigh of irritation, Gabriel cut the call without leaving a message.

24

"Did you notice how hyped up Laure was tonight?" Iris asked, once Laure had gone to bed. "Almost feverish."

"It's understandable," Gabriel said, carrying their empty wine-glasses to the sink and running water into them. "She's angry."

When Iris didn't say anything, he turned to her. "What's up?"

"You'll think it's nothing."

"Tell me anyway."

"It's just that when Laure came back, she wasn't wearing the same clothes that she was wearing when she left this morning."

He gave a wry smile. "Not something I would notice. But maybe she changed when she got to the apartment."

"That's what I thought. But when I complimented her on the dress, she told me she'd bought it while she was in Paris. And the cardigan. Even her sandals were new."

"I suppose she felt like treating herself." Iris frowned and Gabriel raised his eyebrows. "What am I not getting?"

"She said she bought the clothes before catching the Eurostar back to London. But when she called me from Gare du Nord, she was distraught."

"And?"

"I wouldn't go shopping if I was distraught."

"Hm." Gabriel thought for a moment. "Maybe she only became distraught after? You know—she left the apartment angry, went to buy something to cheer herself up and then, when she got to the station, it all caught up with her, especially when she heard your voice."

Iris nodded. "You're probably right."

Gabriel looked toward the door, then lowered his voice. "I'm going to Paris on Monday but I don't want Laure to know."

"Okay. But why not?"

"Because the last time I was meant to go, I think she told Pierre, even though I asked her not to. And I think that was what pushed him into telling Laure he wanted to see her."

"So maybe he never intended on turning up to their meeting," Iris mused. "Maybe it was a tactic to stop you from going over. Laure thinks he was at Claire's. She's convinced that Pierre is Mathilde's father."

"What do you think?"

"Like I said before, it fits." She paused. "If you're not going to tell Laure that you're going to Paris, you'll have to invent somewhere you need to be, otherwise she'll wonder where you are. You can say you have a meeting at the surgery to talk about when you'll be going back to work." He looked taken aback. "You've been off for six weeks now, Gabriel, so it's feasible."

"Is it really? Yes, I suppose it must be." For a moment, he looked like a cornered animal.

"You're only going to pretend to Laure that you have a meeting," Iris said gently. "You don't have to think about going back yet."

"I agreed to take a couple of months because that's all I thought I'd need. But I'm not ready to go back, not in two weeks' time. There's too much going on, Pierre, and now this business of Maggie wanting to meet me."

His voice trailed off. It was the first time he'd mentioned Maggie since she'd confronted him about the letter last Tuesday. "It's okay, Gabriel," she said. "You can take off as long as you want, they said so."

He nodded, but she could see how shaken he was by the prospect of going back to work.

"Have you decided yet about Maggie?" A closed look came over his face. "You can't refuse to see her, Gabriel."

"Technically, I can," he said. And without another word, he left the room, closing the door behind him.

25

Iris looked through the kitchen window and saw the end of a perfect Sunday afternoon; Gabriel and Hugh sitting together at the table, Gabriel laughing at something Hugh was telling him; Esme sprawled on a sunbed under the apple tree, a protective hand on the mound of her stomach, her straw hat shading her face from the fingers of sun poking through the branches. The only one missing was Laure, who had lain in the sun for an hour after lunch, then had gone to lie down with an almighty headache.

It wasn't just the sun that had caused Laure's head to pound, Iris knew. Before lunch, she'd had a couple of G&Ts, and during lunch she'd drunk several glasses of white wine before moving onto red. Iris didn't blame her for wanting to drown her sorrows. She was putting on a brave face, but her *I don't care about Pierre anymore* attitude was only self-preservation. Inside, she'd be breaking.

Iris put a pot of coffee on the tray, ready to carry it out to the garden. She was about to step onto the terrace when she heard Joseph's voice. She froze, only her eyes moving as she searched the garden. He was there, talking to Esme. She moved quickly back into the kitchen and with fumbling hands, put the tray down on the countertop.

"Get a grip, Iris," she hissed. But there was an image she couldn't get out of her mind.

Yesterday, after she'd arrived back from fetching Laure at the station, she had left her talking to Gabriel and had gone to find Joseph to invite him for lunch today. As she'd headed to the walled garden, she'd heard the sound of running water coming from behind the shed, and had presumed he was washing his hands. Instead, she found him stark naked under a makeshift shower he had rigged up by looping the hose over a large iron hook.

Her instinct had been to retreat. But something had prevented her. Joseph hadn't seen her; his eyes had been closed and his head tilted back under the water cascading onto him. Transfixed by the sheer physicality of him, her feet had refused to move. It wasn't the first time she had seen a naked man, but it was the first time she'd seen one as beautiful as Joseph. It was only when he'd lifted his hand to sluice the water from his hair that she'd managed to move away.

Thinking about it now made her cheeks flame. She gave herself a moment, then took another cup from the cupboard, retrieved the tray, and walked out to the garden. Joseph had joined Gabriel and Hugh at the table, and as she approached, he looked up.

"Hi, Joseph!" Iris called casually.

"Iris." He raised a hand, shading his eyes. "I hope you don't mind me coming by, but I needed to speak to Hugh about something."

Iris set the tray down. "No problem at all." She risked looking at him and with an effort, held his gaze. "Have you time for coffee?"

He hesitated, and Hugh jumped in. "Yes, he does." He looked at Joseph. "You said you've stopped the leak for now, so have a coffee and I'll come back with you and we can look at it together."

He pulled Esme up from her sunbed and they settled around the table, Joseph next to Iris. She couldn't help being conscious of the heat emanating from his body. The sun was intense; a trickle of sweat formed between her breasts and she pressed the cloth of her dress to her chest to absorb it.

"How's Laure doing?" Joseph asked quietly as Gabriel poured coffee.

"It's hard to tell."

"Has she been able to speak to Pierre, find out why he didn't turn up?"

"Nobody has been able to speak to him, so we don't know what happened, what made him change his mind about seeing her," Iris replied. "I'm not defending Pierre but it's obvious he's going through some sort of crisis. He would never normally behave in such a way."

"You have to feel sorry for Laure, getting her hopes up, then having them dashed. She's lucky to have you and Gabriel."

Gabriel turned to them. "Did I hear my name?" he asked, and Iris felt a spark of annoyance at his interruption.

"I was saying how lucky Laure is to have you and Iris looking out for her," Joseph explained.

"It's about doing the right thing," Gabriel said, a little pompously, Iris thought. "Laure's like family, we would always be here for her."

Iris couldn't help herself. "Talking about doing the right thing, have you decided whether or not to meet Charlie's mum?"

Gabriel stared at her with such disbelief that Iris wished she could take the words back. The uncomfortable silence was broken by Esme laying a hand on his arm.

"You don't have to talk about it if you don't want to. But maybe we can help?"

His hands clenched and for a moment, Iris thought he was going to push away from the table. But then his shoulders sagged.

"I had a letter from the counselor who is helping Charlie's mum. Apparently, she—Charlie's mum—wants to meet me."

"How do you feel about that?" Hugh asked carefully.

"I don't know." Gabriel rubbed his chin. "I mean, I don't see what good it would do. It would be painful for both of us."

"But it might give you both some sort of closure," Iris interjected, repeating what she'd said when she and Gabriel had first spoken about it.

"I don't see how it can ever be closed. It's not as if either of us is ever going to forget Charlie."

"But it's understandable that his mum wants to meet the person who was with her son when he died," Iris persisted.

"From a mother's point of view, I would want to, if it were me," Esme said gently. "Just to say thank you for being there, for my son not dying alone."

"She's already passed on her thanks, via the police. Anyway, I don't need her thanks, I didn't do anything."

"You allowed him to tell his mum he loved her," Iris said. "That's huge."

Gabriel looked at her with such loathing that she physically flinched. She didn't know why, but she had gone too far.

"There's no obligation for you to meet his mother, is there?" Joseph said, breaking another uncomfortable silence.

Gabriel looked as if he had been thrown a lifeline. "No, no obligation."

"Then stop putting yourself under pressure. Do what's best for you."

Iris frowned. "Shouldn't it be about doing the best for a mother who's lost her son?" There was a flare of panic in Gabriel's eyes. "I'm sorry," she said quickly. "I really shouldn't have brought this up. Can we change the subject?"

"Good idea." Hugh clapped Gabriel on the shoulder. "Why don't you and Joseph show me how the walled garden is coming along?"

Iris waited until they'd left. "I shouldn't have said anything," she groaned, putting her head in her hands. "It's just that I can't believe Gabriel is refusing to meet Charlie's mum. It seems cruel. And Gabriel isn't cruel, he's the kindest man I know."

"Stop beating yourself up," Esme said firmly. "It's probably helped him to hear a few opinions." She paused. "I've been meaning to ask—

I'd love your help in choosing the soft furnishings and color schemes for the house. As a client, of course. Is it something you'd be interested in?"

A warm glow spread through Iris's body. "Definitely."

"I know you're waiting to hear back about the town house. I thought it might fill in the time while you're waiting."

"It would, thank you."

"Great." Esme gave her a smile. "Maybe we could have a day out in London together to look at furniture for the nursery. Do you have a free day this week?"

"How about Thursday?"

"That works for me."

"Perfect," Iris said. And it would be—as long as Laure didn't ask to go with them.

26

Gabriel watched the French countryside speed by, glad to be out of the house for the day.

Away from Iris too. He still couldn't understand why she'd brought up Maggie at lunch yesterday. He knew she was frustrated with him—but what had she been hoping? That everyone would come down on her side and tell him that he had to meet Charlie's mum? That hadn't happened. Although Esme seemed to think that he should meet Maggie, Joseph had said he should do what was best for himself, and Hugh had remained neutral.

Deep down, Gabriel knew he was going to have to bite the bullet, because Iris was right. Despite what Joseph had said, he needed to do what was best for Maggie, not what was best for him.

The controller announced their imminent arrival at Gare du Nord. Gabriel pulled his overnight bag from the rack and stuffed his earphones into his pocket, both excited and apprehensive about seeing his friend. It was a thirty-minute walk to Pierre and Laure's apartment from the station, and, as it was only five o'clock, and Pierre wouldn't be home before seven, Gabriel stopped at a café on the Place de la Republique and sat on the terrace, an espresso in front of him.

While he watched the world go by, his thoughts returned to Maggie. On the train, he'd come up with a plan. If all she wanted to do was thank him, and go over Charlie's last moments, he would maintain the *Tell Mum I love her* scenario. If she insisted that Charlie would never have said such a thing, he'd tell her that Charlie hadn't said anything, but that he'd made up the lie hoping it would bring her comfort. If Maggie accepted either of those versions, and went away happier, he would feel vindicated.

His coffee drunk, Gabriel walked to Oberkampf, the area where Pierre and Laure lived, stopping at a boulangerie for a *pain au chocolat*. He felt surprisingly relaxed considering what lay ahead of him, because he didn't doubt that any conversation with Pierre would be difficult.

He arrived at Pierre and Laure's apartment block. The code for the outer door hadn't changed so Gabriel didn't have to ask someone to let him into the building. He glanced at the rows of letter boxes that lined the left-hand wall of the entrance hall, pressed the release button for the inner door and made his way past the lift and up the staircase to the first floor. He'd never understood why his friends had chosen to live in such a sterile building when they could have afforded a flat in one of the beautiful buildings on the main boulevard.

On the first floor, he rang their doorbell. As he expected, there was no answer, so he sat on the floor to wait, his back against the wall. He took out his phone, prepared to while away the next hour or so catching up on the increasingly depressing news. Whenever the downstairs door clicked open, he looked up, hoping to hear Pierre's footsteps on the stairs. Instead, he would hear the whir of the lift running down its shaft in response to the call button in the hall below.

Seven o'clock came, and went. Gabriel shifted his position, stretching his legs out in front of him. Doubts were beginning to set in. What if Pierre had a dinner tonight? What if, as Laure suspected, he was with Claire, or whoever the mother of his child was? In Laure's absence, he might have moved in with her. He cursed his friend under his breath. *You'd better not let me down, Pierre. You'd better turn up.*

The downstairs door clicked open again and this time, Gabriel heard someone coming up the stairs. He pushed to his feet, but the man who appeared wasn't Pierre, and after a curious *Bonsoir*, he continued along the corridor and up to the second floor, then to the third. There was the distant rattle of keys, followed by the sound of a door slamming shut. Then silence.

It was now eight o'clock. If Gabriel had had the keys to their flat, he might have been tempted to go in and wait there. But he hadn't thought to take them with him; it was one thing to go into their apartment with Laure and Pierre's permission, but a completely different thing to walk in without their knowledge.

Gabriel looked around. There were five other apartments on this floor of the building and he knew, from conversations with Pierre and Laure, that they didn't socialize with their neighbors. That was why they'd chosen to live in such an impersonal building, Pierre had joked. He didn't want to live in the sort of place where neighbors popped in and out of each other's homes. Pierre was an enigma in that sense. When he had to socialize, he did it very well; he would talk to everyone in the room and generally be the life and soul of the party. But he wasn't interested in small chat, and wouldn't normally choose to talk to someone he didn't know. An introverted extrovert, Gabriel supposed.

On a couple of occasions, when he and Iris had been using the apartment, they had bumped into the elderly woman who lived opposite. He stood up, brushed himself down, and went to ring on her doorbell.

For a while, the only sound inside was from the television, the volume turned up so loud that Gabriel knew she was watching the news. Eventually he heard someone on the other side of the door and guessed she was looking through the spyhole to check who was there. There was a rattle of bolts and the door opened a crack.

"I'm sorry to disturb you," Gabriel began, stooping so that she could see his face. He spoke reasonable French, and what he had to ask wasn't difficult, so he carried on. "I'm looking for Pierre." He pointed to the door of Pierre and Laure's apartment.

She nodded, and he knew that she had recognized him.

"I haven't see him for a while," she said. "His wife was here on Saturday, I saw her go into the apartment. But I didn't see him."

"When was the last time you saw him?"

She thought for a moment. "Last week, when I went down to take my rubbish to the bin in the courtyard. He was on his way out." She paused. "I haven't seen his wife for a while, apart from on Saturday."

"She's with us, in England."

"Ah!" A smile crossed her face.

He debated whether to ask her to tell Pierre, if she heard him come in later that evening, that he was looking for him. But he didn't want to put her out.

"If I see him, I will tell him you were here," she said, as if she had seen his inner struggle.

He smiled. "Thank you. Have a good evening."

Gabriel waited until she'd closed the door, then took out his phone and called Pierre. It went straight through to voicemail. *"Pierre, it's me, Gabe. I'm here in Paris, waiting outside your apartment. Can you give me a call, let me know what time you'll be back?"* For good measure, he sent more or less the same message to Pierre's WhatsApp.

There was a brasserie on the other side of the road. He crossed over, chose a seat on the terrace and ordered *steak frites* and a glass of red wine. It came so quickly that he stretched out his meal by ordering dessert, and then a coffee. At nine thirty, with no sign of Pierre going into his building, and no message from him, Gabriel resigned himself to spending the night in a hotel. Tomorrow, he would go to Pierre's workplace and confront him there.

27

Iris snatched up her phone. Gabriel had called last night to tell her that Pierre hadn't been at the apartment and that he was staying in Paris overnight.

"I'll go to his office tomorrow morning," he'd said. "I'm not leaving Paris until I know where he is."

"He is with Claire," Laure had declared, when Iris told her.

"You don't know that. But if you give him the address, Gabriel can go and check, if you like."

Laure had shaken her head. "It would only make things worse."

"Did you see him?" she asked Gabriel now. "Pierre?"

"No."

"Why not?"

"Hang on a moment and I'll tell you. So, I went to his workplace this morning, like I said I would, and asked for him at reception. The receptionist buzzed through to his extension and one of his colleagues answered and said that Pierre was away on holiday. I asked if they knew where he'd gone, and of course they were reluctant to tell me until I said that I was an old friend of Pierre's and that I was worried about him because I hadn't been able to speak to him for weeks. I added that his wife staying with us in England, and that I'd come to Paris to try to see him, so eventually one of his work colleagues Arnaud—Pierre's boss, I think—came to speak to me."

"What did he say?" Iris asked impatiently.

"He said he only agreed to talk to me because he'd recognized my name—apparently, Pierre had mentioned us over the years. Basically, he said that it was obvious to everyone in the office that Pierre was going through some kind of crisis, because he'd become very withdrawn. He hadn't confided in anybody, but one of his colleagues moved in the same circles as Laure's friend, Victoire, and she had heard on the grapevine that Laure had left Paris several weeks before and was somewhere in England. From that, they deduced that there were problems in the marriage."

"I don't suppose you asked Arnaud if he knew anything about Pierre having a daughter?"

"No, because I didn't want to be indiscreet—and because I'm not even sure if it's true."

"What do you mean?"

"Well, when you think about it, we've only heard it from Laure. What if it isn't true? What if there isn't a daughter, what if Laure made it up to cover something else?"

Iris felt herself frown. "Like what?"

"I don't know. But what if she left, not because of something Pierre did, but because of something she did?"

"No." Iris shook her head. "Laure wouldn't lie to us." She paused. "Would she?"

"Maybe." Uncertainty hung in the air for a while. "Anyway, it seems that Pierre messaged Arnaud and said he was sorry, but that he'd decided to take some leave after all, and would be back in the office on Monday the first of August."

"When was that?"

She heard Gabriel draw a breath. "Friday afternoon." He sounded almost triumphant.

It took a moment for Iris to catch up. "So does that mean he never intended being there on Saturday to meet Laure?"

"I think he intended to be there, but then, like you said, he got cold feet. He was at the office on Friday morning but he didn't return after his lunch break. Arnaud wasn't too surprised by his message because only that morning, he'd been persuading Pierre to take some time off. He didn't expect it to be quite so immediate, but he was fine with it."

"Did he say where Pierre had gone?"

"No, but I think he must be in Brittany, and Arnaud thought so too. It's where he always heads when he goes off-grid."

"True. So what are you going to do? Will you go to Brittany? Laure might know where he'll be staying."

"Pierre has made it clear that he doesn't want to see me. He'll have seen my messages telling him I'm here and I also left him a couple of voicemails. So no, I'm not going to Brittany." He hesitated. "I've been thinking—what if he's annoyed with us for allowing Laure to stay with us for so long? What if he thinks we're taking sides? If the story of him having a daughter is a pack of lies, and their problems are because of something Laure did, he might think we're condoning her behavior."

"I never thought of that. But if Laure has made it up, how can we find out? It's not as if we know any of their other friends. We met some of them once, at his fortieth birthday party, but I don't know where any of them live. Funnily enough, I asked Laure if she wanted you to go to Claire's, to see if Pierre was there. But she said it would only make things worse."

"Interesting. The only thing we can do is ask Laure again about his supposed daughter. If it is a lie, she'll trip herself up in the end. Liars always do."

28

Iris pushed her feet into her trainers and went quietly out of the front door. It was only six thirty in the morning, but she'd had a restless night. She was going to London later with Esme, and she needed a clear head.

She climbed over the stile and took one of the routes up the hill. It was much steeper than any of their usual running routes but the view from the top was spectacular. When she was almost at the summit, she found a convenient stone and sat facing the early morning sun. From her viewpoint, she could see their end of the village with the quarry behind it, the fields in front and the wood that lay to its right. She traced the ribbon of road past the duck pond, past Esme and Hugh's house, and all the way to The Watershed. It looked so utterly peaceful. A wave of depression took hold; the beautiful scene in front of her only accentuated the ugliness she felt inside.

Laure had been with them for six weeks now, and sometime during those six weeks, Iris had lost her way. Before, she had known who she was: Iris Pelley, wife to Gabriel, mother to Beth, home enhancer. But things had changed. She was still Gabriel's wife, but not in the same way as before. The physical side of their relationship had gone, and his rejection of her was having repercussions she found alarming. She had never fantasized about anyone before, but now her dreams were haunted by Joseph. If she was honest, she even found herself daydreaming about him. It made her ashamed, because she loved Gabriel and that should have been enough. But it wasn't, not anymore.

Maybe if she and Joseph hadn't started their morning ritual of waving to each other, he wouldn't be on her mind so much. On the surface, it was innocent enough. It had begun last week, on Tuesday morning, when she'd happened to glance out of the bedroom window and had seen him standing in the garden, gazing up at the house. She had watched for a moment, wondering what he was thinking about. Was he contemplating its elegance as the sun climbed over the gray slate roof? Was he contemplating what it would be like to live in it, own it? It was only when she'd moved nearer the window and had given him a little wave that she had broken the spell the house had put him under. He'd raised his hand in acknowledgment, then walked to the shed to prepare for the day ahead.

She had thought it a one-off, so she'd been surprised to see him standing in exactly the same place when he arrived for work on Thursday. Again she had waved, again he had waved back. When Saturday came around, he'd been there again and she had watched surreptitiously from behind the curtain for a while, wondering how long he would stand there, how long he would wait for her to wave. Quite a while, it seemed, because it was at least a minute before she'd made herself visible. Even though he was quite a way from the house, she'd been able to see that he was smiling, as if he knew she'd kept him waiting. And two days ago, on Tuesday, they had gone through the whole ritual again. She wasn't sure what it meant, or if it meant anything at all. It was only a wave—but it gave her a frisson of excitement. It was only a wave, but it felt illicit, intimate.

And then there was Beth. Although Iris had come to accept that they would never have a close mother-daughter relationship, the physical distance between them—because Beth was in Greece—had amplified that emotional distance. It was only now, in the cool breeze stirring the air around her, that Iris finally acknowledged her disappointment when Beth had told them she'd be spending her gap year in Greece, and wouldn't be back until the following August. The three weeks that Beth would spend with them at the beginning of September, before starting at university, would be taken up with seeing her friends before they all went their separate ways again, leaving very little time for her and Gabriel. She might have a couple of shopping trips with Beth, but that was about it.

And Laure. It was two weeks since Laure had come back from Paris and to Iris's dismay, she seemed to have no intention of ever going back. On the contrary, she'd settled even further into their lives by deciding to help in the walled garden, as if she had sensed their eagerness for her to leave and was trying to make herself indispensable.

"Has Laure said anything to you about leaving?" Gabriel had asked the other night.

"No. I've tried to find out, I asked her if she'd made any plans and she replied that for the moment, she wanted to take each day at a time."

"For how long? A week, a month, a year? Why can't she take each day at a time at the apartment in Paris? It's not as if she has nowhere to go."

Iris had laid a placating hand on his arm. "Let's give her another couple of weeks. If she hasn't shown any sign of moving on, then we can ask her to leave."

"Has she really given up on Pierre?"

"I think so. She's convinced he's playing happy families with Claire and her daughter. Apparently, the day he sent the message to his workplace saying he was taking the whole of July off was the start of the school summer holidays."

Remembering that conversation, Iris sighed. Although it was a relief not to have Laure constantly at her side—it was Gabriel who had to put up with her now—it made her dwindling workload all the more evident. Thank God she had Esme's commission, because there'd been no news from Samantha Everett about the town house. Beth had told her to give Samantha a nudge, but the truth was, while there was no news, there was hope, and Iris needed a bit of hope in her life.

Sudden tears pricked her eyelids. She blinked them back; this was not the time to break. She closed her eyes, and let the silence wrap itself around her.

When Iris arrived back at the house, Gabriel was in the kitchen making coffee.

"You were up early," he said, raising his eyebrows.

"I couldn't sleep so I went for a walk."

"Why don't you go back to bed for a while?"

She took bread from the cupboard and put a couple of slices in the toaster. "I can't, I'm going to London with Esme."

"Looks like Laure is going to be here on her own, then."

"Why, where are you going?"

He reached behind her for the kettle. "I thought I'd take a break from gardening and go out on my bike for the day, find a pub for lunch, then cycle back. I feel like getting out, spending some time on my own. It can get a bit crowded around here."

"I know what you mean. Make sure you take plenty of water with you; it's going to be hot."

He left after breakfast and Iris went upstairs to get ready. It was almost nine o'clock and she was picking up Esme at nine thirty so that they could take the nine forty-five train to London. In the bedroom, she crept to the window and peeped out. Heat rushed to her cheeks. Joseph was standing in his usual position.

Her mobile rang. Turning to her bedside table, she picked up her phone and checked the screen. It was Esme.

"Iris, I'm sorry, I've waited as long as possible before phoning you, hoping I'd feel better, but I don't. I seem to have caught some sort of bug, I've been sick all night. I'm afraid I'm not going to be able to go to London."

"Oh no, that's awful," Iris said, immediately worried. "Is there anything I can do? Is Hugh around?"

"He's going to see his brother today but it's not a problem. I'm so sorry to let you down."

"Don't be silly, it's fine."

"You'll still go, won't you?"

"Oh—I don't know."

"I hope you will. I'd really appreciate it if you could take photos of anything you think I might like."

"Yes, I can do that. Or we can reschedule until you're feeling better."

"We could, but I'd like to get ahead before the baby arrives."

Iris frowned; it wasn't like Esme to be stressed. "All right, I'll go."

"Maybe Laure could go with you."

"Good idea, I'll ask her. Are you sure there isn't anything I can do?"

"No, really, I'll be fine. I was up all night so I'm hoping the worst of it has passed and I'll be able to get some sleep." She laughed. "It's almost worth it to be able to spend the whole day in bed."

"Make the most of it. I'll phone this evening to see how you are."

"Thanks, Iris. Have a nice day."

Iris was about to go and find Laure, then remembered that she hadn't waved to Joseph. But he was already walking down the path, a rake balanced on his shoulder. She swallowed her disappointment. Coupled with Esme not being able to go to London, her day had already got off to a bad start.

Outside Laure's bedroom, Iris found herself pausing, Gabriel's remark about wanting to spend time on his own suddenly resonating with her. Did she really want Laure to go to London with her? She didn't—but the prospect of going on her own was somehow worse.

Iris tapped on the door. "Laure? Can I come in?"

"Yes, of course."

Iris opened the door and nearly went out again. Laure was standing in the middle of the room wearing a pair of skimpy knickers and nothing else. Her cheeks were unusually flushed, as if she'd been caught doing something she shouldn't have been doing.

"I can't believe it's so late," she said. "I must have overslept."

"It's fine, there's no rush. I wanted to see if you'd like to come to London with me. Esme is ill, but she wants me to go anyway."

"Poor Esme! What's the matter with her? It's not the baby, is it?"

"No, she has a sickness bug."

Laure nodded slowly. "Thanks, Iris, but if you don't mind, I'll stay here. I need to find a divorce lawyer."

"Oh Laure. I'm sorry it's come to this. Do you want me to stay with you?"

"No, no, this is something I have to do myself. Why doesn't Gabriel go with you to London? It would be good for you to have a day out together."

"He's gone out for the day, on his bike."

"Really?"

"Yes, but don't worry, I'm fine going on my own. I've missed the nine forty-five so I'll get the ten fifteen. I may as well have another coffee before I go."

"Just let me put some clothes on and I'll have one with you."

By the time Laure joined Iris in the kitchen, the coffee was made. Iris poured them both a cup and they drank it standing by the window.

"What time do you think you'll be back?" Laure asked.

"End of the afternoon, probably."

"And Gabriel?"

"The same, I should think. He said he would have lunch in a pub somewhere."

"I could make dinner, if you like."

"That would be great. But you'll have to go shopping, the fridge is almost empty."

"I can do that." But Laure sounded distracted, as if her mind was on something else, and Iris resigned herself to there being no dinner ready when she got back.

"If you don't have time to shop, let me know."

Laure nodded. "Shouldn't you be going? You don't want to miss your train."

Iris drained her cup and put it in the sink. "See you later."

Laure gave her a hug. "Have fun."

She accompanied Iris to the door and closed it behind her, and Iris imagined her trudging upstairs to get her laptop so that she could start looking for a divorce lawyer. She was surprised that Laure was already thinking of divorce, but if she'd learned anything about Laure over the last six weeks, it was that she was mercurial. In a few days' time, she could be talking about reconciliation.

29

Iris drove through the village toward the station. As she passed Esme's house, she looked down the driveway and was alarmed to see Esme getting into her car.

She slowed down and pulled in to the curb a little further down the road. An hour before, Esme had told her she wasn't well enough to go out. Maybe she was going to see her doctor.

She was about to get out of the car and tell Esme she would take her, when Esme's car pulled onto the road. She prepared herself to flag her down—but to her surprise, Esme turned the other way, toward her end of the village. Iris frowned. Maybe Esme was feeling better and had decided to go to London with her after all. But if that was the case, wouldn't Esme have phoned to let her know? And why drive to her house when it would have been logical for Iris to pick her up, as they'd originally planned? She dug in her bag for her phone, in case she hadn't heard it ring. But there were no missed calls, just a message from Laure, asking if she had made it to the station in time for the ten fifteen train.

Pulling out from the curb, Iris drove to the station. She found a place to park and sent a reassuring message to Laure, telling her that she was in plenty of time for the train. But instead of going onto the platform, she stayed in the car, unable to shake the feeling that something wasn't right. Esme's insistence that she went to London without her was strange. She'd said she wanted everything ready for the baby, but the baby wasn't due for another seven weeks. Then there was Laure; not only had she seemed in a hurry for Iris to leave that morning, there was also the message she'd just sent, checking that she was in time for her train. It crossed her mind that maybe Esme and Laure wanted to spend the day together without her. But why not say so? Why pretend that Esme was ill? Yes, she might have been hurt that they'd planned a cozy day together. But being lied to was worse.

The heat hit her as she got out of the car. She looked along the track and saw the train approaching the station. She would need to run—but she stayed where she was. She wasn't sure whether it was the thought of running in the heat that had glued her feet to the spot, or the need to know if there was something going on. Even Gabriel's decision to go out for the day on his bike was unusual. He hadn't been out on his bike since Charlie Ingram, so why today?

She got back in the car and drove slowly toward the house. She let herself in quietly, and listened. There was no sound, which meant that Laure was already outside. She went upstairs and looked out of the window. She could see Laure's sun hat hanging off the tree by the entrance to the walled garden. She should go and tell her that she'd decided not to go to London.

She changed out of her dress and into shorts and a T-shirt. The ground shimmered in the heat as she walked down the path. The silence was palpable, as if no living thing had the energy to move. As she passed the shed, she heard a noise and guessed that Joseph was there, taking a break. She made her way over, intending to say hello. She was about to push the door open when she heard a groan. She paused. Was Joseph ill, had he caught the same bug as Esme? More sounds followed, and understanding what she was actually hearing, she took a quick step back, her cheeks flaming. How could she have been so stupid, how could she not have realized that Esme had engineered the whole thing so that she could spend the day having sex with Joseph? All the signs had been there; her insistence that she went to London without her, and took Laure with her; her mention of Hugh being out for the day. Anger flooded Iris's body; she wanted to fling open the door, shout at them, shame them. But she couldn't bring herself to.

As she backed farther away from the door, two things registered themselves in Iris's mind. The first was that she hadn't seen Esme's car parked outside, the second was that Esme wouldn't have known that Gabriel was out for the day. At that moment, urgent words came to her from behind the shed door, words of love, of desire, of passion, words spoken not in English, but in French.

30

Gabriel put his bike in the garage and went into the house. It was the best day he'd had for a long time.

It was the gentle sunshine coming through the window this morning that had tempted him to go out on his bike—that, and the unappealing prospect of spending the day with Joseph. And babysitting Laure, who had decided to play at gardening.

His trip out had given him the space to think. He still hadn't replied to the request from Maggie's grief counselor, subconsciously hoping that if he didn't, the problem might go away. But he couldn't stall indefinitely; it wasn't fair to Maggie, and anyway, hadn't he worked out what he was going to say? When he'd stopped for a beer and a sandwich, he'd taken out his phone and made the call.

On the way back to the house, he'd stopped at the surgery to talk about taking more time off. He told his partners the truth, that he didn't feel up to returning to work in two weeks' time. To his relief, they'd said that they hadn't been expecting him to, reminding him gently that he was the one who'd insisted two months would be enough.

He found Iris in the kitchen, stirring something in a pan.

"Good day?" he asked, going to wash his hands at the sink.

"Not really."

He flicked the excess water from his hands and reached for the towel.

"Why, what happened?"

"Esme was ill so I went to London on my own." Her voice was short, clipped.

"You should have asked Laure to go with you."

"I did. But she wanted to stay here and contact divorce lawyers."

Gabriel looked at her, relieved to have found a reason for her low mood. "It might not come to that."

"I don't really care one way or another."

Gabriel frowned. "You don't mean that, do you?"

"Yes, I do. Laure and Pierre have taken up too much of our time and energy."

It wasn't like Iris to be in such a bad mood. He looked for something to cheer her up. "I called Maggie Ingram's grief counselor; she's going to contact Maggie and arrange a date for us to meet."

She turned from the cooker and shook her head, as if she was disappointed in him. "I can't believe it took you so long to do the right thing." She took the wooden spoon from the pan and threw it into the sink. "Right, I'm going for a bath. I'll see you later."

Gabriel stared after her. Something had happened, and he guessed it was to do with Laure. He scowled; she was definitely overstaying her welcome. He felt suddenly angry that she was taking advantage of their friendship by putting them in a position where they were going to have to ask her to leave. But there was no way he was going to tolerate Laure upsetting Iris. If Iris didn't do something about it, well, he damn well would.

31

Iris was in the bedroom, getting ready to go to Esme's, when she glanced out of the window and saw Laure and Joseph walking up the garden path, Gabriel some yards in front of them. As she watched, Laure slowed her pace and with a quick look at Gabriel, she grabbed Joseph and kissed him full on the mouth, while Gabriel marched on oblivious.

She turned away, hating the embarrassment that flooded her body whenever she caught sight of Joseph. How could she have been so stupid as to think he'd been watching for her at the window? It was Laure he'd been watching, she understood that now. Their bedrooms were next to each other; the morning she'd gone into Laure's bedroom to ask if she wanted to go to London, and had found her practically naked, she guessed Laure had been parading in front of her window, putting on a show for him.

A week had gone by since she'd heard Laure and Joseph together and whenever she saw them from the window, it was so obvious from Laure's behavior that they were in a relationship that Iris couldn't believe Gabriel hadn't noticed. She heard him come into the house. Maybe it was time to bring him up to speed.

She went downstairs and found him with his head in the fridge.

"Hungry?" she asked.

He jumped at the sound of her voice. "I just need something to keep me going until lunch," he said, turning toward her with a guilty smile.

She squeezed in front of him, and took out a foil package. "A slice of pork pie, will that do?"

"Perfect," he said, unwrapping it with the same excitement as a kid unwrapping a birthday present.

She waited until he'd had a couple of bites.

"I think Laure and Joseph are in a relationship."

Gabriel stopped mid-chew, then swallowed quickly. "Did you say what I thought you said?" Iris nodded. "But—how can she have got over Pierre so quickly?"

"I don't know. Maybe she's not thinking straight, maybe she's trying to make herself feel better by having an affair with Joseph."

Gabriel scratched his head. "Are you sure? About them being in a relationship? I spend most of the day with them and I've never noticed anything."

"I've seen them," she said. "From the window. When they think nobody is looking."

"How long has it been going on?"

"I first realized about a week ago. But I presume it's been going on longer than that."

She didn't want to tell Gabriel that she'd heard Laure and Joseph having sex. She had left the house quickly that day, and had sat for hours in a café in Markham, returning to the house at 5 p.m. Everyone had presumed she'd spent the day in London, even Esme—Iris had picked some photos of furnishings from various websites and had sent them to her—and she had seen no reason to tell them the truth. For the moment, she didn't want Laure to know that she knew about her relationship with Joseph. She wanted to see if Laure would tell her herself. Laure owed her that, at least.

Gabriel put the rest of his pork pie back in the foil, his appetite gone. "What are we going to do about it?"

"There's nothing we can do about it," she said, exasperated. "They're adults, Gabriel."

His brow darkened. "It doesn't seem right. Pierre—"

"Doesn't have a leg to stand on."

"You're right—if it's true about him having a daughter." He glanced toward the garden. "I don't want to go back out there now. Do you think Hugh and Esme know?"

"I have no idea."

"Should we mention it to them?"

"It's not really any of our business."

He unwrapped the foil again and took a half-hearted bite of the pork pie. "Do you think it was going on before she went to Paris? Maybe that's why she didn't hang around to wait for Pierre, because she was already involved with Joseph."

Iris stopped in the middle of filling the kettle.

"I don't know. She was pretty distraught that Pierre hadn't turned up."

"She wasn't distraught when she got back though, only when she phoned you from Paris. And didn't you say that she'd been shopping before she got on the train? You found that strange."

She turned to face him. "What are you saying?"

"That maybe when she phoned you, she was only pretending to be distraught. Maybe she did see Pierre, maybe she told him their marriage was over because she was already with Joseph at that point."

"Wow." She considered this for a moment. "It would explain her bizarre behavior that day, and her decision not to stay even one night in Paris. I found it strange that she wanted to come straight back before knowing how it would go with Pierre. It would help if we could speak to Pierre, get his side of the story. But that's not going to happen, is it?"

"Only when he comes back to Paris at the beginning of August." Gabriel paused. "What are you doing for the rest of the day? How about we go out for lunch, just the two of us? Get away from here for a bit?"

"Thanks, but can we make it another time? I'm going to see Esme."

"Of course. How's she doing?"

"Bored out of her mind."

"I can imagine. It can't be easy for someone like Esme to be confined to bed."

Esme had called her the day after they were meant to go to London, to confess that she hadn't had a sickness bug the previous day, but had been having contractions. She'd phoned the midwife that morning, and the midwife, who lived in the village, had asked Esme to come in. It was where she'd been going when Iris had seen her leaving her house.

"I'm sorry, I should have told you the truth," Esme had said. "But I didn't want you to worry. It was a bit of a wake-up call; the baby isn't due for another seven weeks."

"What did the midwife say?"

"She sent me for a scan and everything is fine but I have to rest. I'm not allowed to go out, so I'm basically lying on the sofa all day. It's so frustrating as there's still so much to do. The rest of the house can wait, but I'd feel better if the nursery was ready." She paused. "Would you be able to come over and bring some swatches for curtains? Then I can have them made up."

"Of course. I'll bring them this afternoon."

She had been over most days since, happy to see her friend and give Hugh a break, because Esme wasn't supposed to get up at all. In the mornings, she moved from her bed to the sofa in the kitchen, but that was the only walking she did.

Iris hadn't spoken to Esme about Laure and Joseph because she was waiting for Esme to mention it first. If she and Joseph were as close as they seemed to be, surely he would have told her about his relationship with Laure? Unless he didn't want her to know. She had tried, but she couldn't shake the image of him with his head on Esme's stomach, nor the intimacy it had conveyed. There couldn't be many pregnant women who would welcome, or encourage, such a gesture from a man if he were only a friend. So if Joseph was more than that, didn't Esme deserve to know that he was in a relationship with Laure?

She hugged the shade as she walked through the village. Esme's front door was open but Iris knocked anyway.

"Come in!"

She headed for the kitchen and found Esme lying on the sofa.

"I'm glad to see you're resting. How are you?"

"Sooooo bored. But fine, otherwise."

"That's good to hear. Can I get you a drink?"

"I'd love a coffee, a proper espresso. There's one of those Italian things in the cupboard over there."

Iris located the percolator.

"How is Laure?" Esme asked.

"She's doing really well. She's been much happier lately."

"That's good. Has she really decided to leave Pierre?"

"I think so."

"That must be hard for you and Gabriel."

"It is." Iris paused. "I don't blame Laure for wanting to move on, although I'm not sure she would have moved on quite so fast if she hadn't met Joseph." Seeing Esme frown, she rushed on. "She talks to him quite a bit, looks to him for advice."

Esme's brow cleared. "I thought for a moment you were insinuating that there was something going on between them."

The coffee made, she carried it over to Esme. "Would you mind if there was?"

"Yes, I would."

"Why?" she asked, setting the coffee on the table. "I mean, they're both adults."

"Yes, they are. But Laure shouldn't get involved with Joseph."

"Why not? Sorry, I'm curious, that's all."

"Because it wouldn't be good for her." Esme reached for her mug and took a sip. "Just what I needed, thanks Iris. So, how is Gabriel? Has he decided to meet Charlie's mum?"

Noting Esme's swift change of conversation, Iris masked her unease with a smile and updated her on Gabriel's change of mind. For the first time, she felt uncomfortable in Esme's company, and as she walked home an hour later, she couldn't work out if it was because she hadn't been upfront with her about Laure and Joseph, or because Esme's words—*because it wouldn't be good for her*—had sounded like a threat.

32

Gabriel almost wished Iris hadn't told him. At first, he thought she must have imagined it, because Laure spent a lot of her time in the garden now and he hadn't seen anything to suggest that she and Joseph were more than just friends. But now that he knew, the signs were definitely there.

What was making him even more uncomfortable was that the relationship seemed to be one-sided, with Laure sending Joseph hot glances, or draping herself provocatively over the spade before calling for his help. She obviously thought Gabriel was blind and deaf, whereas Joseph was more wary. During the last week, Gabriel had seen him, on more than one occasion, move away from Laure when she got too close, shrugging her off physically when she put her arms around him. Earlier, he had heard Joseph telling her to back off. He got it, Joseph was a good-looking bloke, with the sort of charisma that was probably incredibly seductive to women. What made him even more irresistible to Laure, Gabriel thought, was that Joseph wasn't as interested in her as she was in him. He didn't like the idea of Joseph taking advantage of Laure. She was vulnerable at the moment; Joseph could end their relationship at any time, without any real thought as to the effect it would have on her.

No matter how fed up he was of Laure—she'd been with them for nearly two months, for God's sake—he and Iris had a duty to protect her. And if anyone could protect Laure from Joseph, it was Pierre. Gabriel reckoned that if he told him Laure had moved on, it might spur him into action. July was drawing to a close; Pierre would be back in Paris this weekend, ready to start work on Monday morning. Perfect timing.

He took out his phone and messaged Pierre, telling him that Laure had become involved with someone else and that if he didn't come over and sort out the mess he'd created, he would lose her forever.

Gabriel looked through the window at the gathering clouds. A huge storm was forecast for tonight. Perhaps it was an omen.

33

Iris stared at her computer screen. She had finally plucked up the courage to email Samantha Everett, to ask if she'd made a decision regarding the interior designer for her town house. She pressed send and sat back. It was out of her hands now.

The weather had finally broken. The storm last night had blasted away the stultifying heat of the last few weeks. She welcomed the sudden drop in temperature. It was nine in the morning and rain-filled clouds hung low in the sky. Another storm was in the forecast for tonight, stronger than the previous one.

She hadn't seen Esme since Thursday, and she wasn't sure she wanted to see her today. Esme's reaction, when she'd hinted that Laure and Joseph might be in a relationship, had rekindled her concerns about her and Joseph being more than just friends. The first time they'd had dinner together, Iris remembered, Esme had put a hand on her stomach when she'd said that Joseph had every reason to stay on the wagon. That, coupled with Hugh's comment about being away around the time the baby was conceived had made her wonder if Joseph was the baby's father.

Out of the corner of her eye, she saw Joseph go into the shed. Two minutes later, Laure came out of the house and followed him inside. She was wearing Iris's wellingtons.

Her phone rang. "Iris? It's Samantha Everett."

Iris's heart thumped. This could be the phone call she'd been waiting for. She was right to have emailed.

"Samantha, hi. I hope you didn't mind me emailing. I was wondering if you'd had a chance to make a decision yet?"

"Yes, I have. I'm sorry you didn't feel able to revise your quote."

"No, I can certainly take another look at my figures."

There was a puzzled silence. "I think there might have been a misunderstanding. I did say that if you felt you could, I needed to know within the next couple of days. That was a month ago." Samantha paused. "I was quite clear in what I said."

"When was that?" Iris began scrolling frantically through her emails. "Can you tell me the date? I don't seem to have received an email about revising my quote."

"It wasn't an email. I called you on—let me see, I noted it down—on the twenty-ninth of June in the afternoon. I spoke to a friend who was staying with you at the time; she said you were out and asked if she could she take a message. I told her that I loved your designs but wanted to discuss your quote with you and that if you felt you could revise it, to call me as soon as possible. When I didn't hear back from you, I presumed you weren't interested."

"But—I didn't get the message. My friend, she didn't give it to me. I've been waiting, wondering why I hadn't heard from you." Iris knew she was gabbling but she couldn't stop herself. "I can't believe it, I-I don't know what to say. I feel awful that you thought I wasn't interested. I'd love to work on your town house, I was so excited about it." She stopped, feeling near to tears. "I suppose it's too late now."

"Yes, I'm afraid so. I'm so sorry, now I feel awful."

"Please don't, it's not your fault. Perhaps—I don't know—if you know anyone who needs an interior designer, you could point them my way?"

"Yes, I can certainly do that. I really am sorry. If it's any consolation, I was massively disappointed when you didn't get back to me."

"Thank you. Anyway, good luck with everything. I'm sure your house will be beautiful." Iris barely knew what she was saying.

"I hope so. Goodbye Iris, maybe our paths will cross in the future."

Iris cut the call and burst into tears, her phone still in her hand.

34

Gabriel went to find Iris in her office.

"I think I might go out on my bike today, find a pub for lunch like I did last time."

"Okay."

"Is everything all right?" he asked, puzzled by the way she was staring straight ahead, as if she barely knew he was there.

"I emailed Samantha Everett."

"Good, well done. At least you'll know."

"I already do. She called me."

"Ah." He perched on the edge of her desk. "What did she say?"

"That I would have got the contract if I'd been able to revise my commission a bit."

"Couldn't you?"

"Yes, I could have, only I didn't get the chance." She met his eyes. "She rang on the twenty-ninth of June. Laure answered my phone, Samantha explained and asked that I call her as soon as possible. I never got the message." Her voice rose. "A month ago, Gabriel. Samantha called over a month ago and Laure never told me. So the contract went to someone else."

"What? Oh God, I'm so sorry, Iris. Laure—I mean, I suppose she just forgot?"

"Probably."

"What are you going to do?"

"There's not a lot I can do. It's too late."

"Yes, but Laure. She shouldn't be allowed to get away with it. You are going to say something to her, aren't you?"

Iris shrugged. "What good would it do? She forgot, that's all. She had a lot on her mind at the time. She would only feel awful."

"And so she should," Gabriel said indignantly. "She lost you a contract, Iris, a contract you really wanted. All the effort you put into it, including going to see Samantha Everett twice."

"I know."

"Do you want me to say something to her?"

"No, but thank you."

"I think she should know."

"Maybe, but not now. I want a quiet day. If you tell her, she'll feel bad and will hang around me, apologizing."

"Come out with me," he urged. "We don't have to take the bikes, we can take the car, go to the coast."

"I'm fine, really."

"I can stay here, I don't have to go out."

Iris smiled. "Go out on your bike, Gabriel. I've got some tidying to do and I'm going to have a nice, long bath. I'll see you later."

"If you're sure. But I still think Laure should know," he added scowling. "And it would be a good excuse to get rid of her, tell her it's time she left. From what I can see, even Joseph seems to have had enough of her. Pierre will be back in Paris this weekend; she needs to go back, sort it out with him."

Iris nodded. "Okay, we'll talk to her about it tonight."

"Promise? She's invaded our lives enough, Iris."

"Promise."

He left, his desire to go and tell Laure she'd messed up so strong that if Iris hadn't been watching him, he'd have headed straight for the walled garden instead of the house. He felt bad leaving Iris alone, but he knew her well. If she said she didn't want company, it meant she didn't want company. It annoyed him that she'd now spend the day thinking about what could have been while Laure spent the day with Joseph, oblivious to the harm she'd done. A mean thought slipped into his consciousness, that maybe Laure hadn't told Iris about Samantha's call on purpose.

The roads were wet from last night's rain, and as he cycled, his legs already splattered with dirt from the puddles he rode through, his thoughts turned to Pierre. He had never received a reply to his WhatsApp message telling him that Laure had moved on and when he'd checked his phone, there was only one gray tick, which meant that the message hadn't been delivered. Which meant that Pierre had turned his phone off. He pedaled harder, taking his frustration out on the bike, and thought instead about Maggie, and his meeting with her, scheduled for Tuesday. Ever since Maggie's grief counselor had got back to him with a date and time, it had hung over him like a black cloud, looming ever nearer. The good thing was that he'd managed to arrange for Maggie to come to the house, rather than meet in the grief counselor's office. The grief counselor had agreed because he and Maggie knew each other from the past, and because Maggie had been fine with it. All he could hope was that once it was over, he would finally be able to get his life back to how it had been before.

35

The sound of raised voices drew Iris from the bathroom to the bedroom window. From behind the curtain, she saw Laure and Joseph on the terrace below. They were facing each other, but there was a distance between them, as if Laure had stepped back.

"I can't." Laure's voice traveled to her through the open window.

"You have to," Joseph insisted, grabbing her arm.

"No." She pulled away from him. "Not now. I'm going for a run."

"Laure!" But Laure was already running toward the gate.

Joseph stared after her, then took his phone from his pocket. He had his back to Iris but she could see his head bent over the screen. The next moment, he broke into a run and disappeared around the side of the house. Intrigued, she hurried through to the bedroom at the front of the house and saw him run out of the gate.

She hadn't seen Laure since lunchtime, when she'd come to see if Iris wanted to join her and Joseph for a sandwich. Shuddering internally at the thought, she had smiled her thanks and said she wasn't hungry. She barely saw Laure on the days that Joseph came to work, as she spent all her time in the garden. How much use she really was, Iris had no idea.

"How about a run later on, then?" Laure had asked, aware perhaps that she'd been neglecting her in favor of Joseph.

"Thanks, but I've got some tidying to do and I plan to have a long bath," she'd replied.

She'd been tempted to say that she was waiting for a call from Samantha Everett, to see if it would jog Laure's memory. But what was the point? The damage had already been done.

"Okay." Laure hadn't seemed to mind, and Iris couldn't help thinking how much had changed since she'd first arrived.

"Pierre should be back in Paris this weekend. Do you have any plans to go and see him?"

"Not at the moment. I'll wait to see if he contacts me."

As Iris returned to her bedroom, her phone rang. It was Gabriel.

"Just checking to see how you are," he said.

"That's nice of you. I'm fine. I'm about to have a bath."

"Good. Did you see Laure at all?"

"Yes."

"And?"

"I didn't mention Samantha Everett, if that's what you mean." She paused. "I think she had a row with Joseph."

"Really? That doesn't sound good. I hope we don't have even more pieces to pick up. I heard him telling her to back off earlier."

"Her place is with Pierre, not Joseph. I asked her earlier if she planned to go and see him, given that he'll be back in Paris this weekend. She said she didn't. Sometimes I wonder if she'll be with us forever."

"There's absolutely no way," Gabriel said so fiercely that Iris could imagine his face darkening. "Forgetting to tell you about Samantha is the last straw. We can't tiptoe around her anymore."

"How about you?" Iris asked, hurriedly. "Have you had a good day?"

"Not bad. If I'd stuck to the main roads it would have been better, because the state of the smaller roads are atrocious after the storm last night, with broken branches everywhere. Anyway, I'm on my way home." He paused. "So where is Laure now?"

"She went for a run. She's probably gone to the quarry as I'm not with her."

"At least you'll be able to enjoy your bath in peace."

"True."

Iris was in the bath when Gabriel arrived home.

"Is Laure back from her run?" she asked when he came to find her in the bathroom.

He ran water into the sink and bent to drink from his hands. "I didn't see her when I came in."

"What about Joseph?"

Gabriel straightened up. "He'll be in the garden, won't he? It's only five o'clock, he's got another hour to do."

"I thought I saw him go after Laure."

"I'll check once I've had a shower. Shall I use the other bathroom?"

"No, it's fine, the water's cold, I'm getting out."

He dipped his hand in the bath. "It's freezing. No wonder you've got goose bumps."

She stood up, water sloshing up the sides of the bath, then climbed out, water dripping off her. Gabriel handed her a towel.

"Thanks. So, where did you go today?"

"I rode to Faradale."

"That far? Did you have lunch there?"

"No, I didn't bother. I had a sandwich with me."

Iris swapped her towel for her dressing gown and shrugged it on. "Right. Well, I'm going to get dressed and pour myself a glass of wine. Do you want one?"

"After my shower. I'll put my clothes straight on a wash, there was so much mud on the roads that they're filthy."

"Okay. I'll meet you in the garden. It's lovely out there now."

"The calm before the next storm."

Iris smiled. "We should make the most of it, then."

36

"Laure isn't answering her phone," Iris said, hoping to provoke Gabriel into conversation. "Do you think I should phone Esme?"

Dinner had been ready since seven, but Iris had insisted on waiting for Laure. There'd been no news from her since she'd left on her run.

She wasn't sure if it was Joseph's no-show—because he hadn't returned to work this afternoon—that had caused Gabriel's grumpiness, or if his meeting with Maggie Ingram on Tuesday was playing on his mind. He'd hardly said a word since coming back from his bike ride.

He reached for his glass of wine. "Why do you want to call Esme?"

"To ask if she's seen Laure."

"Does she know about Laure and Joseph?"

"No, I don't think so."

"Then if you do phone her, be careful what you say."

But Esme didn't answer her phone either.

"I expect they're all having dinner together and can't hear their phones," Iris said, a little sourly. "Laure could have at least let me know." She paused. "Will you try Hugh?"

"If Esme didn't answer, I doubt Hugh will."

"Please, Gabriel. I just want to check that Laure is there."

He stifled a sigh, took out his phone and called Hugh.

"You're right, they must be having dinner," he said, when Hugh didn't pick up.

"How's she going to get home? It's pouring!"

"I expect Hugh will drive her back. Or maybe she'll stay the night with Joseph," he added. "Can we eat now?"

They had their dinner in near silence. The only time Gabriel responded with any enthusiasm was when Iris spoke about Beth. But even her mind was only half on the conversation and after another couple of unanswered calls to both Laure and Esme, she couldn't stand the uncertainty anymore.

"Gabriel, would you mind phoning Joseph?"

He scowled. "Yes, I would, very much."

"Please. I mean, we're just presuming Laure is with him. What if she's not?"

"Where else would she be?"

"I don't know. It must be muddy out there; if she went over the fields she might have slipped and hurt herself."

"All right. But if she is with him, it's going to be embarrassing for everyone."

"Put him on loudspeaker so I can hear what he says."

To her surprise, Joseph answered immediately.

"Joseph, it's Gabriel. I won't keep you. We've been trying to get hold of Esme and Hugh. You're not with them by any chance?"

"No, they've gone for dinner at The Watershed."

"Do you know if Laure is with them? We've been trying to get hold of her but she's not answering her phone."

"No, I don't think so."

"Did they mention that they'd seen her, that she had called around, or anything?"

"No, they didn't. But I can ask them when they get back. I shouldn't think they'll be long."

"That would be great, thanks." He paused. "I don't suppose you've seen her, by any chance?"

"Laure? No, I haven't seen her since this afternoon at yours."

"Okay, thanks."

Gabriel hung up. "Well, that explains why Esme and Hugh didn't answer their phones; they're having dinner at The Watershed. Laure is probably with them."

"I'm not so sure. I really don't think she would have accepted to go for dinner with them and not let us know." Iris paused. "I'm surprised Esme has gone out when her doctor said she had to stay home."

"Stop worrying about everything. Joseph said he'll call when they get back."

"That could be ages. Maybe I should go down there, see for myself."

"If it will put your mind at rest."

But before Iris had made it out of the door, Joseph called back.

"I went to The Watershed to check." His voice came down the line. "Laure isn't with them."

Iris reached for her phone. "Right, I'm calling the police."

"Thanks for doing that," Gabriel said to Joseph.

"Did I hear Iris say that she's phoning the police?"

"Yes."

"Why?"

"Because we haven't seen Laure since she went for a run this afternoon. We weren't too worried at first because we thought she might be with Esme and Hugh, or with you." He paused to let his words sink in. "But when she didn't turn up for dinner," he continued, "we began to get worried."

"Are you saying that nobody has seen her since she went for her run—what, about six hours ago?"

"Yes."

"Something must have happened." Iris could hear the alarm in his voice. "I'm going to look for her. Do you know where she went?"

"I'll come with you," Gabriel said, as if suddenly realized the seriousness of the situation. "Come to the house and we can try and trace her steps. She and Iris usually take the track over the fields."

"Be with you in ten."

Gabriel hung up. He might not have been worried before, but he was now.

37

Iris stood by the window, her arms wrapped around her body, shivering at the storm raging outside. Worry gnawed in the pit of her stomach. Gabriel and Joseph had been gone over an hour, and she'd been calling Gabriel every fifteen minutes to check if they'd found Laure.

"It's impossible!" he'd shouted over the noise of the wind and the rain when she'd last phoned. "We're on our way back. We'll come out again when the wind has dropped!"

The police had been helpful when she'd called to report Laure missing, but not so helpful as to send out a search party. This may have been partly because, when she had explained about Laure—who she was, why she was staying with them—the police had suggested that Laure might have decided to return to Paris. Iris had pointed out that Laure wouldn't have gone without letting her know but they hadn't seemed convinced.

Hearing a noise, she pressed her face to the window and saw Gabriel, almost doubled over against the wind, fighting his way up the driveway. She rushed to open the door. Gabriel pushed his way in and she slammed the door behind him.

"Here, let me help you." She pulled his sopping jacket from his shoulders. His hair was plastered to his forehead and water ran down his face. "I'll get you a towel."

"We only made it to the top of the hill," he said, his voice hoarse. "We called and called but even if she'd been ten feet away, I doubt she'd have heard. It's vicious out there." He bent to take off his boots. "Don't bother with a towel, I'll jump in the shower. I need to get some heat into me. But I could murder something hot to drink."

While he was in the shower, Iris made tea. They sat at the kitchen table, Gabriel eating his way through a packet of biscuits.

"The police said something," Iris said. "I dismissed it at the time but now I'm wondering. They said Laure might have decided to go back to Paris. But she wouldn't have gone without telling us, would she?"

Gabriel frowned. "I don't think so."

"She knows we would worry about her if she suddenly disappeared. And wouldn't she have said something to Joseph about leaving?"

"Not if they'd had an argument. Maybe that was why she left, because of the argument."

"But where would she have gone, if she's not at Esme and Hugh's? She doesn't know anyone else."

"Maybe she went to a hotel."

"But not without telling us, surely?"

Gabriel scrunched the empty biscuit packet in his hand. "Let's try and get some sleep. As soon as it's light, I'll go out again."

"What if she turns up when we're in bed? How will we know?"

He scratched his head. "I'll stay up. You go to bed."

"Are you sure?"

"Yes, of course. I'll keep trying her phone. If I hear anything, I'll wake you."

38

Groggy with sleep, Iris pushed open Laure's bedroom door. Her bed was still empty.

"Iris?" Gabriel's voice came from downstairs. He was standing in the hallway, rubbing his eyes. "Is she back? I nodded off for a few minutes."

She moved to the top of the stairs. "No. What time is it?"

"I don't know. Last time I looked it was four o'clock and I don't think I was asleep for very long, so four thirty maybe? I'll check." He went back into the sitting room. "It's four thirty-five!" he called. "It's light, I'm going to look for her."

"I'll come with you. Just let me get dressed."

The sky was a watery blue as they walked across the fields, the air completely still, as if the wind had exhausted itself with all the blowing it had done during the night. Evidence of the havoc the storm had wreaked was everywhere; twigs littered the footpaths and several times Gabriel had to stoop to lift branches out of their way. They took the route over the fields, but an hour later—the time it took for them to walk it—they hadn't found a single trace of Laure.

"Maybe we should try the quarry," she said, as they made their way home.

Gabriel came to an abrupt stop. "Why?"

"I don't know. It's just—I told you, she was always trying to get me to go there."

He ran a hand through his hair. "It's out of bounds, we're not allowed. Besides—" he stopped, but Iris knew what he was going to say, that he didn't want to go there.

"It's okay," she said, laying a hand on his arm. "I'll go."

"Why don't we leave it to the police?"

She snatched her hand away in irritation. "Because by the time they do anything it might be too late! What if she went there and fell and hurt herself, broke her ankle or something? What if she's been lying injured all night, in the pouring rain?"

She saw Gabriel swallow. "You're right. Let's go and see."

They took the path through the woods in silence, then took the track up to the top of the quarry, calling Laure's name and checking the dense woods, which acted as a barrier between the path and the edge of the quarry, in case she'd taken refuge there. Water dripped down their necks as they pushed branches heavy with rain out of the way. At one point, the woods thinned out and the edge of the quarry was just feet away.

"This must have been where Charlie came off the path," Gabriel said, his face ashen.

Iris gave an involuntary shudder. "Is that where you found him, down there?" she said, craning her neck.

He grabbed her arm. "Keep away from the edge!"

"It's okay."

"No it's not! Have you seen how slippery the ground is?"

She heard the fear in his voice. "Sorry."

"Come on, let's go home. She's not here. I think it must be as the police said, and she went back to Paris."

She shook her head. "If Laure had gone to meet Pierre, she would have told us. I think something has happened to her." She picked up her pace. "Police stations don't shut, do they?"

39

Gabriel closed the bedroom door quietly behind him, relieved that Iris was finally sleeping, mentally and emotionally exhausted from hours of weeping. He still couldn't believe it. No matter how often he said the words, it wouldn't sink in.

Laure was dead.

Iris was distraught, blaming herself because Laure had asked her to go running, but she'd wanted to have a bath. She said that if she'd gone with Laure, Laure wouldn't have gone to the quarry.

When questioned by the police, Iris had told them how Laure had been curious about the place where Charlie Ingram had fallen. So that was what they thought had happened—Laure had gone to see for herself and had stumbled over the edge.

It was the police who found her, not far from where Gabriel had found Charlie. But her body had been farther back, behind a boulder. Unlike Charlie, she hadn't been propelled over the boulder by the speed of a bike, she had simply fallen straight down.

Gabriel couldn't bear to think about it. It was too horrific.

40

There was a ring at the door. Iris closed her eyes.

"Please let that be Laure," she murmured. "Please let there have been a terrible mistake."

Gabriel squeezed her shoulder and went to answer the door. When Iris opened her eyes again, a police officer was standing in front of her.

"How are you doing, Iris?" the police officer, tall, blond hair tied back in a neat ponytail—PC Locke, Iris remembered—asked.

Iris shook her head. "I keep hoping there's been a terrible mistake."

PC Locke gave her a sympathetic smile. "May I sit? I have a few questions I'd like to ask you."

"Yes, of course. But I was just going to call Beth." Iris looked at Gabriel, standing behind PC Locke. "I've been thinking about what she said, about coming home tomorrow. Don't you think it might be better if she waits until the funeral? I know we don't know when that will be, but she would only be sitting here waiting. At least in Greece she has her job to keep her busy."

Gabriel nodded. "You're right."

"You mentioned yesterday that Laure was Beth's godmother," PC Locke said.

"Yes, she's so upset. Could you call her, Gabriel?"

"Of course." Iris sensed his relief at being able to leave the room.

PC Locke waited until he was gone. "I'm sorry to intrude but I'd like to ask you a few more questions about Laure."

"Does Pierre know yet?"

"As far as I know, he wasn't at his flat when the police called there. They're speaking to neighbors and drawing up a list of his friends."

Iris leaned forward. "Did you give them Claire de Vaillant's name? She was his best friend. He could be with her."

"Yes, we passed on all the information you gave us. They're doing everything they can to find him."

Iris nodded and slumped back in her chair.

"If I can just backtrack to the last time you saw Laure." PC Locke glanced at her iPad. "It was two days ago, on Saturday afternoon. You were in the bedroom upstairs and you saw her from the window talking to Joseph, your gardener. Then you saw her leave."

"Yes. She had told me earlier that she was going for a run."

"Yesterday, you said that you wished you'd gone with her."

"Yes, I felt guilty that I hadn't. But I'd planned to have a long bath, something I don't often get the chance to do."

"How did she seem?"

Iris hesitated. "Fine."

"You don't seem very sure."

"It's just that I'd heard raised voices. That was why I went to the window and looked out." Her words came out in a rush.

"Laure and Joseph were arguing?"

"I thought so. I thought they might be having a lovers' tiff."

"Laure and Joseph were in a relationship?"

"Yes."

"For how long?"

"A couple of weeks. Maybe longer, I'm not really sure."

"So when you looked out of the window, it was because you heard the sound of raised voices?"

"Yes."

"Did you hear what was said?"

"Laure was saying something about not wanting to do something and Joseph said that she had to. He grabbed her arm and Laure pulled away and said she was going for a run."

"What did Joseph do?"

"He called after her but she didn't come back and then he left too."

"Immediately?"

"Not immediately, because he took out his phone and he looked at it for a moment. Then he left. I was surprised because he was meant to be working."

"How did he seem?"

"In a hurry."

"When he was talking to Laure, how did he sound?"

Iris thought for a moment.

"Annoyed."

"Not angry."

"No." She twisted her hands together. "I really don't feel too good."

"I'm almost done. You said Laure left the house at about four o'clock?"

"Yes. I remember checking the time before I got in the bath and it was ten past four. I had started filling it just after she left, and it takes around five minutes to fill, so she must have left at around four."

"Gabriel mentioned he was out on his bike that day, that he cycled over to Faradale. Do you remember what time he got back?"

"It must have been around four fifteen because I'd only just got into the bath."

PC Locke nodded. "Thank you for your time, Iris. As soon as we locate Pierre, I'll let you know."

Gabriel waited until PC Locke had gone before going to find Iris.

"Everything okay?" he asked.

"Not really. How's Beth?"

"Still upset. But she agreed that it's probably better if she waits to see when the funeral is before rushing back." He shook his head as if to clear it. "The funeral. I mean, how can we be going to a funeral, how can we be going to Laure's funeral?"

Iris looked at him nervously. "I'm worried I might have said something to PC Locke that I shouldn't have. She was asking about Joseph and I told her about the argument I'd overheard, and about him running off."

Gabriel sat down and took hold of her hands.

"You only told her what you heard."

"But it sounded bad, for Joseph. What if they think—"

"They probably think lots of things, it's their job. Until they know exactly what happened, we're probably all suspects."

She raised her eyes to his. "PC Locke asked about you, about what time you got back from your bike ride. I said you got back just after I got into the bath, around four fifteen. But you actually got back at five o'clock."

He frowned. "So why did you lie?"

"Because if—God forbid—there was foul play involved, I could see how it might look."

He stared for a moment, then rubbed his chin. "Shit," he said softly.

"Exactly."

41

Gabriel sat on the wooden bench in the walled garden, his head tipped back, his eyes closed against the sun.

If their world hadn't suddenly imploded, he'd be waiting for Maggie Ingram to arrive. He felt guilty at the relief he'd felt when he'd realized Laure's death had given him an excuse for postponing their meeting. The counselor had sent her condolences and said to let her know when he felt able to meet with Maggie. It would be a long time before that would happen.

He'd come to the walled garden to try to get his head straight. The house was too heavy with the sights and sounds of Iris's grief—her drawn face and red-rimmed eyes, her quiet sobs and, sometimes, a roar of disbelief—to be able to think straight.

At first, he'd thought Laure's death was an accident, because of her ghoulish fascination with the quarry. But then he'd begun thinking about her mental state. Her trip to Paris had been an emotional disaster. In not turning up to their arranged meeting, Pierre had effectively rejected her. In retaliation, she'd thrown herself into a relationship with Joseph. The argument Iris had overheard—Laure saying she didn't want to and Joseph saying she had to—could have been about him telling her she needed to leave him alone. There had already been the "back off" comment and the way Joseph physically shrugged Laure off when she got too close. In Gabriel's mind, it suggested that he had tired of her.

Iris felt bad for having mentioned their argument to the police, but in his view, she'd been right to tell them because the police instinctively knew when people were trying to hide something. Thank God Pierre had turned his phone off, had never seen the message he'd sent him last Thursday telling him that Laure had moved on. If he had seen the message, the police might think he had come over and murdered Laure. What he couldn't understand was why Pierre hadn't turned his phone back on yet. Today was the first of August; by rights, he should be back at his desk. A part of him was glad that he hadn't been able to get through to him, because the thought of having to tell him Laure was dead was truly terrible. But he didn't want his friend to hear it from the police. The number of voicemails he'd left, always with the same message—*Pierre, you need to call me urgently. It's about Laure*—were stacking up.

Gabriel turned his thoughts to Joseph. There was something that hadn't added up, something that had seemed a little strange at the time. But so far, he hadn't been able to work out what it was. He cast his mind back to Saturday, when they'd first been worried about Laure. They had tried to get hold of Esme and Hugh, but couldn't, and Joseph had told him they were having dinner at The Watershed. He'd said he would ask them about Laure when they got back, and then he'd called to say that he'd gone to The Watershed to speak to them, and that they hadn't seen her.

"Here you are." He opened his eyes and Iris came into view, her eyes red-rimmed and swollen. "I've been looking for you."

He sat up. "Has something happened? Have the police managed to get hold of Pierre?"

"No." She came over and sat down beside him. "It's just that I don't like being alone. The house is too silent without Laure." He heard the sob in her voice and pulled her toward him. "What were you thinking about?" she asked.

"Joseph," he admitted. "There's something bothering me."

"What?"

"He said he went to The Watershed to speak to Esme and Hugh." She looked confused. "When no one was answering their phones. You know, on Saturday."

"Oh, yes. What about it?"

"I don't think he went."

"What do you mean?"

"There wasn't enough time, I'm sure of it." Releasing her, he dug his phone from his pocket and scrolled through his calls. "Seven minutes. Joseph called back seven minutes later to say he'd been to The Watershed to speak to Esme and Hugh. That's not enough time to get to The Watershed and back, even if he had run."

"Maybe he called you from the pub. Or when he was walking home."

He shook his head. "I didn't hear any background noise. Anyway, there's something else. When I think about it now, neither Hugh nor Esme called us when they got home to see if Laure had turned up. They only messaged yesterday. And they messaged, not called."

Iris frowned. "What are you trying to say?"

"That they didn't know until yesterday that Laure was missing because for some reason, Joseph didn't tell them? I don't know. It just seems a bit weird."

Iris's eyes welled with tears. "Everything's weird. I feel awful that Pierre doesn't know yet."

He tightened his arms around her, cursing himself for upsetting her, for seeming to point the finger at Joseph. He'd be suspecting Hugh and Esme next. But that's what happened when somebody died unexpectedly. If it wasn't an obvious accident, it was human nature to look at those who knew the victim. For all he knew, people in the village might be looking at him, wondering if he'd had anything to do with it. To an outsider, it could have seemed a strange set-up, Laure moving in with them. People might be asking themselves if there'd been something going on between him and Laure.

It was why he'd been glad that Iris had had the presence of mind to tell the police he'd arrived home from his bike ride on Saturday forty-five minutes before he actually had. When the police had asked him about his movements that day, he'd stuck to what Iris had told them, that he'd arrived home at four fifteen. But now, Gabriel couldn't help wondering if it had been the right thing to do, because if the police decided that murder was a possibility, and they made inquiries, someone might have seen him cycle past their house after four fifteen, when Iris had told the police he was already home.

Which would make things incredibly difficult for him.

42

"Have you found him?" Iris asked PC Locke, when she saw her standing on the doorstep the next morning. "Pierre?"

"All I've been told by the French police is that he didn't turn up for work yesterday."

Iris's shoulders sagged. "So where is he?"

"That's what they're trying to establish."

"I can't bear the thought that he doesn't know about Laure. It seems wrong."

"I know how difficult this is for you, Iris, so I'm not going to keep you. I just stopped by to tell you that Mr. Sullivan has been taken in for questioning, so he won't be at work today."

"Mr. Sullivan?"

"Joseph."

She stared, shocked. "You've arrested him?"

"No, we just need to ask him a few questions."

Iris buried her head in her hands. "I wish I hadn't said anything."

"You did right to tell us what you overheard," PC Locke said firmly. "It's about eliminating him from our inquiries."

"But Laure's death was an accident, wasn't it?"

"It's our job to look at all possibilities." She turned to leave. "As soon as I have any news, I'll be in touch."

Iris waited until she'd gone, then went back to the kitchen.

"What did she want?" Gabriel asked.

She sank into a chair. "Everything is such a mess. They've taken Joseph in for questioning." She looked up at him. "Do you think they'll tell Joseph that I said I'd overheard him and Laure having an argument?"

Before he could answer, her phone rang. She snatched it from the table.

"It's Esme," she said, her heart in her mouth.

"You'd better answer it."

She nodded, accepted the call.

"Iris, how are you?" Esme's voice was both warm and worried.

Iris glanced at Gabriel. "Not great, but we'll get there. Thank you for your messages, it was lovely to know you were thinking of us."

"We're so sorry about Laure. It's just heartbreaking."

"I know."

"Iris, I hope you don't mind me calling at such a difficult time, but Hugh has just told me the police have taken Joseph in for questioning. Do you know why?"

"No." Iris searched for something to tell her. "But maybe it's because he was with Laure before she left on her run?"

"I don't understand. Her death was an accident, wasn't it?"

"Yes, as far as I know."

"How do you know Joseph was with her before she went on her run?"

"Because I saw them from the bedroom window, just before she left the house. I suppose the police want to know what they were talking about to get an idea of the frame of mind she might have been in."

"Why couldn't they ask him that at the house? Why take him down to the station?"

Iris knew she needed to be honest. "I overheard them arguing."

"Arguing?"

"I might have got it wrong," she said hastily. "But if I did, I'm sure Joseph will explain. Anyway, how are you?"

"Well, I'm no longer pregnant." Iris heard the smile in her voice but it took a moment for Esme's words to register.

"You've had the baby?"

Gabriel's mouth formed a "*What?*"

"Yes!"

"When?"

"Um, on Saturday," Esme said carefully, and Iris felt a huge wave of emotion. The day Laure died.

"But that's wonderful!" she said, pulling herself together. "Congratulations, Esme! Boy or girl?"

"A beautiful baby boy. Hamish."

Gabriel sat down beside her. "Congratulations, Esme!" he shouted down the phone. "To Hugh too. That's wonderful news, just what we need."

"So how did it happen?" Iris asked. "I want to know everything!"

"Well, I started having contractions during the morning. By the time I thought I should get to hospital, Hugh was halfway up a mountain on a walk. So I called Joseph and he brought me to the hospital, which was lucky because Hamish was born pretty quickly after I arrived. I felt terrible for not being able to hold on, because it meant Hugh missed the birth. But at least I had Joseph with me."

"You should have told us," Iris protested.

"We were going to tell you that evening but then Joseph phoned Hugh at the hospital to say that you were looking for Laure because she hadn't come back from a run and you were worried about her, so it seemed a bit misplaced to tell you at that point. After, once she'd been found, it was even more difficult." Esme paused again. "I wasn't even sure I should tell you now."

Iris choked back a sob. She need to focus on Esme, not Laure. "Of course you should have! Gabriel is right, it's exactly what we need, some lovely news to take our minds off everything else." She paused. "But that makes Hamish about five weeks early, doesn't it? How is he?"

"He's fine, but we're still in hospital. They're keeping us in until he's gained some more weight."

"Will you let me know when I can come and see you?"

"Why don't you wait until we're home? I'm sorry, I need to go, it's time for Hamish's feed."

"Bye Esme, give Hamish a kiss from me. See you soon."

"Wow," Gabriel said, when Iris had cut the call. "I wasn't expecting that."

"Neither was I."

"It explains a lot, like Joseph pretending he'd been to The Watershed to speak to them. They weren't at the pub, they were at the hospital, he will have called them there to ask about Laure." He looked over at her. "You must be relieved."

"Why?"

"Because if Joseph drove Esme to the hospital on Saturday afternoon, and was with her for the birth, he has the perfect alibi for when Laure went missing."

43

Iris stared at the blank screen in front of her. Joseph's testimony, that Laure hadn't been upset that afternoon, only exasperated, plus the fact that he had a solid alibi for that afternoon, meant foul play seemed to have been ruled out in relation to Laure's death. Her obsession with the quarry—repeatedly asking to see the spot where Charlie Ingram had fallen—also supported the accidental death verdict. Nobody came out and said it, but it had been implied on the local news that it was another sad case of curiosity killing the cat.

Sometimes, Iris wondered what would have happened if she hadn't given Gabriel an alibi by saying he'd come back from his bike ride minutes after Laure had left on her run. If the police knew he'd only arrived forty-five minutes later, would they have investigated him, still be investigating him? It didn't bear thinking about and she didn't feel bad for lying, because she knew how easy it would have been to build a case against Gabriel, for the police to start speculating about whether or not there had been something going on between him and Laure. She herself might have been investigated, they might have wondered if she'd found out about an affair, or had suspected an affair, and had wanted rid of Laure. Even if they hadn't been able to make anything stick, everyone knew that mud stuck anyway. It was better this way.

The door to her office opened and Gabriel came in, followed by PC Locke.

"Please tell me that the French police have found Pierre," Iris said. "It's been three days."

"I'm afraid they haven't, not yet." PC Locke pulled up a chair and sat down. "You may already know that Mr. Sullivan has given us a satisfactory explanation for the argument you overheard between him and Laure." She paused. "It seems that he wanted Laure to tell you they were in a relationship and Laure didn't want to, because she didn't think you'd approve, because of Pierre. And the reason he disappeared after was because he was called away urgently to take a friend to hospital."

Iris nodded. "Esme. I know, she told me." It occurred to her that PC Locke might think she'd been trying to pervert the course of justice. "I'm sorry if I misled you," she added.

"No, not at all. You were right to mention it." There was another pause. "Mr. Sullivan mentioned that he thought Laure might have been getting under your feet. Had she been? Getting under your feet?"

"No, not at all. We were happy to have her with us."

"What about you, Gabriel? Did you feel the same way?"

"Yes, absolutely."

PC Locke smiled. "Well, I won't keep you any longer. Don't get up, I can see myself out."

44

Gabriel came clattering down the stairs and burst into the kitchen.

"It's the police," he said. "I've just seen their car pull up outside. PC Locke and someone else, a man."

Iris's hand flew to her heart. "Maybe they've found Pierre."

"Let's hope so."

They waited until the police rang on the bell, then waited some more. Gabriel went to let them in and Iris stayed in the kitchen.

"Hello, Iris," PC Locke said, appearing in the doorway. "This is PC Ramesh, my colleague." She turned to Gabriel. "I don't suppose we could have some tea, could we?"

"Sure."

Alarm bells started ringing as Gabriel lifted the kettle from its base and filled it with water. PC Locke had never accepted their offer of tea before. And she usually came on her own.

PC Locke pulled out a chair and sat down opposite Iris. PC Ramesh took the place next to his colleague, leaving the place beside Iris for Gabriel.

"Do you take sugar?" Gabriel asked, taking four mugs from the cupboard and placing them on the countertop. Iris watched as he maneuvered them into a straight line, a sign that he too sensed that something wasn't right.

"One, please," PC Ramesh said.

"No, thanks." PC Locke gave Iris a smile but it didn't reach her eyes.

The kettle clicked off and they all watched Gabriel as he poured water into the mugs, then stirred the teabags around for a moment before lifting them out, one by one, and putting them in the bin, one by one. By the time he'd placed the mugs on the table, along with some sugar, a carton of milk, and four teaspoons, the tension in the kitchen was palpable.

"Thank you," PC Locke said, once Gabriel had sat down and they'd passed around the milk. She lifted her mug and took a small sip of tea and they all did the same, even though it was too hot to drink.

"The French police have found Pierre," she said.

Breath whooshed out of Iris. "Thank God."

"It's not good news, I'm afraid."

"What do you mean?" Gabriel's voice had risen sharply.

Iris reached for his hand and squeezed it, as much for her sake as for his.

"There's no easy way to say this," PC Locke said. "I'm sorry to have to tell you that Pierre is dead."

There was a terrible silence. "What?"

"Our French colleagues found his body earlier today."

Iris's chair clattered back.

"No. No, he can't be. You must have got it wrong!"

"Iris—"

The room spun and she groped for the edge of the table. She felt Gabriel's arms around her, stopping her from falling, then hands on her shoulders.

"Please, sit down," PC Locke said, pressing her into her chair. "You too, Gabriel."

They sank into their seats and Gabriel buried his face in his hands.

"How?" he asked, choking back a sob. "How can he be dead? How can there be so much tragedy? It's too much to bear."

"I'm sorry," PC Locke said, her voice gentle.

"What happened?" Iris's teeth were chattering. She reached for her mug, needing some warmth, but when she tried to pick it up, tea slopped over the side.

"Why don't you take a minute?" PC Ramesh suggested. "There's no rush."

Iris nodded numbly and pressed her hands together to try to stop them from shaking. Gabriel stood up abruptly, grabbed the kitchen roll from the side, tore off a sheet and blew his nose.

"Right," he said, his voice unsteady. "I'm ready."

He sat down. Iris found his hand again, and held it tightly.

"His body was found earlier today in the basement of his apartment block. Apparently, each apartment is assigned a small storeroom in the basement of the building."

Gabriel nodded. "Pierre and Laure kept their skiing stuff and bikes there. And a spare freezer. And tools—he had a chain saw. Jesus." He rubbed his face. "Is that what happened? He had an accident down there?"

"No, it wasn't an accident."

"Then—what are you saying? Are you saying he killed himself?" Gabriel's voice rose, then broke. "Oh God, was it because of the message I sent him?"

PC Locke frowned. "What message was that?"

Gabriel looked as if he didn't want to tell her. "A few days before Laure died, I sent him a message telling him that she had moved on, and that if he didn't come over, he'd lose her forever."

"And did he reply?"

"No. That's why I didn't mention it to you." He stared at her, his distress evident. "Is that what pushed him over the edge? It was marked as unread so I thought he hadn't seen it."

"It must be why he told Arnaud that he was going away until the beginning of August," Iris said, her voice breaking. "He didn't want anyone to find him."

Gabriel buried his head in his hands. "It's my fault. I should never have said anything to him."

"Gabriel." PC Locke laid a hand on his arm. "Pierre didn't take his own life."

Gabriel raised his head. "What?"

"May I see the message?"

Gabriel nodded, dug out his phone, located the message and passed it to her.

"It's still marked unread," she said.

"I don't understand." Gabriel's frustration was evident. "If Pierre didn't take his own life, how did he die then?"

PC Ramesh cleared his throat. "I'm sorry to have to tell you that he was murdered."

45

Iris stood at the bedroom window, her arms wrapped around her body. It was another beautiful day, mid-thirties she'd heard them say on the radio. They had it on constantly now, to drown out the suffocating silence that permeated the house.

Despite the heat, she was shivering. She'd been cold since PC Ramesh told them that Pierre's body had been found in the freezer he and Laure had kept in the storeroom of their Paris apartment. It was as if her body was mirroring what had happened to Pierre. He had been stabbed in the heart.

She couldn't stop crying, and she needed to, because her tears only added to Gabriel's distress. He was broken, utterly and completely broken. He'd aged almost beyond recognition in the space of a few days, his face pallid and gaunt, his hair streaked with gray. Iris had heard about hair going white overnight with shock. Now she knew it could be true.

Maybe she was the same. She didn't know because she hadn't looked in a mirror. She could barely be bothered to dress; she had showered that morning only because she could smell her own sweat. She'd done it for Gabriel, not for herself. She'd pulled her leggings back on after, and if the shirt she'd been wearing hadn't had coffee spilled down it, she would have probably put that back on too, regardless of the sweat.

She forced herself to move to the wardrobe. She pulled a sweater from the shelf, put it on with difficulty, her body so stiff with sorrow that her limbs no longer bent as they should. She walked to the top of the stairs and went down them slowly, gripping the banister rail for support. There was a casserole sitting on the side in the kitchen, brought by a kind neighbor. Gabriel had gone to fetch Beth at Gatwick, she had left Greece that morning, three weeks earlier than she should have. Even if Iris and Gabriel weren't hungry, Beth might be.

She opened the oven, put the dish on the shelf and closed the door. She was about to sit down, because standing took too much energy, when she remembered she needed to turn the oven on. She reached out, turned the dial to halfway around and sank into a chair.

Beth didn't know that Pierre had been murdered. She and Gabriel had discussed it and had felt it would be too much for her to cope with alone, coming so soon after Laure's death. They hadn't wanted her to find out from social media before they'd had a chance to tell her face-to-face, so they'd told her that Pierre had been found and that he was dead. Beth hadn't asked for any details, just said she wanted to come home. They were dreading telling her the truth. She would have so many questions and they had no answers to give her.

She heard the car pulling into the drive. Gripping the table, she pushed slowly to her feet. There was the clunk of a car door shutting, then another. She moved into the hall and looked through the window. The devastation on Beth's face was clearly visible, and Iris breathed a sigh of relief. Gabriel had already told her.

46

PC Locke was back. It was Monday morning, nine days after Laure had died, four days after Pierre's body had been found in the freezer.

"It seems Pierre was killed earlier than the French police first thought," she said, once they were sitting around the table in the kitchen, in what had become their familiar positions. "Possibly six weeks ago."

Iris's eyes flickered toward the stairs, visible at the end of the hallway. She was glad Beth was still in bed, she preferred her to receive any updates from her and Gabriel. Then PC Locke's words penetrated her mind.

"Six weeks?" Gabriel said, getting there before her. "Pierre's been dead six weeks?"

"Yes, the French police think he was murdered sometime around the beginning of July."

"The beginning of July?" Stunned, Iris turned to Gabriel. "That was around the time Laure went to Paris to meet him. Oh God, do you think that's why he didn't turn up? Because he was dead?"

"Christ," he muttered.

Tears filled her eyes. "She thought he didn't turn up because he didn't care. But what if he was already dead? I can't bear it."

"When was this?" Iris looked up, startled by PC Locke's urgent tone. "When did Laure go to Paris to see Pierre?"

"Um, I'm not sure, exactly."

"Please Iris, it's important."

Iris found her mobile and brought up the calendar. "It was the day after I met my friend Jade for lunch. Here it is—my lunch with Jade was on Friday the first of July, so Laure's meeting with Pierre must have been on the second."

PC Locke frowned. "The second?"

"Yes."

She checked her iPad and a stillness came over her.

"Iris, can you take me through that day, the day Laure went to Paris to meet Pierre? What time did she leave?"

"Gosh, I can't remember. I know I had to get up early because I was taking her to the station. She was meeting Pierre at one o'clock at their flat and with France being an hour ahead, she needed to get the Eurostar around nine, I think. Yes, that's it, she had booked the nine o'clock Eurostar, because the journey takes around two and a half hours, which meant she'd get into Gare du Nord at twelve thirty French time, giving her enough time to get to their flat for one."

"But Pierre wasn't there?"

"No."

"When did Laure tell you that he wasn't there?"

"At about three in the afternoon, when she phoned from Gare du Nord."

"That would have been four o'clock French time."

"Yes. She said she was about to leave, that she had changed her ticket for an earlier train."

"Did she say anything else?"

"No, she just asked if I could pick her up at the station in Markham. I was surprised, as I hadn't been expecting her back until later. To be honest, I wasn't really expecting her to come back even though she'd said she wouldn't be staying overnight. I suppose I hoped she'd patch things up with Pierre. I asked her how it had gone with Pierre and she burst into tears and told me that he hadn't been at the flat."

"Did she say how long she'd waited at their flat?"

"No. But it takes about fifteen minutes to get from their flat to Gare du Nord by metro, and when she phoned me, she was already at Gare du Nord and had managed to change her ticket for an earlier train." With difficulty, she worked backward from four o'clock French time. "To have had time to do that, she must have left the flat at about three o'clock. No, earlier, because in between leaving the flat and arriving at Gare du Nord, she'd been shopping."

"Shopping?"

"Yes, she was wearing new clothes when I picked her up at the station and when I complimented her on them, she said she'd decided to treat herself to something new."

PC Locke frowned. "How was she when you picked her up at the station?"

"I was expecting her to still be upset, but she wasn't, she was—defiant, I suppose. Apparently, she'd got chatting to someone on the train who told her that Pierre didn't deserve her and that she could do better." She gave a small smile. "She obviously decided to take his words to heart."

"Where were the clothes she'd been wearing when she left?"

"In her bag, I presume." Iris thought for a moment. "Actually, they couldn't have been, she only had her handbag with her. She hadn't taken anything bigger because, as I said, in her mind she was only going for the day. It's why she'd bought a return ticket."

"Did she have a carrier bag, from the shop where she'd bought the clothes?"

"No, I don't think so. I don't remember seeing one."

"Do you remember what she was wearing when she left?"

"Yes, a pale blue dress and blue canvas shoes. She liked things to match. We'd bought the dress together, it's why I noticed she wasn't wearing it when she came back."

"Can you show them to me please? The dress and the shoes?"

"Yes, of course."

PC Locke followed Iris upstairs. Iris pushed open the door to Laure's bedroom, then stopped. She hadn't been in since Laure died, although the police had.

"I-I haven't been in yet, not even to take the sheets off the bed," she said, faltering. "I know I'll have to at some point but I can't face it."

"It's probably best to leave everything as it is for the moment."

"It smells of her." Iris's voice broke. "Her perfume."

"Take your time."

Iris nodded, then walked over to the wardrobe. She opened the door and rifled through the clothes on the rail, assaulted by memories of Laure wearing each item. There weren't that many; Laure had arrived empty-handed and had only bought a few pieces the day they'd gone shopping together, two dresses, a skirt, a pair of jeans, some shorts and T-shirts.

"It's not here," Iris said, blinking back tears. "Her dress. It must be in the wash."

"What about the canvas shoes she was wearing?"

The few pairs of shoes that Laure owned were neatly lined up along the bottom of the wardrobe. Iris scanned them quickly.

"Not here either. Downstairs maybe."

They trekked back down the stairs and Iris checked the hallway, the cupboard under the stairs where she and Gabriel kept their shoes, and outside the back door. She even checked the garage. But Laure's shoes were nowhere to be seen. And her blue dress wasn't in the wash.

Iris glanced at PC Locke. She could tell from the policewoman's face that she was reading something into the fact that the clothes weren't there.

"Do you mind if I have another look in Laure's room?" PC Locke asked.

"Not at all."

"Thanks."

Iris returned to the kitchen where Gabriel and PC Ramesh were waiting. Gabriel lifted his head from his hands. "Everything okay?"

"Laure's clothes aren't there. The ones she was wearing when she went to Paris," she added.

"What has that got to do with anything?"

She slumped into the chair next to him. "I don't know."

"Christ."

"Would you like some water?" PC Ramesh asked.

"Please."

"Gabriel?"

"No thanks."

PC Ramesh filled a glass from the tap and brought it over to Iris. She sipped it slowly, wishing that PC Locke would hurry up and come back. All she wanted was for her and PC Ramesh to leave before she and Gabriel broke down completely.

She heard footsteps on the stairs and PC Locke came into the kitchen. She was wearing rubber gloves and had a mobile phone in her hand.

"Have either of you seen this phone before?" she asked, holding it up. It had a navy blue cover and there was a white logo on the back.

Iris shook her head. "No."

Gabriel's face blanched. "I think it's Pierre's," he said.

47

Gabriel had refused to believe it at first. He just couldn't get his head around it. But according to the French police, Laure had killed Pierre.

They said that Laure had lied, that Pierre had been at their apartment that day, and she had killed him and that it had been either premeditated—she had gone with the intention of killing him—or that they'd had a row and she had ended up killing him.

Iris had asked PC Locke how Laure could possibly have lifted Pierre's body and got it into a freezer when she was so slight, and PC Locke told her that it helped that Pierre was also slight; with a lot of lifting and shoving, the French police reckoned it was possible for Laure to have done it. Then there were the clothes Laure wasn't wearing when she came back that evening. The French police were searching for them, but had acknowledged that they were probably in landfill and would never be found. So now Gabriel and Iris had had to accept it; Laure had killed Pierre.

Memories crowded Gabriel's mind; the four of them together on the beach in Normandy, Pierre wading into the sea with Laure in his arms and throwing her in, Laure shrieking and kicking her legs; the four of them at their favorite Parisian restaurant, platters piled high with seafood, Laure and Pierre fighting over the last langoustine; Laure's head on Pierre's shoulder as they watched the sunset from the top of a hill in the Dordogne. How could any of them have ever imagined that she would end up killing him? And why? Because he *had* fathered a child? Because he'd been cheating on her? Because he'd wanted to make a new life with someone else? Because she wanted to make a new life with someone else? How would they ever know when they were both dead?

Gabriel had asked PC Locke if, in the light of Pierre's murder, there'd been a revision as to the cause of Laure's death. She'd looked uncomfortable and said, off the record, that suicide was a possibility. Laure would have known that Pierre's murder would eventually come to light, because at some point, the police would search their storeroom.

He no longer felt sorry for Laure. She had killed Pierre, and they had wept for her, grieved for her. To him, it was the ultimate betrayal.

48

They walked down the road, talking determinedly among themselves, trying to look nonchalant.

In reality, Iris felt horribly conspicuous. In her mind, the inhabitants of every house between theirs and Esme's were watching them surreptitiously from behind their curtains, murmuring about them: *Ooh, look, they've finally come out. But hardly surprising they wanted to shut themselves away. It's not every day a friend staying with you dies— they're saying an accident but I'm not so sure—and then, not long after, you hear that the friend's estranged husband was murdered. I've heard that she did it, the wife. But it all seems a bit strange, don't you think? Sometimes I wonder if there was anything going on—if you know what I mean.* The veritable walk of shame.

For a moment, Iris wished she hadn't given in to Esme's invitation. But they still hadn't met Hamish and, during their daily telephone call yesterday, she had told Esme she was worried about Beth, who, since coming home two weeks before, hadn't ventured out at all. She seemed content to stay close, working alongside Gabriel in the garden before coming in to help her prepare lunch or dinner. Iris knew Beth was worried about them, just as she was worried about Beth. They were all worried about each other, it seemed.

"Come over tomorrow," Esme had said. "Please don't refuse, Iris. Hugh and I would love to see you and Gabriel, and meet Beth. And you need to meet Hamish. And Marcus, Hugh's son, will be here. It will be good for Beth to meet someone around her own age. You don't have to stay for long if you don't want to, but a change of scene will do you good."

Iris knew Esme was right, so she'd agreed. It was only as she'd been getting ready this morning—it had been a relief to be forced into wearing something other than jogging bottoms and a T-shirt—that her mind had looped back to the circumstances of baby Hamish's birth. It had been a welcome respite to be able to think of something other than the horror of Pierre's murder, but Iris wished her thoughts hadn't focused on Esme, and a possible relationship between her and Joseph. The fact that he'd been present at the birth, rather than Hugh, made her uneasy. That he had taken Esme to the hospital made sense. But to have stayed, to have been with her while she gave birth, to have been the one to hold the baby in the first seconds of his life—it felt somehow wrong. It couldn't have been contrived; Esme couldn't have planned to give birth while Hugh was up a mountain so that she could have Joseph by her side. But still.

It made Iris uncomfortable about seeing Joseph, and as they neared Esme and Hugh's, she prayed he wouldn't be there. There was also the problem of what she'd said to the police, about hearing him and Laure arguing. She felt she owed him an apology, but she wanted to talk to him on his own, not in front of everyone.

That morning, Gabriel said he wondered how Joseph was feeling, given that he'd been in a relationship with Laure, and Iris had realized that she'd been so caught up in her own emotions that she'd never once thought of Joseph in all of this. In her defense, she thought that his feelings couldn't have run very deep in the space of a few weeks. It must have been a huge shock, however, for him to learn that Laure had murdered Pierre.

The pavement was too narrow for the three of them to walk abreast so Iris slipped behind and ran a worried eye over Beth. Despite being in shock when she'd first arrived, she had looked wonderfully healthy, her skin tanned a golden brown, her mahogany hair braided into a thick glossy rope. Now, despite spending most of the day outdoors in the garden, her face had an ashen pallor and there were hollows under her eyes. She had lost weight, they all had. Gabriel's clothes hung off him, he needed a belt to keep his jeans up.

In their desire to be away from prying eyes, their pace quickened as they approached Esme and Hugh's house. They were quickly swept into warm embraces and introduced to Hamish and Marcus, who was the image of his father but with a head of hair and no beard. As she watched Beth walking in the garden with Hamish in her arms, laughing at something Marcus was saying, Iris felt some of the tension leave her.

"Thank you," she said, as Esme pressed a glass of chilled white wine into her hand. "I didn't know how much we needed this." She glanced over to where Gabriel was talking to Hugh. "Gabriel especially. He and Pierre had a special bond, and to think of his life ending in such a violent way is torture for him."

"I can't even begin to imagine how hard it must be for you all."

Iris moved to a wicker chair and sat down. "We think that for Laure to have been driven to such an extreme act, there's more to the story of Pierre having a child. Gabriel said he had doubts at one point. The problem is, we'll never know." She took a welcome sip of wine. "I feel so confused about everything, about how I should feel. Despite what she did, Laure was my friend. And I feel partially to blame for what happened. I should have noticed, paid more attention to her state of mind. When she came back from Paris, there was this feverishness about her which was totally at odds with how she'd been when she called me from Gare du Nord. To be honest, I was just glad that she was no longer depressed and crying, and I didn't think to question the change in her mood." Iris paused. "At the time, Gabriel wondered if her distress when she called me was an act. It obviously was."

"You can't blame yourself, Iris. Even if you had realized that Laure was mentally unstable when she came back from Paris, it would never have occurred to you that she had murdered Pierre."

"There must have been a trigger. I don't believe Laure went to Paris with the intention of killing him. He must have told her something that made her spiral out of control."

"We saw her the day after, at yours, and she was as cool as a cucumber. It seems incredible that less than twenty-four hours earlier, she'd killed Pierre in cold blood."

"She'd started drinking early that day, I remember. Maybe she was trying to blank out what she'd done." Iris looked for something else to talk about. "Your garden is looking so much better."

Esme nodded. "Having Joseph working full-time for the last three weeks has certainly helped."

"How is he?"

"Devastated. Her death hit him hard, and being taken in for questioning was a huge shock. A shock to me and Hugh too, as we hadn't known they were in a relationship." She paused. "You tried to tell me but I'd hoped it wasn't true. I didn't think he would be good for Laure—yet it seems that he loved her. He couldn't believe the police thought he might have had something to do with her death."

"I need to apologize to him."

"He's not here today, he's gone to see his mother." She hesitated a moment. "You'll be going to Paris this week?"

Iris nodded. They hadn't gone to Laure's funeral last week, but they were going to Pierre's. "Yes, on Tuesday. The funeral is on Wednesday. Then back on Thursday." Esme nodded slowly. "What?" Iris asked.

"It's just that Joseph doesn't believe that Laure killed Pierre."

"Neither did we. And yet it seems that she did."

"He said she wouldn't have been capable of it."

"There was a lot more to Laure than any of us knew." Iris's voice was sad. "And I'm sorry, but Joseph only knew her for a few weeks. I don't think he could have known the true essence of Laure in such a short a time."

"I agree. It's probably his grief speaking." Esme looked toward the garden. "Beth is lovely. You must be so proud of her."

Iris smiled. "Thank you. Yes, we are, we're tremendously proud of her. It's lovely having her around, although it's probably not so great for her. Gabriel and I aren't much fun at the moment."

"I'm sure she understands. And if she ever needs a change of scene, she can always come here and cuddle Hamish."

"They're so lovely," Beth said, as they walked home two hours later. "Esme says I can go around whenever I want."

Iris nodded. "She's amazing like that. Her door is always open, literally. She's fine about people just walking in."

Beth smiled. "That's so cool. I would hate it. Imagine someone dropping by when you've got a face mask on, or are still in your pajamas."

"Neither of those things would faze Esme at all. Whereas I can't think of anything worse."

"Yet you coped really well when Laure turned up uninvited and made herself at home."

Iris blinked back sudden tears, touched by Beth's compliment but feeling unworthy of it. "On the surface perhaps. But she was beginning to exasperate me. I feel terrible about that now. And we didn't go to her funeral," she added, her voice breaking. "We couldn't. It would have been as if we were condoning what she'd done."

Beth linked her arm through Iris's. "Stop beating yourself up about it, Mum. You were right not to go. And if you do feel bad, just remember that she killed Pierre." Her voice hardened. "That should get rid of any pity you feel toward Laure."

49

Gabriel stared out of the train window. Now that Pierre's funeral was over, the little energy that had carried him through it had drained out of him. They'd soon be at St. Pancras and he felt so bone-weary he wasn't sure he'd be able to make it off the train.

What alarmed him the most was that he didn't seem to be able to give himself the mental shake that he needed. Yes, the last year had been hard; his beloved father and equally beloved dog had died; he had found Charlie near to death in the quarry; his best friend had been murdered by his wife, who had then jumped to her death. He could be forgiven for feeling depressed. But it was his inability to find anything positive to hang on to that worried him. His marriage wasn't in a great place, and he had no inclination to go back to work as a GP. Beth—the only thing that got him up in the morning—would soon be going to university, and the walled garden would soon be finished, so he wouldn't even have that to do.

Beth hadn't wanted to come to the funeral, and he and Iris had been happy to let her stay behind. He hadn't wanted her to see the tears he knew he wouldn't be able to hold back; he couldn't have coped with her distress at his distress. It was also something he felt he and Iris needed to do together, by themselves, because once it was over, their shared relief that they could now get on with their lives would hopefully bring them closer. Except that it hadn't. Last night, in their hotel, they might have been in different rooms for the little they'd said to each other. It seemed there were no words big enough to bridge the gap between them.

It was the same at home. If he walked into the kitchen, and found Iris already there, he would mumble *Sorry*, help himself quickly to whatever he wanted and leave. When had it come to the point, he wondered, where he was apologizing for going into his own kitchen?

He pressed his head into the head rest so that he could see Iris's reflection in the window. She was sitting upright, staring straight ahead of her and the bleakness on her face made him instinctively reach for her hand. She didn't grip his, or even hold it. Her hand lay limply in his, as if she was only tolerating his touch, and because to snatch it away would have been rude.

"Are you okay?" he asked quietly, turning to her.

He saw a flare of anger in her eyes and steeled himself for a *What do you think*? But, perhaps in deference to the other passengers, she gave a tight nod. He saw the woman sitting opposite glance at Iris, and when she turned her eyes on him and gave him a sympathetic smile, he wanted to lean across and shout at her not to judge his wife, because she didn't know everything she'd been through. But he was scared that once he began, the anger and the bitterness and the unfairness of it all would explode out of him, and he wouldn't be able to stop.

Claire had been at the funeral. After, as they'd left the crematorium, he'd wanted to speak to her, but she'd been with friends, and Iris hadn't wanted to interrupt them. But when Iris had got caught up in a conversation with Pierre's work colleagues, Claire had seen him standing alone and had come to speak to him.

"I'm so sorry," she'd said. "I can't imagine how difficult this must be for you and Iris, coming so soon after Laure. I know how close the four of you were. It's hard enough for us." She indicated the group of friends.

"It doesn't seem possible that they've both gone," Gabriel had said. "And in such terrible circumstances." He'd hesitated and then plunged on, because he would probably never see her again, and he needed to know. "Do you know what happened, why Laure left Pierre?"

Claire had shaken her head. "All Pierre told me was that they'd decided to take a break from each other and that Laure had gone to stay with you and Iris in England. He never said why and I never asked because if he'd wanted to tell me, he would have. From the little he said, it seemed to have been a mutual decision." She'd exchanged a rueful smile with him. "You know how private he was, how he never really shared his problems with anyone, preferring to go off by himself when he was feeling low. It's why, when he messaged me and said he was going away for the whole of July, I didn't think anything of it. It was what he did." She'd hesitated then, as if she wasn't sure if she should continue. "I can't believe it of Laure, I really can't. I know I have to, but it seems—I don't know, unfathomable. Even if he was having an affair, which I doubt, why kill him?"

He'd been tempted to ask Claire if she'd heard anything about Pierre having a child. But he hadn't, because the more he thought about it—and he had, a lot—the more he was convinced that Laure had lied. The fact that they would never know the truth, and so never really have closure, made moving on doubly hard.

He was roused from his thoughts by Iris removing her hand from his. He waited to see if she needed it to rummage in her bag, or rub her eye, but she simply folded it into her other hand, lying in her lap. His heart went out to her; he could almost see her inner turmoil and wished he could help. But she seemed so out of reach.

And then there was Maggie Ingram. Acknowledging that he'd kept her waiting long enough, he'd rescheduled their meeting for a week on Tuesday. He could have made it sooner, but he thought he might need some downtime after the grueling, desperate experience of Pierre's funeral. Once he'd seen her, he hoped that everyone would leave him alone, and he'd finally be able grieve in peace for his friend.

50

Iris felt terrible for removing her hand from Gabriel's. She hated that she couldn't bear for him to touch her, hated that she was unable to comfort him, especially at a time like this, when he had buried his best friend. But she couldn't allow him to penetrate the steel barrier she had mentally constructed around herself to contain the terrifying emotions that had piled up inside her, afraid that they would come spewing out in one massive, violent jet. Because if they did, that would be the end of her. Iris Pelley would cease to exist.

She also hated that uppermost in her mind wasn't Gabriel, or Pierre, or even Laure. It was Joseph who invaded her thoughts as she sat on the train on their way back to London. It had been a mistake to go and see him, she realized bitterly, a mistake to think that he would forgive her.

She had gone to see him at Esme's on Monday. The front door had been unusually closed, and Iris remembered Esme saying the previous day that she had an appointment at the doctor's for Hamish the next morning. She had taken the path around the side of the house, expecting to find Joseph working in the garden. There'd been no sign of him, and when she knocked on the door of his cottage, there had been no answer.

She shouldn't have gone in, she knew that now. But when she'd tried the door, it had swung open, almost as if it was inviting her in. She'd been curious; there had been so many jokes about Joseph living in a shed that she'd wanted to see what it was like.

It looked surprisingly comfortable. The door opened onto a main room, with a sofa along the right-hand wall, and on the opposite wall, a kitchen area with a double gas ring and a fridge. In the center of the room, there was a small wooden table and two chairs.

Opening the door to the left of the main door, she'd found a small a bedroom with a double bed and a chest of drawers. Pushing away images of Laure and Joseph there together, she had moved to the door to the right of the bed. As she had expected, it led to a compact shower room.

Back in the main room, she'd pulled open the cupboard doors and found blue and white striped crockery, saucepans and cans of beans, chickpeas and soup. She should have left then, and waited for Joseph outside. Instead, she had sat on the sofa, imagining what it would be like to live there, away from everyone and everything. *Here*, she remembered thinking, *I would find peace.*

"What do you think you're doing?" Joseph's voice, angry and disbelieving, had broken abruptly into her thoughts. He was standing in the doorway, his face dark with something Iris feared might be loathing.

"I-I've come to apologize," she'd stammered, scrambling to her feet.

Before she could say anything further, he had stepped away from the door so that he was no longer blocking it.

"Please leave."

"I just want to explain," she'd said, flustered. "It was an honest mistake, I really did think you and Laure had been arguing. I—" She stopped. Joseph had stepped toward her. "Now!" he had almost shouted.

The memory made her cheeks flame with embarrassment. She

wanted to ask Gabriel something, but it was several minutes before she could summon enough saliva to be able to speak.

"Joseph's not coming back to work for us, is he?" she asked.

Gabriel turned to her, his eyebrows raised, and she knew how odd it must have sounded, that she was talking about Joseph when she'd barely said two words to him since Pierre's funeral yesterday.

"Yes, he should be there now. I asked Hugh on Sunday if we could have him back to finish the garden and he said he would send him around this week. He was probably there on Tuesday too. I should have asked Beth if he turned up."

"Why?" Iris tried to hide her panic. "I mean, why can't you finish it yourself? There's not much to do now, is there?"

"No, but I want it finished before Beth leaves for university and if I don't have Joseph to help me, it won't be."

"Does it matter if it's not finished?"

"Yes, it does." Gabriel lowered his voice. "I promised Beth it would be ready for when she came home and, because of everything, it wasn't. So it's important to me that she can enjoy it for the few weeks before she leaves."

"How long? How much longer is he going to be with us?"

"I don't know, a couple of weeks probably. Look, I know things might be a bit difficult between you, but I'm sure if you explain, it will be fine."

"I would have thought he'd want to avoid being where he spent so much time with Laure," Iris hissed, causing the woman opposite to give her another look before turning back to the book she was reading.

"I hadn't thought of that," Gabriel said. "So maybe he hasn't been around." He dug his phone from his pocket. "I'll message Hugh and ask."

Iris leaned her head back against the seat and closed her eyes, silently praying that Joseph had been so traumatized by Laure's death that he'd refused to come back to work for them.

Gabriel's voice cut through her thoughts. "Hugh just confirmed. He's at the house."

Iris blinked back tears. She had hoped never to see Joseph again. But there was nothing she could do about it except stay out of his way on the days he was there.

51

Gabriel paced the sitting room, waiting for Maggie Ingram to arrive. He glanced at himself in the cracked mirror; his face was deathly pale, but hopefully Maggie would put it down to the trauma he'd been through, and not to his dread at their meeting.

He and Iris had never got around to replacing the mirror, maybe because subconsciously, it had represented their relationship at that point in time, and they would put up a new one only once they were back on track. For a moment, Gabriel wondered if he should smash the mirror to smithereens, because he sometimes felt that he and Iris were broken beyond repair. Once Beth left for university, he wasn't sure how they would survive. She filled the silences between them.

The doorbell rang, rooting him to the spot. He gave himself a mental shake. Compared to everything he'd been through in the past few weeks, this was nothing.

Walking into the hall, he opened the door. He was grateful that Maggie hadn't changed much in the intervening seven years or so since he'd last seen her. Her smile wasn't quite so wide, and her eyes were tinged with sadness. But she was instantly recognizable, which made it suddenly easier.

"I'm so sorry to intrude at such a terrible time," she said, as he led her into the sitting room. "It's kind of you to see me when you have so much else to deal with." She hesitated. "How are you?"

He searched for something that would sum up the utter desolation he felt.

"Bereft. Lost. Unsure if I'll ever feel whole again."

She nodded. "It doesn't get easier," she said softly. "It just gets different."

"Please, sit down. Can I get you tea, coffee?"

"No, thank you."

"I'm so very sorry about Charlie," he said, sitting down opposite her. "I have such good memories of him. I hope he carried on playing football at St. Cuthbert's?"

"He did, and rugby, and tennis. He was sports mad." She gave him a quick smile. "I'm so grateful that you were there with him at the end, that he was with someone he knew, someone he'd liked and admired very much. You can't imagine what a huge comfort that has been." She paused. "I-I'm not sure I'd have been able to bear it if he had died alone. And if you hadn't been there, I would never have known that he'd forgiven me. We'd had a huge row, and he was angry with me, so angry that he wouldn't let me explain. He stormed out of the house and I never saw him again."

"I'm sorry."

"Thank you. Now, tell me about Beth. How is she?"

As Gabriel began telling Maggie about Beth's gap year in Greece, he was humbled by her generosity. He couldn't imagine how painful it must be for her to hear about someone nearly the same age as her son, who was experiencing life to the full and had a bright future ahead of them. He also felt ashamed. Yes, he had lost two friends in terrible circumstances, but Maggie had lost her only child, yet she still managed to get out of bed every day instead of indulging in self-pity, as he'd been doing.

"Are you still practicing as a GP?" Maggie asked, when they had finished talking about Beth.

Gabriel hesitated. "Not at the moment. I've taken some time off."

"Of course." Maggie nodded sympathetically, and Gabriel gathered, to his relief, that she thought his time off was a recent thing, and was related to what had happened to Laure and Pierre rather than Charlie.

"I feel so guilty about Pierre," he blurted out suddenly, wondering why he was telling Maggie about the crushing culpability he carried around with him, when he had never mentioned it to Iris. "He was my best friend, and I let him down. I should have gone to see him as soon as Laure moved in with us, but I didn't, I only went a month later. If I'd gone right at the beginning, it might have changed the course of events." He broke off, realizing that she might not know what he was talking about. "I'm sorry, I don't know if you read about it in the press."

"I did," she said, eager to put his mind at rest. "When Laure was found, the media drew a lot of parallels with Charlie, because they were both found in the quarry."

Gabriel looked appalled. "I can't imagine how hard that must have been."

She smiled. "Going back to Pierre, regret is such a waste of emotion. No matter how much we want to, we can't change the past. We need to acknowledge the mistakes we've made but not allow them to cloud every moment of every day."

"I know you're right. But it's not easy to move on." He paused. "How about you? Are you working at the moment?"

Maggie shook her head. "I'm concentrating on our garden. While I was working at the school, I used to help in the vegetable garden in my spare time and I'd love to be self-sufficient one day, and have some chickens too."

"You're speaking to a convert," Gabriel said. "I never had time to garden before, but when I started looking for something to fill my time, I decided to make a start on an old walled garden that the previous owners had let slide into ruin. I can't tell you how much I love being out there."

"A walled garden," Maggie breathed, closing her eyes for a moment. "The ultimate dream."

"Would you like to see it?" Gabriel asked impulsively. "Unless you're in a rush?"

"No, no, I'd love to see it. Thank you."

Gabriel led Maggie through the house and out onto the terrace, pleased to have someone to show the walled garden to. He was sure that once they'd managed to put the horror of the last few months behind them, Iris would appreciate the garden. At the moment, it was the last place she wanted to be. He knew she no longer felt comfortable around Joseph because of what she'd said to the police about the argument she'd overheard. It was unfortunate that he needed Joseph for a few more weeks, otherwise he would have asked him to leave. But there was still work to be done that he couldn't do on his own, from lack of expertise—and, he hated to admit it, strength.

"This is lovely," Maggie said, admiring the flower-filled borders as they walked down the path. "Do you do all this on your own or does your wife help?"

"Iris usually takes care of the borders and I cut the grass. But I have help in the walled garden."

They arrived at the entrance and Gabriel pushed the door open.

"What a lovely space!" Maggie exclaimed. She stepped inside and looked around. "I love all the paths—and you have quite a lot in here already. I imagine some of these shrubs have been here a long time."

"Yes, we kept what we could, but as you can see, we've got a lot of planting to do. I wish I'd taken some photos of what it was like before, then you could have seen how far we've come in three months or so. It's largely down to Joseph. He's the one with all the knowledge and expertise."

"Joseph?"

"Yes. That's him in the far corner. We poached him from some friends of ours who recently moved into the village—" Gabriel stopped; Maggie had clutched his arm and when he turned to look at her, he saw the blood had drained from her face. "Maggie, are you all right? Do you want to sit down?" Fearing she was about to keel over, he put his arm around her shoulder and tried to lead her to the wooden bench. But wrenching free, she turned, pushed through the open door and began running up the path toward the house.

"Maggie!" As Gabriel caught up with her he could hear her ragged breathing. Iris's face appeared at the kitchen window, then disappeared as she ran to open the sliding door for Maggie.

"Would you like to sit down for a moment? Can I get you some water?" he heard Iris asking.

Moving past her, Maggie made her way to the door. "No, no, I'm sorry, I need to go. I didn't feel well for a moment. But I'm all right now."

"Are you sure you won't sit down for a minute?" Gabriel asked as he caught up with her. "I'm worried about you driving, if you're not feeling well."

"No, really, I'm fine now." She fumbled for the latch and he reached around her and opened the door.

"If you're sure," he said.

"I am. Thank you, you've been very kind." Maggie looked past him to where Iris was standing. "Goodbye." And then she was gone.

They stayed where they were until they heard the car pulling out of the drive.

"What was all that about?" Iris asked, bemused.

"I don't know, she suddenly had a dizzy spell. I hope she'll be all right driving home."

"Me too. So, apart from that, how did it go?"

"Really well."

"Did it help, talking to her?"

"Yes, it really did," Gabriel said, because if the lie he had told had helped Maggie, had allowed her to move on, he was no longer going to feel guilty about it.

52

Iris heard Beth's footsteps on the stairs.

"Is everything all right?" she asked, coming into the kitchen "I just saw Charlie's mum leaving, from my bedroom window. She seemed to be in a hurry."

"I'm not really sure what happened," Iris said, pouring herself a glass of sparkling water. She held up the bottle, offering some to Beth, who shook her head. "She was in the garden with Dad and then she suddenly came running into the house. She said she didn't feel well. I tried to get her to sit for a while, but she wanted to go."

"Did Dad say something to her? Something that upset her? About Charlie, I mean."

"No, I don't think so. He seemed as surprised as me."

"Weird." Beth leaned back against the countertop. "I'm worried about him, Mum. He looks awful."

"I know. But maybe meeting Maggie will have helped."

Beth opened the fridge and took out a carton of juice. "I might go to Esme and Hugh's later. I promised Esme I'd look after Hamish for a while."

Again, Iris wanted to say. "Good idea," she said instead, passing Beth a glass. She didn't blame Beth; being with her and Gabriel twenty-four-seven must be depressing.

"I might go upstairs and read for a while."

"Okay." Iris gave her a smile, looking for something to keep Beth with her a bit longer. "Maybe we could go shopping on Saturday, have lunch out."

"I'd love that," Beth said happily. "It would be really nice to spend some time together."

Beth left and Iris's thoughts went reluctantly back to something Beth had said when she'd come back from Esme's last night.

"It's really sweet how attached Joseph is to Hamish," she'd said, flopping down on the sofa next to Iris.

Iris had put her book down. "In what way?"

"Just that he dotes on him. If Esme needs anyone to hold Hamish, or to go and fetch him from his cot, or put him to bed, Joseph is there before me and Hugh. Even Marcus didn't get a look in over the weekend, and he only really came down to see Hamish."

"Doesn't Hugh mind? About Joseph?"

Beth had laughed. "I think he's relieved. He and Esme are pretty exhausted at the moment. They're still getting up a couple of times a night for Hamish, so they're grateful for any help they can get in the evenings."

"Does Joseph spend every evening with them, then?"

"Not every evening, just some. Where's Dad?"

"In the shower."

Beth had stretched her arms above her head. "I think I'll go to bed," she'd said, yawning. "How about you, are you coming up?"

"In a minute."

She'd leaned across to kiss Iris. "Night, Mum. Don't stay up too late."

Iris had smiled at their momentary role reversal. "I won't."

But she had stayed up, her doubts about Esme and Joseph resurfacing. The thought that Esme might have been in a relationship with Joseph, and might be having an affair with him now, had made her indignant on Hugh's behalf. Unless they had an open marriage. But if that were the case, wouldn't Hugh wonder whether Hamish was actually his?

She began to make salad to go with the steaks she'd bought for their dinner. She already guessed that Beth wouldn't be eating with them, not if she was going to Esme's. She and Gabriel had taken to having the news on while they had dinner, something they'd never done before, and something they didn't do during meals with Beth. Iris told herself that it was normal they didn't have much to say now that neither of them were working. Before, they would chat to each other about their respective days. Now, they ran out of conversation before they'd even sat down.

"Penny for them."

Gabriel was standing in the doorway, trying to hide his worry behind a smile.

"What's up?" she asked, taking the steaks out of the fridge so they could get to room temperature.

"It's Maggie. I've been going over it my mind. When we were in the walled garden, Joseph was working at the far end. It was when I pointed him out that she suddenly seemed unwell."

She frowned. "A coincidence, surely? She can't possibly know Joseph."

"What if his job took him to the school where Maggie worked and where Charlie was a pupil? Their paths might have crossed there." He came farther into the kitchen and stood across from her. "The thing is, before coming to work for them, Hugh told me that Joseph worked for a landscaping company called Jarmans. I looked them up, and it said that one of their contracts had been for landscaping the grounds of St. Cuthbert's. So I asked Joseph if he had worked on that contract, and he said that he hadn't. But what if he lied?"

"Why would he?"

"I don't know. Maybe because he doesn't want anyone to know he worked there." He paused. "I don't suppose you're going to see Esme anytime soon?"

"I was thinking of going tomorrow morning. Why?"

"Could you try and find out where Joseph worked before coming to them? Don't ask her outright, I don't want him to know that we're checking up on him."

"You really think he and Maggie knew each other?"

"I can't think of anything else to explain her sudden distress."

"Okay," Iris said. "I'll see what I can do."

53

Iris pushed open the door to Esme's kitchen.

"It's only me," she called.

"Iris!" Esme crossed the room and gave her a hug. "What a lovely surprise! It's so good to see you."

"I'm not disturbing you, am I?"

"Never. Come and sit down. It's been ages." There was a slight hint of reproach in her eyes.

"I didn't want to cramp Beth's style," Iris explained, moving to the sofa. "It's done her so much good, spending time with you and Hugh these past few weeks."

"We love having her here and she's a great help with Hamish. Now, what can I get you? Tea, a cold drink, or something stronger?" Esme fluttered around her like a bird.

"A cold drink would be lovely. Where's Hamish?"

"Sleeping, thank God. On the terrace."

Esme brought a jug of cordial and two glasses over to the table and sank into the sofa. "So, how are you?" she asked, picking up the jug.

"Getting there. Having Beth around has helped so much. It's made us strong in the sense that, for her sake, we can't allow ourselves to sink into depression, which we might have done if she wasn't with us. I think we're both dreading her leaving."

Ice clinked into the glasses as Esme poured the cordial.

"I'm glad you're here, Iris, because I want to ask you something. Or rather, Hugh and I do, but he's not here at the moment and I know he won't mind me asking you on his behalf." She took a breath. "We'd love you to be Hamish's godmother."

Iris felt her eyes widen. "Me?"

Esme laughed. "Yes, you. If it's something you think you'd like. You might already have enough godchildren, so please say if you'd rather not."

"I don't," Iris said, still feeling dazed. "I only have two, and one of those I don't see very often. It's just that you barely know me."

"Not in terms of time, but in my heart I feel as if I've known you for ages, and I know we'll always be friends."

"Are you sure there's no one else you'd rather have? One of your sisters?"

Esme shook her head. "Hugh and I would really like it to be you."

"Well, then, I'd be delighted. Thank you."

"Really? Oh gosh, I'm so glad. Now we really will be like family!"

"Who's the godfather?" Iris asked. "Marcus?"

"No. We've asked Joseph."

The euphoria flooded from her. "Joseph?"

"Yes. I mean, he practically delivered Hamish, so it was an easy choice." A frown crossed her face. "You seem shocked."

"It's just—I don't know—he seems maybe too involved with the baby."

Esme's frown deepened. "What do you mean?"

"Okay, I'm just going to say it." Her words came out in a rush. "I saw him once with his hand on your stomach and it seemed a bit familiar. Then he was there with you at the hospital when you gave birth, which again is quite intimate. And Beth said that he does a lot with Hamish, that in the evenings he's often the one who looks after him."

Two spots of color appeared on Esme's cheeks. "You think Joseph is Hamish's father."

"No, but—" Iris stopped, her cheeks as red as Esme's.

"He isn't."

Iris nodded. "Right."

"But we were in a relationship at one time." Esme met Iris's eyes. "I've never told anyone."

"You don't have to tell me," Iris said quickly.

"I don't mind telling you, Iris, but Hugh doesn't know that Joseph and I have ever been anything more than friends. And I'd rather he didn't know, because he might think there's something going on between me and Joseph, which there isn't, and it would only complicate things." She reached for the jug and refilled their glasses. "It began when I went back to live with my parents after I split up with my partner of three years, and I think I told you I was in a bad way, both emotionally and psychologically."

"Yes, I remember."

"Joseph used to come around and do a bit of gardening for my parents; they knew his parents, and because Joseph was training to be a landscape gardener, they were happy to let him try out ideas on their garden. It was the summer, and because I'd given up my job, I spent most of my time sunbathing on the lawn and generally getting in Joseph's way, because he was putting a border in. He was just a kid to me at first, but the more I got to know him the more I understood that like me, he was going through his own personal trauma and we began to share our problems with each other. I told him how it felt to be dumped at thirty years old, he told me how it felt to be a recovering alcoholic at twenty-three."

"But isn't that when you met Hugh? When you went back to live with your parents after your relationship broke down?"

"Yes, but I only worked for him at first. Falling in love with him was a gradual thing, it didn't happen until two years later."

"How long did your relationship with Joseph last?"

"Not long." She paused a moment, and dropped her head. "Three months later I realized I was pregnant and against Joseph's wishes, I had an abortion. So that was that, really."

Iris heard the pain in her voice and reached for her hand. "I'm sorry."

Esme raised her head, her eyes bright with tears. "I've never told anybody before. It's something I can't forgive myself for, especially since I had Hamish, because I can't help thinking what that child would have been like if I'd gone ahead with the pregnancy. But at the time, I couldn't see that I had any other choice. Joseph was only twenty-three, he wanted us to get married, have the baby—it was an impossible situation. In the end he supported me in my decision; he came with me to the clinic and looked after me afterward. And then, when he felt I was better, he left. I didn't see him again until a few months ago, at my parents' house."

"What happened?" Iris asked.

"Even though we'd both moved on, because nearly a decade had gone by, and I was married, we hit it off straight away. He told me he'd had a couple of long-term relationships and admitted that it was his alcohol problem that had caused them to end. He'd also crashed his car while drunk and had lost his job as a result. He'd—"

"That must have been a blow," Iris interrupted quickly, seizing the opportunity to find a way into what Gabriel wanted to know. "Where was he working?"

"For Jarmans, landscaping the grounds of a public school."

"Which one?"

Iris sensed her hesitate. "St. Cuthbert's."

"St. Cuthbert's? Wasn't that the school Charlie Ingram went to?"

"Yes, but Joseph didn't know him."

"It's strange he's never mentioned to Gabriel that he worked there when he knows it was Gabriel who found Charlie."

"Probably because he didn't want to upset him. We all know Gabriel doesn't like talking about it. Anyway," Esme said. "After he lost his job, Joseph went back to live with his mum, and my dad, seeing what a mess he was in, gave him a job. But after the incident with the gas bottle, my parents didn't want the responsibility of him anymore—they're in their late seventies and don't need the worry—so my dad asked if I'd be interested in having Joseph over to sort out the garden, and also to get him away from some friends of his who he felt were a bad influence. I called Hugh, told him about Joseph, said he was a recovering alcoholic who needed a place to stay for a while, and he agreed to give him a job."

"Do your parents know that you and Joseph were in a relationship all those years ago?" Iris asked, her heart still racing from the news that Joseph had worked at the same school as Maggie Ingram.

Esme shook her head. "No."

"And you didn't mention it to Hugh?"

"No. In retrospect, I should have, because if I had, Hugh would still have allowed Joseph to stay, because if he'd refused, it would have been as if he was saying that he didn't trust me. But I didn't want him worrying that something was going on every time I spoke to Joseph, so I decided to say nothing. I knew Joseph wouldn't be with us forever, and neither he nor I have any problem with each other. There's nothing between us anymore, except for friendship and the memory of our unborn baby."

"That can't be easy."

"It isn't. When we met up again, he didn't mention it so I thought that he'd forgotten about it, or at least put it from his mind. When he saw that I was pregnant, he just asked the normal questions about when the baby was due. It was only a week or so later that I realized how much he was still affected by it."

"Why, what happened?"

Esme got up and walked to the window, then stood looking out at the garden for a moment. "I was upstairs in the bedroom when Hugh came to tell me that he thought Joseph had been drinking. Apparently, he'd asked him to do something in the garden and when he saw it hadn't been done he went to find Joseph, who spun him some yarn about not feeling well. Hugh reckoned he was hungover and I was really disappointed, because Joseph had been doing so well and hadn't touched a drop for weeks. So I went to see him." She paused a moment. "Hugh was right, Joseph had been drinking, and I was really angry with him, I told him he had let himself, and my dad, down. And that's when he told me that the news of my pregnancy had really upset him because he'd never stopped thinking about the baby we might have had." She turned to face Iris. "It's strange, isn't it, the way people presume men are less affected by abortions and miscarriages than women. Although Joseph had spent a long time making sure I was okay after the abortion, I had given very little thought to how he might be feeling. Do you know what he told me? That all those years before he'd calculated approximately when the baby would have been born and that every year since, on the twenty-ninth of March, he's imagined what it would be like to have a two-year-old, or a four-year-old, or a seven-year-old, and so on. I felt so sad, and guilty, because he had thought about our baby more than I had." She moved back to the sofa and sat down. "He's never had a child and he's always longed for one. So I can understand why my pregnancy destabilized him. Anyway, we talked for ages and he promised that he wouldn't start drinking again. As far as I know, he hasn't. I think the fact that I allowed him to be involved with my pregnancy helped. You know, he liked to put his hand on my stomach and feel the baby kicking, and sometimes, when I was lying down, he would lay his head on my stomach to see if he could hear him moving. But only when no one was around, because it could have looked a bit strange."

"Yes, I don't think there're many women who would let a man other than their husband lay their head on their pregnant stomach," Iris said. "As long as he doesn't start thinking of Hamish as his."

"No, of course he won't. But as he was there at the birth, he's obviously going to feel a connection with him, which is why we asked him to be Hamish's godfather." Esme stopped. "You're frowning again."

"I just think that if Hugh knew about your past relationship with Joseph, he might not be so keen on him being the godfather, that's all."

Esme raised her eyebrows. "I can't imagine Hugh being that petty."

"You're right, of course," Iris said hastily.

"We'd like to have the christening quite soon," Esme chattered on. "We've spoken to the vicar and we're thinking Sunday the second of October. Would that work for you? And Beth? We'd love her to be there, but I know she'll only just have left for university. Do you think she'll be able to come back for it?"

Iris made a quick calculation—just over three weeks away—and gave Esme a smile. "That should be fine."

54

"Joseph did work at St. Cuthbert's," Iris said, handing Gabriel a glass of wine. "I asked Esme. I also asked her why Joseph had never mentioned it to you and she said he probably hadn't wanted to upset you."

Gabriel supposed it was a reasonable explanation. He still didn't like that Joseph had lied to his face—but hadn't he himself lied to Maggie?

He took a sip of wine. "How's Esme?"

"She's good. She and Hugh are having Hamish christened and they've asked me to be his godmother."

"Gosh, that's nice of them. It shows how much they appreciate you as a friend. You accepted, I presume?"

"Yes, but I might not have if I'd known that they'd asked Joseph to be Hamish's godfather."

"Joseph?" Gabriel raised his eyebrows. "Isn't that a surprising choice? You'd have thought they'd have asked Marcus. Or maybe they did and he didn't want to?"

"No. They asked Joseph because he was there at the birth."

"Right." He looked closely at Iris. "There's something else, isn't there?"

She put her glass down on the side, then leaned back against the countertop, facing him, as if she wanted to be able to gauge his reaction.

"Esme and Joseph were in a relationship."

"What! When? I mean, is he—"

"No, it was years ago, before she met Hugh. She was staying at her parents' after splitting up with her partner and he was doing some gardening for them. Hugh doesn't know."

"Why hide it? If it's over."

She reached for her glass. "I think she was worried that if she told Hugh, he might not have wanted Joseph to come and work for them."

"But if he finds out now, he'll wonder why Esme wasn't up-front about it."

"He won't find out. It's not as if there's anything between Esme and Joseph now."

"Hm. I still would have told Hugh, if I'd been Esme."

"That's because you're honorable."

Gabriel smiled but he couldn't make it reach his eyes.

"I'm going to take a walk around the garden," he said. "Ease the muscles in my back a bit. I never knew digging could be such hard work."

"You've been out there all day."

"Yes, I like it when Joseph's not around."

"You and me both."

He held up his glass of wine. "I'll take this with me."

"There's only the two of us for dinner tonight, so take your time."

"Beth at Esme's?"

"Yes."

He nodded distractedly and carried his wine out to the garden, thinking about Joseph. A relationship with Esme, a relationship with Laure—and a possible affair with Maggie? Was that why Joseph had actively encouraged him not to meet Maggie, the day Iris had told everyone that he'd been contacted by her grief counselor? Had he been worried that his name might come up in conversation? He reminded himself not to get carried away. It was pure speculation that Maggie and Joseph had had an affair; there could be a million other reasons why Maggie had fled when she saw him. Still, Gabriel didn't like that Joseph's relationships with both Esme and Laure had happened when they had been vulnerable; Esme had split from her long-term partner, and Laure had left Pierre. Was that what Joseph was? A man who preyed on vulnerable women when they were at their lowest?

With that thought in his mind, Gabriel couldn't help questioning Joseph's version of events the day Laure had died. What if it hadn't been as he'd said, what if their argument hadn't been about Laure telling him and Iris that she and Joseph were in a relationship? What if it had been as he'd first thought, that Joseph had told her it was over between them? It didn't change anything; whether Laure took her own life because she knew Pierre's murder would eventually be discovered, or because Joseph had broken up with her, the fact was that she was dead. But if it was the latter, surely Joseph bore some responsibility for her death.

55

"Mum, Dad, can I talk to you a minute?"

Gabriel and Iris turned from where they were standing in the kitchen, and replied simultaneously, "Of course."

There was relief in their voices at another silence between them being broken. Their concerns about Joseph having known Maggie, and their attempts to find out if he had worked at St. Cuthbert's had brought them together briefly. But now the distance was back.

Beth moved from the kitchen doorway and they followed her onto the terrace, Gabriel carrying his mug of coffee. A million possibilities flew through Iris's mind at what Beth could possibly want to tell them that merited sitting down at a table. She watched Beth closely as she pulled out a chair and sank onto it. She'd seemed happier lately and Iris knew she had Esme to thank for that.

Gabriel threw Iris a look, telling her to hurry up and sit down. From the way he was running his hand through his hair she could tell how nervous he was and guessed that the thought uppermost in his mind was that Beth was going to tell them she had some terrible illness.

"What's up, Bethie?" he said, when he couldn't bear the suspense any longer.

"Okay—well, I've asked to defer for a year. I don't feel ready to go to university yet."

"Oh," Iris said, unable to keep the surprise from her voice.

"I will go," Beth said quickly. "Just not this year."

Relief whooshed out of Gabriel. "That's fine, Beth, we completely understand." He turned to Iris. "Don't we?"

"Yes, of course, if you don't feel ready. Are you sure they'll agree to defer you?"

"I hope so. I emailed and explained everything—you know, about Pierre and Laure—and I think they will, on compassionate grounds."

"And do you have any plans? Will you try and get some work experience? I don't mean straightaway, I know you probably want to chill for a bit."

Beth reached up, pulled the scrunchie from her ponytail and shook out her hair. "Chill for a bit, definitely. If you and Dad can bear having me stay a while longer," she added with a smile.

"That goes without saying," Gabriel said. "You know you can stay for as long as you like."

Iris nodded. "I think you've made the right decision, Beth. You've been through a lot, you need some downtime."

Beth got to her feet and hugged each of them in turn. "Thank you for understanding. Why don't we go out for lunch? My treat, for you being the best parents in the world."

Iris smiled. "That's a lovely idea. But I don't think your dad will let you pay."

"You're absolutely not paying." Gabriel couldn't hide his delight at Beth's decision to defer for a year, and Iris realized that if she stayed with them that whole time, it would be the longest she'd ever lived with them since she was eleven years old. Her heart flickered at the thought that this would be the chance to really get to know her, a chance for them to forge the mother-daughter bond she'd always felt was missing. She glanced at Beth as she chattered happily to Gabriel about where to go for lunch, and wondered if Beth had ever felt that there was something lacking in their relationship, if she'd ever felt the slight holding back on her part. She pushed the guilt away. Beth was happy and confident; she must have done something right.

Gabriel took out his phone and managed to find a table for three at a pretty pub they liked. There was a choice between a table at twelve fifteen or a later booking at two.

"Two o'clock would be better," Iris said. "We'd have to leave now otherwise."

"Actually Mum, would you mind if we go for the twelve fifteen?" Beth asked. "I told Esme I'd go and give her a hand with Hamish this afternoon."

Iris gave her a quick smile. "No problem."

"Great. Is that okay with you, Dad?"

"Yes, of course. Hold on, just let me book it. Done." He looked up from his phone. "Right, let's get in the car."

Beth pushed up from the table. "I need to get my bag!" she called, disappearing into the house.

Iris looked at Gabriel. "That's the pub where we used to go with Laure and Pierre."

A shadow passed over his eyes. "I know. But we went to a lot of places around here with them. We can't avoid them forever. We need to get on with our lives, live for the moment. We've seen firsthand how things can change in an instant. Let's enjoy life while we can, make the most of Beth being here, get our lives back on track." He reached for her hand. "What do you think?"

For the first time in a long time, Iris felt a small tug of something positive. "I think that's a very good idea," she said.

56

Gabriel's phone rang. He stopped digging, rummaged in his pocket, brought out his phone and glanced at the screen. The call was from an unknown number. He wasn't going to bother answering but remembering that Beth had borrowed their car to go and visit one of her school friends, he accepted the call, his heart already racing.

"Gabriel?" He couldn't place the voice, and his fear that Beth had had an accident increased.

"Yes?"

"It's Maggie, Maggie Ingram. I hope you don't mind me calling. I got your number from Annette, my grief counselor."

Tension seeped out of Gabriel's body. "No, of course I don't mind." He paused. "How are you?"

"I'm fine, thank you. I just wanted to apologize for the other day, for rushing off as I did. I owe you an explanation."

"You don't owe me anything at all," Gabriel replied.

"You're very kind. But I'd like to explain anyway. It has a bearing on Charlie, you see." She paused. "I don't suppose you'd meet me for a coffee somewhere? I could come to Markham."

"Of course."

"Does The Burnt Cherry café still exist?"

"Yes, it does."

"Shall we meet there, then? Tomorrow, if you're free."

"Yes, I am."

"Three o'clock?"

"I'll see you there. Bye, Maggie."

He cut the call and stood for a moment, relieved that Maggie had called. He'd been worried about her since she'd left so suddenly last week and he'd been tempted to ask Maggie's grief counselor for her phone number. But he hadn't wanted to answer questions about how their meeting had gone, or why he wanted to contact her.

A mix of excitement and apprehension flowed through his veins, wondering what she was going to tell him. He was sure it had something to do with Joseph; if Maggie had really been ill that day, she wouldn't have felt obliged to give him an explanation. And she'd said it had a bearing on Charlie. It was just as well that Joseph was leaving. When he and Hugh had met for a drink the other day, Hugh had mentioned that Joseph was going as soon as the christening was over.

"I hope that's all right for you," Hugh had said. "Will the garden be finished?"

Gabriel had made a quick calculation. "That's another seven or eight days' work. That should be fine."

He left the garden and went to find Iris, his phone still in his hand. She was on the terrace reading a book, the same book she seemed to have been reading for weeks, as if she kept having to go back over what she'd read because she hadn't taken it in the first place. He was worried about her, worried that despite her seeming desire to get their lives back on track, she seemed to be making little effort to do so. He understood her apathy, he had experienced it, was still experiencing it, but having the walled garden helped. Iris had nothing. He had tried to talk to her about looking for new contracts, but she hadn't wanted to engage, mumbling about taking time off now that Beth had decided to defer for a year, a prospect that had delighted him and had helped lift his depression. But it didn't seem to be working for Iris, and he guessed it was because Beth spent a large part of most days at Esme and Hugh's, helping with Hamish. It had now become her job, as Esme and Hugh had insisted on paying her. There was still much to do in the house and as they both enjoyed painting and decorating, they were happy that Beth was there to take Hamish off their hands.

"Everything okay?" he asked Iris.

She shaded her eyes against the sun as she looked up at him. "Yes, fine. You?"

He pulled up a chair. "I just had a call from Maggie. She wants to meet for a coffee to explain why she left so suddenly the other day."

Iris nodded. "Good. At least that will be one mystery cleared up."

He smiled. "Why, are there other mysteries that need clearing up?"

"Yes. Laure."

"What do you mean?"

"Do you think Esme might have given Joseph an alibi the day that Laure went for her run? Just said that he was at the hospital, or that he'd arrived earlier than he actually had, like I did for you?"

Gabriel frowned. "What are you saying, Iris? That Joseph killed Laure?"

"It's possible."

"If you're working on that theory, then it's also possible that I killed her."

"I know."

Gabriel's mouth dropped open. "Seriously? I mean, did you ever seriously think that I killed Laure?"

"Why do you think I gave you an alibi?"

"Jesus, Iris."

"It's all right, I know you didn't. But for a fraction of a second it crossed my mind."

"But what motive would I have had?"

"Come on, Gabriel. You were fed up with her, and annoyed that she'd lost me the contract by not passing on the message from Samantha Everett. If we had mentioned that to the police, they would have looked at you a lot more closely, believe me."

Gabriel knew she was right. But her words had shocked him.

"And you weren't keen to go and look for her when she hadn't come back that night," Iris went on. "You only went because Joseph said he was going to look for her."

"Because until then, I thought she was with him! And there was a bloody storm blowing, if you remember!" He ran his hand through his hair. "Christ, Iris, where has all this come from?"

Iris shrugged. "From mulling things over."

"Then why don't you stop mulling and do something useful instead?" he said angrily, pushing his chair back. "Laure took her own life, Iris. She knew that Pierre's body would eventually be discovered and she was afraid of the consequences."

"But she was happy. She had Joseph."

"Well, maybe he was just a calculated last fling. And your reasoning is complete bullshit. One minute you're saying that Joseph murdered her, the next you're saying that she was happy with him. Oh, maybe you think he murdered her because she refused to tell us about their relationship. Is that it, Iris, is that what you think?"

"Why are you getting annoyed? I'm just putting forward theories."

Gabriel shook his head. "You'll be accusing Esme next, saying that she wasn't really in hospital giving birth, that she was out murdering Laure because she was jealous of her relationship with Joseph. Or what about Hugh? Maybe he knew about Esme and Joseph and killed Laure hoping to frame Joseph for her murder and get him out of their lives. Have you thought of that?"

Iris turned away from him. "Now you're being ridiculous."

"Me?" He looked at her in astonishment. "You really need to get your life back in order, Iris. All this sitting around staring into space isn't good for you."

Cursing under his breath, he walked off.

57

Iris felt bad for goading Gabriel as she had. But she hadn't been able to help herself. She was jealous that he seemed to be moving on when she wasn't able to.

She had thought she could do it. The day they'd gone for lunch with Beth, when Gabriel had said they needed to move on, she had agreed, because she was tired of the guilt and the regret and the sheer awfulness of everything. She'd thought they would do it together, that little by little, day by day, she and Gabriel would limp slowly forward and get themselves back to where they were before Charlie Ingram had died.

But Gabriel hadn't waited for her. The news that Beth was taking a year out had given him new purpose. And now this thing with Maggie. His mood had been lighter since their meeting, as if a huge weight had been lifted from his shoulders. Perhaps it really had been about him not being able to save Charlie, despite his medical skills. If Maggie had relieved him of that guilt, she should be happy for him. But she felt nothing but resentment.

Beth had told her yesterday, when she'd found her sitting in the garden, staring into nothingness, that she should be in therapy.

"You've had so much to deal with, Mum," she'd said, putting her arm around Iris's shoulders and giving her a hug. "A lesser woman would have crumbled under the strain of the last few months. First Dad, then Laure, then Pierre. It's not surprising that you're finding it difficult to focus on anything."

And that was the truth of it. It had started with Gabriel. If he hadn't crumbled so dramatically after finding Charlie in the quarry, if she hadn't had to carry him, worry about him, then she would have been able to focus on Laure. And if she'd been able to focus on Laure, then the disaster that had followed could have been averted. Because of Gabriel, she had taken her eye off the ball. And because she had taken her eye off the ball, Pierre had been murdered and Laure had found solace in Joseph's arms. These were the thoughts that went around and around in her head, building her resentment, rendering her incapable of putting everything behind her and moving on. And now there was Hamish's christening to get through.

Pulling her laptop toward her, she opened her search engine and checked the responsibilities of a godmother. To her relief, apart from at the christening itself, there was nothing that involved any interaction with the godfather.

Checking the time on her mobile, she saw it was already six thirty, time to start preparing dinner. But she couldn't be bothered. There would only be her and Gabriel, because Beth had gone out for the day. And after their conversation earlier, she doubted Gabriel would want to eat with her anyway.

Maybe she'd go to bed instead.

58

Gabriel walked into The Burnt Cherry café, relieved to see Maggie already there, sitting at a table wedged along the left-hand wall, set a little apart from the other customers. She had chosen it for privacy, he guessed, raising his hand in greeting.

"How are you?" he asked, taking the seat opposite her.

"Fine, thank you. Nervous about what I'm going to tell you," she added.

"Please don't be. What can I get you?"

He ordered a tea for Maggie and a coffee for himself and while they waited for it to arrive, he tried to put her at ease by asking if it was the first time she'd been back to Markham since leaving to work at St. Cuthbert's.

"I used to drive over every couple of months to catch up with some of the mums whose children were friends of Charlie's, and so had become my friends. But I haven't been back since Charlie died. I think it would be a bit awkward." She gave him a smile. "If you have a child who's died, it's hard to continue being part of friendship groups. Everyone feels they have to tiptoe around you and not mention their children. It makes it unnatural because if you're a mum, your main topic of conversation is often your family." She paused as the waitress placed their drinks on the table. "Thank you for agreeing to meet me. I wanted to explain about last week." She picked up her spoon and began to stir her tea. "That man, your gardener—I know him. He was employed by the company St. Cuthbert's contracted to landscape the school grounds." She looked up. "Does he know that you're the person who found Charlie in the quarry?"

"Yes. Iris and I talked about it one day with some friends, and Joseph happened to be there."

"Did he ever mention Charlie to you?"

"No. To be completely honest, when I heard he'd been sacked from Jarmans, I looked them up and saw that one of their projects had been landscaping the gardens at St. Cuthbert's. So I asked him if he'd worked on that contract and he told me that he hadn't. I suppose he had to lie because I would have found it strange that he hadn't mentioned having worked there once he knew I was the person who had found Charlie."

"Or he didn't want you to know why he'd lost his job." Maggie took a sip of her tea and sat back. "He was sacked because of me. One of the students came to see me in my role as head of pastoral care and told me she was concerned about her friend, who was completely in love with Joseph and had been corresponding with him about the two of them traveling around Thailand together this summer. I knew who Joseph was, I'd seen him working in the grounds, and I could see the effect he was having on some of the students, who were thrilled to have a good-looking man to say hello to on their way to and from their classes. Anyway, I went straight to the head and told him. The fact that Joseph had given one of our students his mobile number meant he'd already crossed a line. The head called Jarmans and Joseph was sacked immediately." Her eyes filled with tears. "And then he took his revenge."

"How?" Gabriel asked, simply to fill the silence while Maggie took a couple of deep breaths.

"He came to the staff cottage in the school grounds where Charlie and I lived. It didn't occur to me that the head would name me as the person who had brought Joseph's indiscretions to light—but then, I would never have expected Joseph to come to my door and begin shouting at me. He was making so much noise that I brought him inside. At first, I didn't realize he was drunk; if he hadn't been, I don't think he would have been so cruel. He told me I should have come to him first, because he would have told me that the friendship between him and the student was exactly that, an innocent friendship, and that he had only given her his number because she said her parents wanted to speak to him about his offer to show her around Thailand if she happened to be there at the same time as him. There had been no question of them going there together, he said. The student had discovered, through the conversations they'd had in the school grounds—in full view of everyone, he'd added—that he went to Bangkok every August, and the student had said that she was also going to be there in August, and asked him if he would show her around. He had apparently said that he would, but only if her parents gave their permission." She paused for breath. "I asked him if he knew that the student in question was in love with him and that she possibly thought, or hoped, that it might be reciprocated, and he dismissed it as me trying to cause trouble. I also pointed out that she was only seventeen, and that he was putting himself in a precarious position by engaging with her. But he couldn't see that he'd done anything wrong." She took a breath. "Anyway, Charlie was upstairs and he came rushing down to see what all the shouting was about. So Joseph told him that I had just lost him his job, that I was an interfering bitch, and asked him if he knew that I was having an affair with his chemistry teacher. Charlie laughed and waited for me to deny it. But I couldn't, because it was true. When Charlie realized, he went completely white, and Joseph began taunting him, saying that everyone knew except him, and asking him how it felt to know that everyone was laughing at him behind his back, especially during chemistry lessons, and that if he was getting good grades in chemistry, well, now he knew why. That sort of thing. And then Charlie went for him, he knocked Joseph to the ground, and Joseph was swearing and calling me and Charlie all sorts of names. He was so threatening and frightening that I took out my mobile and said I was phoning the police. So he left, and then there was just Charlie and me."

"I'm so sorry, Maggie."

"I don't know how Joseph found out about my relationship with Andrew. We've been seeing each other for about three years now, but we make sure that our paths never cross at school, or at least as little as possible. All I can think is that Joseph saw us together in Winchester one Saturday evening on one of our few evenings out. My marriage to Angus, Charlie's dad, was over long ago but we agreed to stay together until Charlie went to university, because Charlie absolutely adored his father and it was easy to do with Angus being away for most of the year. Angus and I get on really well, so we have a lovely time whenever he's here. A few years ago, he met someone and was upfront about it straightaway, and I was happy for him, just as he was for me when I started seeing Andrew."

"Did you explain all that to Charlie?"

"I tried to, but he wouldn't listen. He was shouting at me, asking how I could have betrayed his dad, and made him a laughing stock at school. I told him that I was sure that nobody knew, that nobody was laughing at him behind his back, but he was saying that he wouldn't be able to go to classes the next day, and that he was going to have to leave St. Cuthbert's. I tried to call Angus so that he could speak to Charlie and explain everything to him, but he was on a training exercise and by the time he phoned back, Charlie was gone. I'd tried to stop him from leaving, but he said he didn't want to be anywhere near me." She raised her eyes and Gabriel saw the anguish in them. "That's why the message he gave you meant so much to me. It allowed me to carry on living."

"I'm grateful that I was there," Gabriel said quietly.

Maggie picked up her cup and he saw that her hand was trembling. "I went after him on my bike, but it was already dark and I couldn't see which way he'd gone. I called his friends, including Gina, his girlfriend, but she hadn't heard from him. I asked her, I had to, I asked her if she'd heard any rumors about me at school, and begged her to tell me if she had, telling her it had a bearing on Charlie storming off. But she assured me that she hadn't, and I believed her because she seemed so surprised that I'd asked. When Charlie hadn't come back by ten o'clock, I called the police." She took a sip of tea and carefully placed the cup on its saucer. "You know the rest."

"I understand why seeing Joseph had such an effect on you. I'm truly sorry, Maggie, for everything you've been through."

"I know he was drunk, but he shouldn't have told Charlie about me and Andrew. If he hadn't, Charlie would still be here. The worst thing is, a few months later Angus and I would have told Charlie about our respective relationships; we'd planned to tell him during the summer holidays, before he went to university." She gave a small smile. "It's hard not to think that in seeking to protect him, we effectively killed him."

"Please don't think like that," Gabriel said, shocked. "It's not your fault, it's Joseph's. I wish I'd known; I would never have employed him and I don't think our friends would have either. If he wasn't leaving soon, I'd ask him to go immediately. I might anyway," he added.

Maggie's head jerked up. "Please don't tell him that we've met. I know he doesn't know where I live now, but he was so threatening that night. At one point I was afraid that he might physically attack me."

"It's a shame you didn't call the police."

"I was just glad that he'd left."

"Thank you for telling me." A headache had suddenly come on, and he had to resist rubbing his temples to ease the pain. The last of Charlie's words—*He shouldn't have told me*—made sense now. He'd been talking about Joseph.

He turned his attention back to Maggie and moved the conversation on to other things to take her mind off what she'd just told him. When they parted company forty-five minutes later, he told her she could call him if she ever needed to talk. And then he drove home, anger toward Joseph simmering inside him.

59

Iris had woken that morning feeling slightly more positive. It was Saturday, and she was going shopping with Beth.

This would be their third Saturday in a row. She treasured these mother-daughter outings and hoped they'd become a regular thing now that Beth was going to be around for another year. She enjoyed Beth's company and Beth seemed to enjoy hers. They chattered away happily together, laughed together and talked about Gabriel and Esme and Hugh, but never unkindly. Saturdays had become the highlight of Iris's week.

As she stood eating a bowl of muesli by the kitchen window, waiting for Beth to come down, she caught sight of Joseph, and her mood instantly soured. She resented that Gabriel had insisted he carried on working for them until the walled garden was finished, especially now that Beth wasn't leaving. She resented that on Tuesdays, Fridays, and Saturdays, she had to avoid going into the garden for fear of bumping into him. Thank God he was leaving soon.

She wasn't the only one who feared him, it seemed. Gabriel had told her about his meeting with Maggie, and how Joseph had verbally attacked her because she'd reported him to the head of the school for giving one of the students his personal telephone number.

"Then I hope you're going to ask him to leave?" Iris had said.

"I would, but he's leaving after the christening, so we only have to put up with him for another two weeks."

She'd felt a flood of relief. "Is he?"

"Yes, I thought I'd told you. Hugh mentioned it when we met for a drink last week."

Now, all that stood in the way of her peace of mind was the christening.

Her appetite gone, she put her bowl on the side and went to see if Beth was ready. Her bedroom door was still closed and, remembering that Beth had come back from Esme's in the early hours of the morning, Iris knocked softly. "Beth?"

"Hm." Her reply came sleepily. "Come in."

Iris pushed open the door and Beth emerged, tousle-headed, from under the bedclothes.

"Morning," she said, propping herself up on her pillows. "What time is it?"

"Coming up for ten thirty."

"What?" Beth grabbed her mobile to check. "How can it be so late?"

"You didn't come back from Esme's until after one," Iris reminded her.

Beth grimaced. "Did I wake you? Sorry."

"No, I was awake and heard the door." Iris sat down on her bed. "Dad's gone out and he won't be back until this afternoon, so we can have lunch out."

"On his bike?"

"Yes."

"He seems better lately. Not so depressed."

Iris smoothed Beth's bedcovers. "I think he knows that life has to go on. Maybe having seen so much death in such a short space of time has made him realize how precious life is." She gave Beth's leg a nudge. "What time do you think you'll be ready?"

Beth lay her head back against the pillows. "Actually, Mum, do you mind if I take a rain check? I feel like a lie-in this morning. But feel free to go without me."

"Oh." Iris's happiness deflated like a balloon. "I need to buy a dress for the christening next week, so yes, I'll go." She paused. "I was hoping you'd help me choose."

"Sorry Mum. I'm really tired."

"It's fine." Iris moved from the bed, hiding her disappointment. "Is there anything you need? I'll stop off at the supermarket on the way home."

Beth shook her head. "I can't think of anything."

"Okay—well, enjoy the rest. Will you be having dinner with us tonight?"

Guilt flooded Beth's face. "I told Esme I'd have dinner with them."

"Okay, no problem. See you later maybe."

She left the room, swallowing down tears of self-pity. Were she and Gabriel really so hard to be around? Iris thought about how they pounced on Beth whenever she came into the room, eager to have someone else to talk to, because they were unable to talk to each other. Had Beth worked out that she was the glue holding her and Gabriel together? It was a huge weight to carry. Iris couldn't blame her for preferring to spend time with Esme and Hugh.

She felt it then, a massive mix of loss and jealousy.

Half an hour later, Iris parked her car in town and began the hunt for a dress. She was coming out of a boutique when she spotted Hugh on the other side of the road.

"Hugh!" she called over the sound of the traffic.

He looked up, gave a wave and made a sign that he was coming over to talk. He waited at the curb until there was a break in the traffic and crossed over.

"Lovely to see you, Iris," he said, giving her a hug.

"It's lovely to see you too. How are you? How's Hamish?"

"I'm good. And Hamish is growing so fast that I've had to come and buy more sleepsuits for him. Esme wanted to finish painting the guest bedroom, which is why she's had to entrust me to buy the right size," he added with a smile.

"Has she nearly finished? Gosh, she works fast."

"She does. Her parents will be staying with us for the christening, so she wants the bedroom finished for then."

"Of course."

"She loves that shade of green you suggested."

"Oh good."

Hugh peered at her from under bushy eyebrows. "Are you all right?"

"Yes, I'm fine. I was just thinking that I should be helping Esme. But I don't seem to have the energy."

"You need to give yourself a break, Iris. You've been through a lot."

"I'll get there." She gave him a smile. "I'm surprised to see you looking so chipper after your late night."

"Not me," Hugh said cheerfully. "I was in bed by ten."

"I suppose Esme and Beth were putting the world to rights," she said, trying not to sound wistful.

"No, she was chatting to Marcus and Joseph. Esme was asleep before me."

"Marcus and Joseph?"

"Yes, the three of them get on really well. That's one of the best things about having had Hamish; we get to see Marcus a lot more often." He paused. "Beth has been good for Joseph. He's been understandably subdued since Laure died, but Beth manages to make him laugh. She's really great, Iris. You and Gabriel must be very proud of her."

"We are," Iris said. "I'm sorry, Hugh, but I need to dash. I'm on the hunt for a dress for the christening. Give my love to Esme."

"Will do. See you next Sunday, if not before."

Iris forced her legs to move and in a daze, she walked back to where she'd parked the car, raising her face to the sky to greet the drizzle of rain that had started to fall. She tried to shake off the feeling of impending doom, but couldn't.

60

Since his meeting with Maggie the previous week, Gabriel had avoided working in the garden with Joseph. Instead, he messaged him first thing in the morning on the days he was due to work, detailing any specific tasks that he wanted done.

It had been hard not to go and confront him straight from the café that day. But Gabriel had been so full of rage he was worried he wouldn't be coherent, and he knew that what he had to say to Joseph would have more effect if he stayed calm.

He hadn't given Joseph any explanations for his absence in the garden. He'd simply messaged to say that he'd heard he'd be leaving after the christening, and therefore his last working day would be Thursday the twenty-ninth. He added that sometime on Saturday the first of October, he'd like to call in and see him, as they probably wouldn't get much chance to talk at the christening the following day. Joseph had replied, inviting Gabriel to call by at 6 p.m.

From the rough timeline Gabriel had constructed, from when Joseph had first arrived at Esme's after spending two months at his mother's house, he was certain that Joseph's drunken car crash had happened in the days following Charlie's death. Had guilt over what he'd said to Charlie partly been the cause of the accident? What Gabriel hated most, he realized as he drove his spade hard into the ground, was that his lie about Charlie's last words might have lessened that guilt. Joseph needed to know the truth, which was that his cruel words had caused Charlie—either on purpose or because, in his distress, he'd been riding without due care and attention—to ride his bike over the edge of the quarry.

"It's not deep enough yet!"

Gabriel looked up, a mound of earth on his spade. Iris was walking toward him. "Sorry?"

"For a body."

He gave a grim laugh, added the earth to the pile next to him, then stuck his spade into the ground with a satisfying crunch.

"Is it time for dinner?" he asked, wiping his brow with his forearm.

"Almost."

"Beth at Esme's?"

"Yes." Iris met his eye. "She didn't come in until after one o'clock in the morning. I met Hugh in town and he mentioned that he and Esme were in bed by ten."

"Meaning?"

"That she was with Marcus and Joseph. It seems they get on very well. Apparently, she's been good for Joseph since Laure died."

Gabriel's eyes widened. "Hugh said that?"

"Yes."

"Do you think he was trying to tell us something?"

"Such as?"

"I don't know. That Joseph and Beth are closer than they should be?"

"I think if he had any real concerns, he'd just come out and say it. But we need to keep an eye on things. She's around there a lot."

Gabriel ran a hand through his hair. "Is that why she spends so much time with them, do you think? Because he's there?"

"Maybe. But mainly to get away from us. Let's face it, we're not much fun to be around, are we?"

She left, and Gabriel went back to digging, the thud of the spade hitting the earth echoing the thud of his heart.

61

"Can I talk to you and Dad a moment?"

Iris looked up and saw Beth hovering uncertainly on the terrace, her hair still damp from her shower.

She pushed away the present she'd been wrapping, a beautifully carved Noah's Ark, a gift for Hamish. "Of course."

"As long as it's not to tell us that you've decided against university altogether," Gabriel joked, wiping his hands on his jeans. "Actually, even if it is, I'm not worried. You'll make your own way in life, I know that."

"Thanks, Dad," Beth said, coming over to give him a hug. "I'm still intending to go to uni, but I do want to speak to you about my future. My immediate future," she added.

"Oh, right." Gabriel smiled at her. "How can we help with that?"

"I've decided to go traveling." She pulled out a chair and sat down opposite Iris, and Gabriel did the same. "See something of the world before I go to uni."

"Traveling?" Gabriel asked. "Where? I mean, have you got it all planned or is it something that you're thinking of doing?"

"I've got it more or less planned. It's just that I feel like getting away for a while."

"I can understand that," Iris said. "You've been through a lot lately, and your dad and I aren't much fun to live with at the moment."

"That's not why," Beth said quickly. "I love being here with you and Dad. But it seems a bit of a waste to stay in Markham for a year when there are so many places to see."

"So where are you thinking of going? Europe?"

Beth shook her head. "No, Asia. Then maybe South America."

"Asia?" Gabriel jumped on the word. "Where in Asia?"

"I'll probably start in Bangkok and take it from there."

"By yourself?"

"At first, yes. But I'll meet up with people and if they're going in the same direction, I can travel with them."

Gabriel rubbed his chin. "We need to talk about this, Beth."

"Of course. But my mind is pretty much made up. I need to get something good on my CV. Future employers will want to know what I did during my second gap year and if I say that I stayed with my parents, babysitting for friends—well, it would look a bit lame."

"When are you thinking of going?" Iris asked.

"Next month."

"Next month?" Gabriel's dismay was apparent. "Why do you need to leave next month? Can't you wait until after Christmas?"

"No, because the flights will be more expensive then."

"I'll pay the difference."

"Gabriel." Iris managed to catch his eye. "Stop. You're making Beth feel bad."

"Sorry." Gabriel looked at Beth. "It just feels a bit rushed, as if you haven't really thought it through."

"Can we talk about it tomorrow, Dad? It's that I'm meant to look after Hamish tonight. Esme and Hugh are going out for dinner."

"Can't Joseph babysit?" Iris couldn't help herself. "You told me he loves looking after him. It would be nice if you could have dinner with us for once."

"I'll have dinner with you tomorrow, I promise." Beth was already backing toward the house. "We can talk more about it then. I just wanted to give you a heads-up." She blew them a kiss. "See you later."

Iris glanced at Gabriel. His whole body had sagged, as if his world had come to an end. But then, Beth was his world.

"You didn't really expect her to spend a whole year here, did you?" she asked.

Gabriel looked up. "Why, didn't you?"

"I didn't really think about it. But now that I have, I can understand her wanting to do something useful with her year out, have something to show for it."

"How do we know she's not going with Joseph?"

"Joseph?" She looked at him in alarm. "What do you mean?"

"She said Bangkok. You know I told you that he had given his phone number to a student at the school? According to Maggie, he'd offered to show her around Bangkok. He's very familiar with Thailand apparently, and usually spends the summer there." He found her eyes. "Will you still be as blasé about her going if she tells us tomorrow that she's going to Thailand with Joseph?"

"That will never happen," Iris said from between gritted teeth. "There's no way she's going anywhere with that man. He's an alcoholic! He might be on the wagon now, but I bet it wouldn't take much for him to fall right off."

"I wish we'd never met the guy," Gabriel said bitterly. "I wish you'd never brought him into our lives. He's nothing but trouble. Charlie would probably still be alive if it wasn't for him. And Laure. And if she hadn't met him, Pierre might still be alive."

"She killed Pierre before she started a relationship with Joseph," Iris reminded him.

"We don't know that. Maybe she told Pierre that day in Paris that she'd met someone else, maybe their argument started from there. Maybe Pierre told her that he'd never let her go, so she killed him. We don't know, Iris. That's the absolute tragedy. We just don't know." He pushed his chair back. "The only thing I know is that if Joseph is at the root of Beth's decision to go to Asia, I will bloody kill him."

62

Iris carried a tray laden with bowls and cutlery into the sitting room. They were having a takeaway tonight in front of a film chosen by Beth. A family Saturday night in, of which there had been too few.

She and Beth had gone shopping that morning, to buy her a backpack for her trip to Thailand. When Beth had told them last week that she was going traveling next month, neither of them had realized that they were almost at the end of September, and that "next month" was just days away.

During the week, they had talked to her about her trip, and that's when she'd told them she was planning to leave around the twentieth of October. It meant they only had three weeks left with her. Iris had managed to soften the blow for Gabriel by suggesting that they met up with Beth wherever she was at Christmas.

"Yes!" Beth had jumped on the idea. "That would be brilliant. What do you think, Dad? Would you like to do that?"

"Yes, of course."

"You don't sound too sure."

"What I'm not sure about is you traveling on your own."

"Plenty of people do it, Dad. And I told you, once I get to Thailand, I'll meet up with people and we'll move on together. That's what it's all about, making friends, sharing experiences with them and seeing something of the planet we live on." She'd put an arm around his shoulders. "I need you to get behind me on this."

"You're right, Beth." Iris could see the effort it took for Gabriel to rally some enthusiasm. "It will be a great adventure for you, and I agree, it would be a shame not to do something more interesting than staying in Markham."

"And will you come out and meet me at Christmas, like Mum said? I'll probably still be in Thailand at that point so we could spend it on one of the islands, Koh Samui or Phuket."

"Yes," Gabriel said. "We'll definitely do that. It will give us something to look forward to."

"I'll only have been gone for two months. You'll hardly have time to miss me."

As soon as Esme had heard that Beth was leaving, she'd hired a nanny to replace her. It meant that Iris and Gabriel would see a lot more of Beth in the run-up to her departure, as the nanny was starting on Monday.

"If there was only Hamish, I could cope," Esme had explained to Iris over the phone. "But there's still so much that needs doing in the house."

"Esme, nobody is going to judge you for having a nanny."

"We'll miss Beth. How are you feeling about her leaving?"

"Worried, but proud that she's doing her own thing. I'm going to miss her tremendously, it's been so lovely having her here. Gabriel is putting a brave face on it, but he's devastated."

"I can imagine. Iris, I have a favor to ask." Esme had sounded uncharacteristically nervous. "It's about Joseph. Would you keep an eye on him during the christening, especially at the lunch? There's going to be alcohol, and I don't want him to be tempted."

Iris's heart had sunk. She'd been planning to avoid Joseph as much as possible once the service itself was over.

"Yes, of course," she'd said. "Although if he decides to start drinking, I'm not sure I'll be able to wrestle the glass from him."

"Just tell my dad. Or Hugh and Marcus. They'll sort him out."

Iris set the tray on the table and checked the time. It was six thirty. Beth was having a shower and Gabriel had gone to see Joseph; he was picking their takeaway up on his way home. When she had asked if he was going to mention Beth to Joseph, Gabriel had shaken his head.

"Why not? Why are you going to see him if it's not to talk about Beth?" she'd asked.

"Because I've got other things I want to talk to him about. Anyway, if I tell him to keep away from Beth, he'll only tell her, and that will cause trouble between us and Beth. For what it's worth, I don't think her decision to go traveling has anything to do with him. Yes, he might have talked about Thailand and sparked an idea in her. But I think if she'd been meeting up with him, she would have told us. And Esme and Hugh would know, and they'd have mentioned it to us."

She hadn't bothered replying. She guessed that Gabriel wanted to speak to Joseph about Charlie. Once again, it seemed, Charlie Ingram was taking precedence over everyone else, even their daughter.

63

"First of all, I want to thank you for all your hard work," Gabriel said. He was sitting at the table in Joseph's cottage, a glass of juice in his hand.

"I enjoyed it," Joseph said. "I just regret that Iris came between us."

Gabriel frowned. "Iris? Any problems you have with Iris are no concern of mine." Seeing the puzzlement on Joseph's face, he carried on. "Iris isn't the reason I haven't worked in the garden with you for the past two weeks." He paused. "You know, don't you, that it was me who found Charlie Ingram in the quarry?"

"Yes."

"So why didn't you mention you had worked at his school? More to the point, why did you lie when I asked you if you'd worked there?"

Joseph shrugged. "I didn't think you wanted to talk about it," he said. "Anyway, I hadn't known the boy."

"That's not quite true though, is it? You went around to the house where he lived with his mum. You were abusive and threatening and cruel."

Joseph tried to hide his shock. "She cost me my job. She had no right to interfere."

"She had every right to interfere. She was head of pastoral care. A student was worried about her friend, who was in love with you, a teenage girl to whom you had given your personal number and who you had promised to show around Bangkok."

"It was completely innocent!"

"You need to grow up. You shouldn't be allowed around young people. What you said to Charlie was unbelievably cruel. It wasn't just what you told him about his mum having an affair with his chemistry teacher. What really did the harm was you telling him that everyone knew about the affair, and were laughing at him behind his back."

"How do you know?" Joseph asked, stunned.

"I was with Charlie before he died, remember?"

"He told you?" Gabriel kept silent. "I shouldn't have said it, I know that, I shouldn't have told him that everyone was laughing at him. I regretted it afterward."

"Especially as it wasn't true. Nobody knew about the affair because his mum and the chemistry teacher had been ultra-discreet. Not even their colleagues knew. Charlie's father did, and he had no problem with it, because he and Maggie had agreed years ago that although their marriage was over, they would stay together until Charlie left St. Cuthbert's. Then they would tell him, and introduce him to their respective partners. That was going to happen this summer. But you got their first, with your lies and cruelty. How could you? How could you have said those things to Charlie?"

"I was drunk."

"Yes, you were, and a few days later you crashed your car while drunk and pretended to Esme and Hugh that it was why you lost your job. But you had already been sacked. You're a liar, and a coward."

Joseph dropped his head and stared at the table. "If it's any consolation, I came off the road because when I heard that Charlie had died, I felt in some way responsible. I thought that if I hadn't said those things to him, he might have been riding more carefully."

"It's not any consolation at all. You came off the road because you were drunk. And please don't feel 'in some way responsible' for Charlie's death. You are one hundred percent responsible."

Joseph's head jerked up. "What do you mean?"

"I lied, Joseph. I lied about Charlie's last message. He didn't ask me to tell his mum he loved her. What he actually said was, 'Tell Mum I'll never forgive her. This is her fault. She shouldn't have done what she did.'" Gabriel paused to let Charlie's words sink in. "And then he said, 'He shouldn't have told me.' To me, that sounds like Charlie rode off the edge of the quarry on purpose because of what you told him."

He watched impassively as the blood drained from Joseph's face. And then he left to collect the takeaway that he and Iris and Beth were having that evening.

64

Iris woke with a rumbling stomach, and dashed to the bathroom.

"You okay?" Gabriel asked, as she climbed back into bed. "You don't look too good."

"I'm fine," she said. "I'll have to be. It's the christening today."

He pulled a face. "Don't remind me."

"What did you say to Joseph yesterday?" Iris asked, sinking back against the pillows and pulling the covers under her chin. Although he'd tried to hide it, his anger had been simmering below the surface all evening. He'd barely touched the takeaway they'd ordered, or concentrated on the film, and she had left him alone, afraid that his anger was directed at her, that Joseph had told him she'd gone into his house uninvited.

"I just thanked him for his hard work," he said, and some of her fear dissipated.

"Did he tell you what his plans are, where's he's going? He's meant to be leaving tomorrow."

"I didn't ask," he said, his voice curt. "The sooner he's gone, the better. He's a dangerous predator."

A wave of pain had her clutching her stomach. Throwing back the covers, she ran to the bathroom again.

"I think it might have been that curry last night," she said, when she finally made it out. "Are you feeling all right?"

"Yes, but I didn't have the same as you." Gabriel paused. "Beth did, though. She had prawns like you."

Iris moved to the door. "I'd better check that she's okay."

She padded woozily down the landing and tapped on Beth's door.

"Mum?" The word, accompanied by a moan, told Iris that Beth wasn't feeling great. She went in, and found Beth in a worse state than her. Her face was as pale as her bedsheet, and gleamed with sweat.

"I feel terrible," she groaned. "I think I've got a bug of some kind. I've lost count of how many times I've been to the loo."

"I think it might be the takeaway we had last night," Iris said, sitting down on her bed and putting a hand on Beth's forehead. "I've got it too. But not as badly as you."

"Serves me right for being so greedy. I had about twice what you had. How's Dad? He had something different, didn't he?"

"Yes, he had the beef. He's fine, which is why I think it must be the prawns." Beth groaned and turned her head away. "Sorry," Iris said hastily. "Shall I get you some water?"

"I've got some, thanks. What about the christening, Mum? If I'm still feeling like this, I'm not sure I'll be able to make it." Tears leaked from her eyes. "Sorry. it's just that I really wanted to go."

Iris reached out and smoothed her hair from her face. "You might still be able to. It's only eight thirty, so you've got another couple of hours. I'm going back to bed for a while. Let's see how things go. If neither of us feel better, we'll spend the afternoon huddled under a blanket watching television."

"Sounds lovely," Beth said, making an effort to lift her head from the pillow. "But you have to go to the christening, don't you? You're Hamish's godmother."

"Yes, but I suppose if I really can't make it, someone will stand in for me."

When eleven o'clock came, Iris couldn't pretend she wasn't feeling better. Beth, though, was still horribly ill.

"Maybe I should stay with her," Gabriel suggested, looking glumly at the suit he'd taken from the wardrobe.

"She's ill but not that ill," Iris said, giving him an exasperated smile. "Just a few hours, and then it will be over." She paused. "By the way, I invited Hugh and Esme to come here after the christening. I thought we could have a light supper this evening and crack open a bottle of champagne. I invited Marcus too, but Esme said he'll probably hang out with his cousins."

"As long as Joseph doesn't have the gall to come with them," he growled.

"If he does, we'll have to make the best of it. It's good that they're coming because Beth might be feeling well enough to join us by then. At least she won't feel she's missed out on everything."

"True."

The ceremony was scheduled for twelve, so Iris got ready, pulling on the yellow dress she'd bought especially for the christening, along with a light jacket. It was one of those beautiful autumn days, with bright sunshine and little wind. They arrived at the church and found it half full of villagers who'd been invited to stay behind for a glass of champagne after the morning service. Esme was already there, beautiful in an emerald green dress and matching shoes, with Hamish asleep in her arms. Iris and Gabriel made their way over.

"Thank God," Esme murmured, when Iris mentioned how good he was being. "I don't think I could cope with a screaming baby right now."

"Is something the matter?"

"It's Joseph." Esme's voice was grim. "He was meant to leave with us, but he wasn't ready. And he's still not here. I'm going to have to ask Hugh to go and look for him."

Gabriel craned his neck. "Where is Hugh?"

"Over there, chatting to the vicar with Marcus. I don't suppose you could go and interrupt them, ask him to go and get Joseph?"

"Why don't I go and see where Joseph is?" Gabriel offered. "Hugh should really be with you."

A sigh of relief whooshed from deep inside Esme. "Would you? Thanks so much, Gabriel, I really appreciate it."

"Let me take Hamish from you," Iris said, as Gabriel left the church. "Then you can go and say hello to people while we wait for Joseph."

"As long as he doesn't keep us waiting too long." Her voice was tight with annoyance. She slipped Hamish into Iris's arms, then looked around suddenly. "Where's Beth?"

"She's ill," Iris explained. "She's so upset not to be here. We had a takeaway curry last night that didn't agree with her."

"Oh no, poor Beth! What about you and Gabriel? Are you both okay?"

"Gabriel didn't have the same as me and Beth, so he's been spared. I wasn't great this morning but I'm feeling better now."

Esme laid a hand on her arm. "Thank you for making the effort to come when you'd probably rather be tucked up in bed." She rolled her eyes. "Can you imagine if there was no godmother or godfather?"

Iris moved to the front pew reserved for the parents and godparents, and sat down, cradling Hamish. "It'll be fine. Joseph will be here any minute now."

65

It was another agonizing twenty-five minutes before a commotion at the back of the church announced Joseph's arrival.

Iris kept her eyes to the front as he walked up the aisle. She could hear everyone laughing good-naturedly as he made fervent apologies, explaining that mice had got into his wardrobe, which was why he was wearing trousers and a jacket rather than a suit. She glanced at Esme, sitting next to her. The tension had left her face and she was laughing along with everyone else.

Hearing Gabriel making his way along the pew behind her, Iris turned, and in the look he gave her, she knew that Joseph's excuse for being late was total fabrication.

After apologizing personally to the vicar, Joseph came to the pew where she was sitting with Esme and Hugh, and with whispered excuses, wedged himself between them.

"I hope you don't mind," he murmured.

She caught the sharp smell of mint on his breath. "Not at all."

Joseph leaned toward Hamish, asleep in her arms. "Isn't he lucky to have the two best godparents in the world? Paragons of virtue, both."

She was saved from answering by the vicar calling them to attention. The service began, and, apart from having to hand Hamish to Joseph at one point, she was able to ignore him until the ceremony was over and they were called through to the village hall for lunch. She hadn't been able to speak to Gabriel yet, so she edged her way over and gently touched his arm. With an apology to one of Esme's sisters, he broke off his conversation with her and moved to Iris's side.

"What happened?" she murmured. "With Joseph?"

"He was drunk," he said, disgust clear on his face. "I had to stick his head in a sink of cold water to get him to sober up. He's still borderline drunk though."

"Esme asked me to keep an eye on him at lunch and make sure that he doesn't drink."

"Good luck with that. How are you feeling? Any better?"

"A bit. But I'm going to take a couple of pills just to be sure. I've got some with me."

Grabbing a bottle of water from one of the tables, she headed to the loo. When she came out, everyone was milling around the buffet table. Moving her bag onto her shoulder, she joined the queue, took a plate and helped herself to a couple of things that she hoped wouldn't upset her stomach, chatting to the people around her as she went.

Two long tables had been set up in the center of the room. Iris scanned the places until she found the card with her name on it and sat down. A quick glance to the name cards to the right and left told her that Esme's two brothers-in-law were her neighbors and, for a moment, she thought Esme had changed her mind about her being responsible for Joseph, until she picked up the card for the place opposite and saw his name. She checked the place cards on either side of him; Esme's two sisters. Esme had cleverly surrounded Joseph with people who probably knew about his alcohol problem and, like her, had been instructed to keep an eye on him.

Reaching over, she picked up his wineglass and moved it farther down the table.

"I saw what you did there, Goldilocks."

She looked up and saw Joseph standing by his chair.

"All right, cards on the table," she said as he sat down. Esme's sisters and their husbands were still at the buffet so there was no one in earshot but she lowered her voice anyway. "Esme asked me to keep an eye on you and make sure you don't drink, so while you're on my watch, the only stuff you'll be drinking is this." She waved a bottle of water in his face.

"I think it might be a case of closing the stable door after the horse has bolted," he said. "And that," he added, jabbing a finger at her, "is your husband's fault."

She heard the slur in his voice and her heart sank. "What is?"

"Me falling off the wagon. He shouldn't have told me."

"Told you what?"

"About Charlie."

Iris frowned. "What did he tell you?"

"That it wasn't an accident."

Her heart thumped. She took a quick glance around; there was still no one in earshot. "What do you mean?" she asked.

"It was my fault."

Her mind began racing. "You need food," she said. "I'll get you some. And while I'm away, do yourself a favor and drink a couple of glasses of water."

She unscrewed the lid from the bottle, filled his water glass and stood up. At the buffet table, she piled a plate high with food and took it back to him. Esme's two sisters and their husbands were sitting down as she arrived.

She placed the plate in front of Joseph.

"You're not so bad after all, Goldilocks," he said, raising his glass.

"Try the quiche," she suggested. "It looks delicious."

Iris turned her attention to her neighbor, and left his wife Nicola to talk to Joseph. At one point, when Nicola turned her head to talk to the person on her other side, Joseph reached surreptitiously for her glass of wine, drained it, then refilled it from a nearby bottle.

"I saw that," Iris hissed.

He picked up the glass and drained it again, then reached for the bottle, daring her to stop him. Annoyed, she leaned over and snatched the wine from him. Joseph grinned, refilled his glass with water and drank it down.

She glanced at her neighbor, both engaged in conversation with other people, as were Joseph's. The room was filled with the sounds of chattering and laughing, interspersed now and then with pattering feet as children left their places and began to play together. Iris smiled.

There was a soft thud, Joseph's head hitting the table. People were looking toward him, so Iris stood up and moved quickly around the table to his side.

"Come on," she said.

He raised his head and gave her a lopsided smile. "Where are we going?"

"I'm taking you home before you disgrace yourself," she said, relieved that he wasn't being aggressive.

"Fine by me."

He pushed up, knocking over Iris's glass of water, and made his way to the door, stumbling as he went. Hugh looked over at her.

"Need help?" he mouthed.

She looked for Gabriel. He was deep in conversation with Esme's mum so she nodded at Hugh.

"Sorry," she said, when he came over. "Joseph's drunk, he needs to go home. I'll go with him to make sure he gets there."

Hugh glanced at Joseph's departing back. "I'll come with you."

"No, you need to be here. Gabriel can help, or Marcus."

He looked around for them, then shook his head. "It's fine, we won't be long. I'll tell Esme."

Iris watched as he went to Esme and whispered to her. Esme looked over, and placed her hands together. *Thank you.* Iris gave her a quick smile.

"You don't have to come," Hugh said as they hurried after Joseph. "I can manage."

"It's fine, I could do with some fresh air. I'm sorry about Joseph. Esme asked me to keep an eye on him, and I tried, but he kept drinking out of Nicola's glass. He was already drunk when Gabriel went to fetch him," she added, in case Hugh didn't know.

"Between you and me, I'm delighted he's leaving," he growled.

They caught up with Joseph and got him to his cottage, Hugh helping him when he stumbled, and settled him at his table with a jug of water and a glass. He slumped forward onto the table, mumbling about Charlie and how everything had been his fault.

"Do you think it's all right to leave him?" Iris asked Hugh, talking over Joseph's mumbles.

"We need to get back to the christening," he said curtly, his annoyance with Joseph obvious. "I'll get Marcus to come and check on him later."

"He needs something to eat," Iris said, opening the cupboards. "He didn't have anything at the christening." She found a can of beans and a pan. "Could you open them, please, while I look for a couple of slices of bread?"

Hugh opened the can, tipped the beans into the pan and put it on the stove. "He can heat them himself," he said.

"Okay." Iris looked at Joseph. His head was on the table. "Joseph!" He opened his eyes. "There are some beans for you, and some bread. Make sure you eat them before Esme gets back. You owe it to her not to be drunk. Do you hear me?"

"Yes."

"Good."

She followed Hugh from the cottage. "Do you know where he's going when he leaves tomorrow?" she asked. "Has he got another job to go to?"

"I don't think he'll be leaving tomorrow, in view of the state he's in," Hugh said. "But no, he doesn't have another job. He's going to Thailand apparently. According to Esme, he spends a month in Bangkok each year, usually during the summer. He missed out this year because he was working for us, so he's going now instead."

They rejoined the christening group and an hour later, Esme and Hugh's family and friends began to leave. By the time the goodbyes had been said, it was almost five o'clock.

"Thank God that's over," Esme said with a heartfelt sigh. "It was lovely though, wasn't it? Despite Joseph."

"Nobody really noticed," Iris said. "And hopefully he'll have sobered up by now. Come on, let's go back to ours."

66

Gabriel handed Iris a glass of champagne, and then gave one to Esme, his fingers shaking slightly on the stem.

"I didn't drink at all at the christening, so I'm allowed this," Esme said. She looked over at Iris. "Thank you for inviting us back here. It's lovely to be able to relax now that it's finally over."

Iris smiled. "You deserve it."

"It was a great day, though." Hugh raised his glass. "Here's to Hamish. And his mum, of course."

"And to you," Gabriel said. "The proud father."

The four of them drank, and Esme gave a contented sigh. "Gosh, I've missed this so much."

Hugh raised his glass again. "Iris, Gabriel, it's been one hell of a summer. Here's to happier times."

A silence fell on the group. Gabriel cleared his throat. "Thank you, Hugh. As you said—"

An almighty explosion, followed by the panicked rustling of birds taking flight from the trees drowned out the rest of his words. Iris's heart thudded, echoing the *boom* still reverberating in the air. And then, deathly silence.

For a few seconds, they were a tableau frozen in time. Gabriel and Hugh standing, their champagne glasses in their hands, their heads turned toward the sound of the explosion; Iris, the alarm in her eyes mirrored in Esme's. Even baby Hamish paused in his nuzzling, and Esme, the instinct to protect her child automatically taking over, tightened her arms around him. Reassured, he went back to drinking, his tiny legs kicking under his blanket, the only movement in the stillness.

"I hope that wasn't the house," Esme joked, breaking the spell the explosion had cast over them. "Not after all our hard work."

"Maybe I should—" Hugh stopped mid-sentence, his attention caught by something. Iris followed his line of vision and saw black smoke billowing into the sky.

In the distance a siren wailed, then became louder.

Gabriel turned to Hugh. "Shall we go and take a look?"

"Good idea. It looks a bit too close to home for comfort," Hugh added, his voice low. He looked over at Esme. "We won't be long."

"As long as Joseph hasn't blown himself up," Esme said, detaching Hamish from her breast and shifting him to the other side. "I'm so disappointed in him." Hamish settled, she stretched out her free hand and laid it on Iris's arm. "Thank you for taking him home before he became completely out of control."

"I only suggested taking him home because I didn't want everyone to see him in that state." Iris paused. "Do you think he fell off the wagon before today and managed to hide it from everyone?"

"I don't know, but I'm furious, and disappointed and everything else in between. I'm beginning to regret asking him to be Hamish's godfather." She looked suddenly nervous. "He didn't say anything, did he, when you and Hugh took him home? He tends to shout his mouth off when he's drunk."

"No," Iris said. "Don't worry."

"I should have been upfront with Hugh in the first place," Esme fretted.

"It doesn't matter now. Joseph is leaving tomorrow, isn't he?"

"If he's sober enough." She moved Hamish to her shoulder and began to pat his back and, as Iris listened to her chattering about the christening, and how lovely it had been, an extraordinary sense of well-being flowed through her body. For the first time in months, she felt at peace.

"Oh, they're back!" Esme exclaimed.

Iris turned her head toward the terrace, but before she could register that anything was wrong, Esme had thrust Hamish into her arms and was hurrying across the lawn toward Hugh. Alarmed, Iris caught Gabriel's eye, and her heart dropped at the desolation on his face. Moving Hamish to her shoulder, she took comfort from the warm, sleepy weight of him and, as she began rubbing his back, her eyes fixed worriedly on Hugh and Esme, he obligingly expelled little pockets of milky air. And then a wail started, and at first she thought it was coming from Hamish.

But it wasn't Hamish, it was Esme, weeping brokenly in Hugh's arms.

67

"Do you think we're jinxed?" Gabriel asked. "Pierre, Laure, and now Joseph. Three deaths in the space of three months. And that's not counting Charlie."

"Stop it, Gabriel," Iris said sharply.

But he couldn't. It was a death too many. Joseph had blown himself up while drunk. Nobody was sure what had happened, but it seemed he'd turned on the gas and had forgotten to light it. The police said that he must have gone back to sleep and had either struck a match when he'd eventually come around, or turned on the light. Either way, there had been so much gas in the room that the explosion had been violent and deadly.

The remains of an empty whisky bottle had been found amid the debris.

"He must have had a secret stash hidden away," Iris said, when Gabriel had told her. "Because it certainly wasn't in sight when Hugh and I were there. We would have taken it away from him."

When Hugh had checked their drinks cupboard, he'd found a bottle of whisky missing. From the remnants of glass found in Joseph's cottage, the police had been able to establish that it was the same brand as the missing bottle. He'd had keys to the house, so the conclusion was that he'd taken it.

Gabriel hated himself for it, but there had been a moment when he'd looked at Hugh and thought—*What if?* He wouldn't have had that thought if Iris hadn't told him about Esme and Joseph. But when he remembered that, he then thought about Laure's death and found himself wondering about Esme, because how well did they really know Hugh and Esme? They'd only met them a few months ago. He and Iris had met Pierre and Laure twenty years ago and had spent count-less weekends and holidays with them, and it turned out they hadn't known them at all.

"I'd better go up and check on Beth," Iris said.

Gabriel raised his head. "Do you want me to go?"

"No, it's fine."

He let out the breath he'd been holding in. It was the first time he hadn't felt up to comforting Beth because he wasn't sure what he could say to make her feel better. She had barely stopped weeping since she'd found out about Joseph.

Admittedly, it had been brutal. She'd come running down from her bedroom, still in her pajamas, drawn by the sound of Esme's sobbing.

"What's happened?" she'd asked, her eyes on Esme. "I heard the explosion, I was trying to work out where it came from."

"It's Joseph," he'd said, still in a state of shock himself. "He blew himself up."

"What?" Her face had bleached white and he'd just had time to catch her before she hit the floor.

"No," she'd wept. "No." And then her voice had risen to a scream. "No!"

Gabriel looked over at Iris.

"Do you think her reaction to Joseph's death was a little over the top?" he asked.

"Whose? Beth's or Esme's?"

"Beth's."

"Not really. She's been through a lot this summer."

"Has she said anything to you? About Joseph?"

Iris leaned back in her chair and closed her eyes. "We were right to be suspicious. She was going to meet up with him in Thailand. But she said they were just friends."

"Do you believe her?"

"Yes. But she's young, and maybe she hoped their friendship would develop into something deeper. It doesn't matter now, does it? He's dead. Through his own stupidity, he's dead."

"Not just his stupidity. Mine too. It's my fault he's dead."

Iris stared at him. "What do you mean?"

"When I went to fetch him yesterday, because he hadn't turned up at the christening, I was angry with him for being drunk. And he said it was my fault, that I shouldn't have told him about Charlie." He gave a dry laugh. "If it wasn't so tragic, it would be funny."

"Why?"

"Because they were the same words that Charlie used about Joseph."

"I don't understand."

"Joseph found out that Maggie was in a relationship with one of the teachers, and to get back at Maggie for him losing his job, he told Charlie that everyone knew about the affair except him and that people were laughing at him behind his back. It wasn't true; nobody knew about it, and Maggie and her husband were going to tell Charlie during the summer that they both had other partners." He rubbed his eyes tiredly. "I lied, Iris. I lied about Charlie's last words. He didn't ask me to tell Maggie that he loved her. He told me to tell her that he would never forgive her, that his accident was her fault because she shouldn't have done what she did. And then he said that he—meaning Joseph— shouldn't have told him."

"Oh, Gabriel." Iris came over and put her arms around him. "I can't imagine what you've been going through these last few months."

"I couldn't tell the truth, you do see that, don't you?" he said, his voice breaking. "If I'd had any sense, I would have said that Charlie hadn't said anything. But when the paramedics asked, I had to think on my feet and all I could come up with was *Tell Mum I love her.*"

"It was the right thing to do. It was absolutely the right thing to do."

"But I shouldn't have told Joseph that Charlie's death was his fault. That's why he started drinking on Saturday night. He couldn't cope with the guilt. And now I have his death on my conscience, as well as Pierre's, because I should have gone to Paris to see him, right at the beginning of it all."

"You are not to blame," Iris said fiercely. "Look at me, Gabriel." She gave his shoulders a shake. "It's important that you listen. Does anyone else know what you've just told me about Charlie's message?"

"No."

"Then don't ever tell anyone. Do you hear me, Gabriel? And you've got to stop saying that Joseph's death is your fault, especially in front of Beth. Do you understand?"

He nodded. "Yes."

"Good. Now I'm going upstairs to see Beth, and when you see her, you're going to tell her that you've just found out that she and Joseph were going to meet in Thailand and that you're devastated for her and are very sorry about what happened to him."

She left, and he sat there, crushed and broken with guilt.

EPILOGUE

IRIS

It's Joseph's funeral today. Beth insisted on going, and there was nothing Gabriel or I could do to dissuade her. So he has taken her to Winchester, where the service is being held.

Everybody understood when I said I'd rather stay behind. Beth told me, in the aftermath of Joseph's death, that the reason she hadn't said anything about meeting up with him in Thailand was because she knew that Joseph and I had fallen out.

"Did he tell you why?" I asked.

Beth was in bed at the time, and she sank back against the pillows, scrunching an ever-present tissue in her fingers. "He said you told the police you'd seen him and Laure arguing on the day she died, and that because of it, he'd been taken in for questioning," she said, with more than a hint of reproach in her voice.

"It was an honest mistake, and I apologized for it," I explained.

"He said there was other stuff. But he wouldn't tell me what."

I had to think quickly. "He knew I wasn't happy about his relationship with Laure. I felt he was taking advantage of the fact that she was in a vulnerable place."

Beth sat up so abruptly that I reared back in alarm.

"He-he had an affair with Laure?" The words stuttered out of her.

My hand flew to my mouth. "Beth, I'm so sorry. Didn't he mention it?"

She shook her head, then lay back down and began to sob, her face turned to the wall, and I felt a real hatred toward Joseph, for not telling Beth about Laure. It confirmed what Gabriel and I had come to realize, that Joseph was predatory. Nothing might have happened between him and Beth, but I suspected that if she'd known about his relationship with Laure, she would have quickly closed down any feelings she might have had for him. Joseph had probably guessed it too.

"Beth, there's something else you should know," I said, acknowledging that I was about to cause her even more anguish. She didn't turn around, but her shoulders stopped heaving so I carried on. "Joseph lost his job at St. Cuthbert's because he'd been exchanging messages with one of the students about meeting up in Bangkok during the summer holidays."

For a few seconds, Beth's body froze. Then she let out a wail that came from deep inside her.

"I hate him!" she cried through a river of tears, and as I rubbed her back, I felt quietly vindicated. She would get over him faster this way.

Although I tried to deter her, I understood why she insisted on going to the funeral. She needed the closure; now, she'd be able to move on.

It's a relief to be on my own in the house where the silence exists only because there's no one else around, not because Gabriel and I are keeping secrets from each other. He finally told me the one he was keeping from me: Charlie's true message to his mum. It explains so much. Now I get why he was so stressed and why he didn't want to talk about what had happened in the quarry, although I would never have condemned his decision to change Charlie's message. But it's a sad irony that just when he'd begun to accept he'd done the right thing, he's now burdened with guilt over Joseph's death.

I will never tell Gabriel the secrets I've been keeping from him. It doesn't matter, because he doesn't know I have any. He doesn't know me, he doesn't know who I really am. He thinks he does, he thinks I'm the person he married all those years ago. I wish I'd been able to carry on being that woman, starting out on an adventure with the man that I loved, excited about our plans for the future, building careers, starting a family. One mistake was all it took to rob me of those dreams.

A mistake, but a mistake I can't regret because it was so beautiful, because it resulted in Beth. A magical night in the Bahamas, where Gabriel and I were celebrating our first wedding anniversary. Unable to sleep, I'd crept out of our hotel at three in the morning and made my way down to the private beach for a deliciously naked swim. Approaching the edge of the water, I'd been surprised by a man emerging from the gentle waves, his body gleaming in the moonlight. I didn't realize at first that it was Pierre, with whom Gabriel and I had become friends, along with his new wife Laure.

I don't know what dark forces were in play that night that made us walk toward each other, sink onto the sand and make love, without any verbal communication, without any previous desire for each other. I had never once looked at Pierre and wondered what it would be like to make love with him, nor he with me. But caught in a whirlwind of desire unlike anything we had experienced before, we could only succumb to what was an almost out-of-body experience. After, as we lay on the cool sand, our bodies still entwined, our minds numb with disbelief, we agreed never to speak about what had happened, and never seek to repeat it. And we never had, until Pierre discovered, twenty years later, that he had fathered a daughter that night.

I can still remember the terrible fear that gripped me as I'd walked back to the hotel, leaving Pierre on the beach. I already knew, with a certainty that now seems strange, that Pierre and I had just created a new life. As I sat on the bed, watching Gabriel sleep, I was more frightened than I'd ever been, frightened not just by what had happened with Pierre, but what it would do to Gabriel, to us, if he ever found out. My mind was in turmoil; since our marriage a year before we'd been trying for a baby without success. If I was right, and there was new life growing inside me, what would happen, in two or three months' time, when I announced that I was pregnant? If the news got back to Pierre, would he suspect that the baby was his? And he would find out. The four of us got on so well together that we'd already exchanged contact details. I could have deleted theirs, but they had our address. We'd been living in London at the time. What if they came to London on one of Pierre's frequent business trips and looked us up, as we had urged them to do?

I was so stressed that I even considered telling Gabriel, once we were home, that I wanted to move to another part of the UK. But he wouldn't have understood; we'd only moved into our flat a year before and we were happy there. I loved Gabriel and wanted to stay married to him at all costs, at any cost. So I took what I felt was the only way out.

The next morning—it was the day before we were due to leave—I told Gabriel that I was pregnant. I said I'd taken a pregnancy test before leaving for the Bahamas, which had been positive, and that I'd wanted to tell him the wonderful news on the last night of our holiday. He was so happy, but agreed we should only tell his parents once the first three months had gone by; mine had died years before. He was so excited that he wanted to share the news with someone, and asked me if we could tell Laure and Pierre, which is what I'd been hoping. That evening, over dinner, we told them I was five weeks pregnant. I managed to make it sound as if Gabriel had known before we left on holiday, and they were delighted for us. It was then that they had told us about their decision not to have children, and I'd felt a mix of relief and guilt, relief that there would be no half siblings to physically compare our child to, guilt that Pierre's decision not to procreate had possibly already been thwarted. It was another reason why he could never know about the baby.

If I'd been wrong about being pregnant, I would have pretended I'd had a miscarriage. A pregnancy test a few weeks later confirmed that I was. By then, I was being constantly sick, a mix of incapacitating fear and hormones. I was frightened of the baby growing inside me, afraid he or she would look like Pierre, and Gabriel would know instantly that it wasn't his. I never considered terminating the pregnancy, because of the values instilled in me by my upbringing, and which still stuck with me.

I didn't see a doctor until I was five months pregnant. Before that, I'd pretend to Gabriel that I'd been for an appointment, and when he wanted to come with me, I'd invent a last-minute change, saying that the doctor had asked me to go in earlier, so that he wouldn't be able to get home in time. When I eventually saw a doctor, I lied about my dates, and the doctor accepted what I told her, that I was six months pregnant, believing that the baby was smaller than it should have been because I'd been so sick. The doctor was sympathetic when I told her that I hadn't been able to accept I was pregnant because I had a fear of giving birth. When the time came, I was so scared to see the child I'd conceived with Pierre that I'd had to have a caesarean.

I was lucky; Beth took after me. Pierre and I were both dark-haired, but Beth had my eyes, my mouth. She was perfect, but I wouldn't let myself love her because I didn't feel I deserved her. Instead, I pushed her into Gabriel's arms, desperate for him to create a bond that he'd never be able to break if, one day, he discovered she wasn't his.

Our only real argument came when Gabriel wanted Pierre to be Beth's godfather. I was adamant that he should choose his oldest friend, citing hurt feelings and a longer friendship. Gabriel stood his ground, saying he wanted to bring Pierre and Laure into our family, and the only way I'd been able to appease him was by suggesting that we asked Laure to be Beth's godmother.

We carried on seeing Pierre and Laure two or three times a year, for weekends and holidays abroad. I hadn't wanted to, but Gabriel and Pierre adored each other and if I'd made a fuss, there was the risk that

Pierre might wonder if there was more to my reluctance to see them than simply being uncomfortable because of what had happened that night in the Bahamas. We had never taken Beth on those trips, choosing to leave her with Gabriel's parents instead.

Because she was Beth's godmother, it was normal that Laure saw more of Beth than Pierre did. She would come over from Paris to take her out for her birthdays, or during the Christmas holidays. On the rare occasions that Pierre saw her, there was never anything in his behavior to suggest that he was wondering if she was his. Until last December, when Gabriel, still grieving over the recent death of his father, invited Pierre and Laure to spend the New Year with us.

Beth had planned to stay with friends over the New Year and I did everything to make her leave before Pierre and Laure arrived. But she'd wanted to see them, and had hung around. I wasn't too worried, until I saw Pierre's eyes rest on Beth more than once as she flitted around the room, laughing and talking with us. And even then, because he didn't look my way with a question in his eyes, or try to contact me in the weeks that followed, I'd thought I was safe.

Until I saw Laure standing at the top of the stairs.

I have this ability to appear calm when I've just received the worst possible news, when my insides are twisting in a frenzy of fear. It served me well when Laure dropped her bombshell about Pierre having a child, and I was grateful that Laure suspected Claire as the mother, as my plan, during that first long night, had been to point my finger in her direction. But when Laure told me about the DNA test Pierre had conducted, I knew that everything I'd sacrificed over the last twenty years had been for nothing.

I tried to stop Pierre from taking it further. I didn't want to risk messaging him or calling him as I didn't want any trace of communication between us. But I needed to contain it before it got out of hand. To do that, I knew I'd have to talk to Pierre face-to-face. But I couldn't just say I was going to Paris without giving a reason. Then Laure asked to see my designs for the town house in London and suddenly, I had the perfect excuse. If I could get to Paris and back in a day, I could pretend I was going to London to see my client Samantha Everett. In reality, I would go to Paris to see Pierre.

Four days after Laure told us about Pierre having a child, I surprised him outside his workplace. It was the first time we'd been alone for any length of time, and it was horribly awkward. I couldn't pretend that Beth wasn't his; he knew that she was. All I could do was beg him to understand why I'd deceived everyone. He was angry that he'd missed out on so many years of Beth's life, and I called him a hypocrite, reminding him that he had never wanted children, and that Laure had sacrificed being a mother for him. To my relief, he understood why I'd done what I had, because he was a kind and decent man, and when I told him that I hadn't let myself get close to Beth and that I'd sent her to a boarding school because I didn't feel I deserved her, he had hugged and comforted me. But more than that, he loved Gabriel, and Laure, and eventually agreed that saying anything, especially after so many years, would do more harm than good. In return for his silence, I promised that whenever he and Laure came to stay, I would do my best to ensure that Beth was there so that he could at least see her.

I explained to Pierre that his refusal to engage with Laure and Gabriel was adding to everyone's stress and asked him to message them, once I was back home. He was to say that after thinking about it, he'd decided not to cause problems for his child and her mother and wouldn't be seeking contact with either of them. Ten agonizing days later, he still hadn't messaged, and I was out of my mind with worry. All he'd done was call Gabriel to say that he wasn't ready to talk because he needed more time. I was terrified; more time for what?

Worried that he was going to renege on our agreement, I returned to Paris, again using a meeting in London with Samantha Everett as an excuse. Laure was due to go back to Paris the following weekend and I pleaded with Pierre not to destroy both our marriages. I pointed out that if Beth knew the truth, there was no guarantee she would accept him as her father. On the contrary, she might resent him for destroying mine and Gabriel's marriage, and he would be left with nothing. I thought I'd got through to him, but when Laure changed her mind and decided not to go, my desperation at having to put up with her for even longer was tinged with relief. I wasn't sure I could count on Pierre not to implode our lives.

It helped that Gabriel was so traumatized by what had happened with Charlie Ingram that he kept losing his focus with regard to Pierre. When he told me that he planned to go to Paris to see him, I realized I'd have to prevent him from going because I knew Pierre wouldn't be able to keep the truth from him. I'd planned to hide Gabriel's passport—but then, two days before he was due to leave, Pierre messaged Laure, asking her to go to Paris, saying he didn't want to lose her. My initial reaction was one of huge relief; Pierre had finally come through. Then Laure dropped a new bombshell; he wanted to tell her everything.

The subsequent dread I felt was like nothing I'd ever experienced. Devastated, my only solution was to return to Paris and try to get to Pierre before Laure arrived. I couldn't use Samantha Everett as an excuse again, so I told Gabriel—who by then had canceled his own trip to Paris—that as a surprise for him, I'd arranged a lunch with my friend Jade on the day he'd planned to go and see Pierre, so that we could travel to London together.

On that Friday, I made the same journey that Laure would make the following day. I went to Pierre's workplace and caught him on his way for his lunch break. He saw me and came over.

"I hope you haven't come to make me change my mind," he said, kissing me on each cheek, because there was no reason for him not to; we were friends. "I've given it so much thought, and it's the only way forward. Life is short, Iris. I want to be a part of Beth's life. I want her to know that I'm her father."

My world crumbled around me. "Okay. I know I can't make you change your mind," I said, wanting him to think that he had won, because I needed time to think. "But could we go somewhere to discuss how we're going to tell Gabriel and Laure? We need to talk this through, Pierre."

"Of course. There's a brasserie over there, we can talk about it over lunch."

As we crossed over to the restaurant, I couldn't help but notice the change in him. There was a lightness about him, as if he'd been relieved of an enormous burden. It was then that I understood there was nothing I was going to be able to say that would make him change his mind.

I played along. When he said that the best thing was for him to come back with me, so that we could tell Laure and Gabriel together, I agreed. He asked the time of my train to London, and when I told him it was leaving Gare du Nord at 4 p.m., he sent a message to his boss, saying that he wouldn't be back that afternoon because he had something to sort out.

"In fact, I will take the whole month off," he said. "They've been bugging me to use up my leave from last year, and Arnaud suggested this morning that I take some holiday." He gave a wry smile. "He knows I haven't been in a good place lately, although he doesn't know why. And after we've told Laure and Gabriel, we'll need time to sort things out."

"Good idea," I said, hiding my rising panic at the realization that if he was going to come back with me, it really was going to happen.

"I'll message Claire too," he went on. "She's been worried about me, so I'd better let her know I'm going away, otherwise she'll think something terrible has happened."

I think it was those words that gave me the idea of killing him. It seems unbelievable now that the thought even entered my mind; it seems unbelievable that I actually did it. But all I could think of was Gabriel and Beth, and a rage began to build inside me at Pierre's disregard for everyone's happiness but his own. He didn't seem to care that he was about to destroy four other lives despite there being no guarantee that it would make his better. I knew Beth; she adored Gabriel, he had been her father for the last twenty years. If the truth came out, she might have rejected me, but she would never have rejected Gabriel.

The waiter came to take our order. My mind was spinning. If I was to kill Pierre, I would need a weapon, and I would need somewhere to do it, somewhere where his body wouldn't be discovered for a while. I thought of the storeroom in the basement of their building where they kept their bikes and tools and bits of broken furniture. There was even an old chest freezer, and Laure had laughed one day that it was the perfect place to hide a body.

"What would you like to eat, Iris?" Pierre smiled at me, and the thought that I was going to kill him made me so dizzy that I had to grip the table to stop myself from falling.

"Steak frites," I said, because somewhere in my subconscious, I connected the need for a murder weapon with a knife. Not just an ordinary knife, but a sharp knife.

Our lunch came promptly. I picked up my knife and let it slip from my hand. It clattered to the floor and I stooped quickly and put it in the tote bag at my feet, then told Pierre I couldn't find it. It didn't matter, he explained. I would be brought a clean one, and someone would fish the errant knife from under the bench when they tidied up after the service.

"I'll need to go back to the apartment to get some things," he said.

I nodded. "Of course. And while we're there, could we go down to your storeroom? The last time I was here with Gabriel, I left my umbrella in the basket of Laure's bike. Beth gave it to me, so I'd really like to get it." He nodded in agreement.

Lunch over, we walked the ten minutes to his apartment, the oppressive heat, with its hint of a storm to come, only adding to the tension inside me.

"Aren't you hot in that?" Gabriel asked, because the weather had been cloudy when I'd left home so I was wearing a long cardigan over my dress. On the train, I'd been annoyed to discover in the pockets, a tissue, a hair clip and a pair of the thin, flesh-colored cotton gloves that Laure wore when she was sunbathing or running. I'd got used to her borrowing my clothes, but had wished on numerous occasions that she would empty the pockets before putting them back in my wardrobe. Now I was glad that she hadn't.

"No," I said. "I'm fine."

We arrived at their building and I suggested going to the storeroom first, to get the umbrella. As I followed him down the stairs to the basement and along the rabbit warren passageways, I took Laure's gloves from my pocket and slipped them on. I felt strangely detached. Pierre was no longer a friend, just an obstacle that had got in my way. My focus was not on him, but on getting done what I had to do as quickly and cleanly as possible.

He unlocked the door, snaked his hand around it for the light switch, and stood back to let me pass in front of him.

"You still have the freezer," I exclaimed, heading for it, noting its lid wedged slightly open by a piece of wood, indicating that it was empty. Using my body to shield my gloved hand I pushed up the lid and peered inside. "I thought you might have got rid of it."

He came into the room. "We keep meaning to," he said. "We've just never got around to it."

The confined space meant that I only needed to turn, take a small step toward him. I already had the steak knife in my hand. He was the same height as me, and narrow-bodied. Without giving myself time to think, I plunged the knife into his chest.

He took a surprised step back, but I followed his movement and drove the knife in farther.

"What—" He shook his head slightly, trying to work it out, and then the pain must have hit, because a gasp of shock expelled from him. I caught him as his legs buckled, and then, in a macabre dance, I twisted our clasped bodies around to the freezer behind me, stooped, hooked an arm under his knees and tipped him in.

He landed on his side, and lay immobile, apart from his eyes, which flickered upward, searching for an answer. I reached in and pulled out the knife and watched as blood seeped from him, staining the floor of the freezer red. Then I took his phone from his pocket and closed the lid.

It was only when I looked down at myself, saw the knife in my hand, its blade red with blood and the red stain on my cardigan, that shock hit me with a force so great I almost collapsed. I closed my eyes, summoned Beth's face and used her image to fight the weakness in my limbs and calm my panicked breathing. I focused on what I needed to do. I took off my cardigan and bundled the knife into it, then added the SIM card from Pierre's phone. I thought for a moment, then dug out the hair clip. Several of Laure's hairs had been caught in the clasp, so I pulled one out and let it drop to the floor. I checked my dress; no bloodstains had seeped through from my cardigan and I was grateful I'd had the presence of mind to remove the knife from Pierre's chest once he was in the freezer. Stooping, I plugged the freezer into its socket, and left the storeroom.

Pierre had left his keys in the door, so I locked it behind me, slipped the keys into my rolled-up cardigan, put it in my bag and walked back through the narrow corridors and up the basement steps. I made it to the front door without meeting anyone; the whole building was silent.

I walked to Gare du Nord, rode the metro north for ten minutes, got off at a random station, took the cardigan from my tote and dumped it in a nearby bin. Then I took the metro back to Gare du Nord, in time for my train to St. Pancras. When I arrived at St. Pancras, I bought, from the shops on the concourse, a bottle green polo shirt for Gabriel, a beautiful silk scarf for Laure, and a skirt and sandals for myself as evidence of my shopping trip with Jade. Then I went home, and waited for the right time to plant Pierre's phone among Laure's belongings. And while I was in her bedroom, I took her blue dress and canvas shoes, and hid them among the rubbish in the bin, due to be collected the next day.

My phone buzzes, interrupting my musings. A WhatsApp from Gabriel telling me that he and Beth have arrived in Winchester. What do you reply to someone who is about to go to a funeral? I message back *I hope everything goes as well as can be expected. Let me know when you're on your way home*, and add two kisses.

I walk to the window and look out, as I've done so many times before, thinking about the day after I killed Pierre. I dropped Laure off at the station in time for her train to London. I hadn't slept all night and my anxiety was acute. What if Laure decided, when she found the apartment empty, to go looking for Pierre in the basement?

I distracted myself by sending Gabriel to the supermarket so that Joseph and I could have lunch together, just the two of us. The lunch was both a distraction and a reward. I needed something to take my mind off Laure and, after everything I'd been through the previous day, I felt I deserved some time alone with Joseph. I thought I was fine, but as I walked to the walled garden to call him, the scarlet flowers that lined the path, the same color as the blood that had spilled from Pierre, haunted me. And when the knife I used to slice the tomato slid so easily into its flesh, I couldn't help but be reminded of the knife that had slid just as easily into Pierre.

When Gabriel interrupted the lunch I'd so carefully prepared, I fled to the bedroom and drew in deep breaths, praying for Laure to phone. I don't know how I managed to sleep, from exhaustion perhaps. When she finally called me from Gare du Nord and said that Pierre hadn't been at the flat, and she was coming straight back, my relief was so immense that I dropped to my knees and gave thanks, although I'm not sure whom to. I went to find Gabriel, and his hangdog look as he sat on the bench moping about the letter he'd received from Maggie Ingram's grief counselor made me want to scream. I had murdered for this man, and here he was, feeling sorry for himself because Maggie wanted to meet him.

It was because he was wrapped up in his own problems that it was easy for me to pretend, later that day, that Laure had come home wearing clothes different from the ones she'd been wearing that morning, to pretend that she'd been feverish and overexcited when she'd only been defiant. He believed what I told him, because he had no reason to believe I would lie.

If I felt any guilt in setting up Laure to take the blame for Pierre's murder, it disappeared when I discovered she was in a relationship with Joseph. The truth was, from simply being intrigued by him and liking the way he paid me attention, I had become obsessed. Everything about him, from his dark good looks, to the lilt of his voice, to his easy, confident stride, awakened something in me, something that I hadn't allowed myself to feel for many years. Pure, uncontrollable desire.

Sometimes I ask myself—if everything had been fine between me and Gabriel when Joseph entered our lives, if Gabriel hadn't started rejecting me both physically and emotionally, would I still have become obsessed with Joseph? If Laure hadn't turned up and, with the mention of Pierre's daughter, unearthed the feelings of profound ecstasy I'd experienced on the night of Beth's conception, would I still have become obsessed with him?

Joseph became my guilty secret. I could have chosen to spend my days helping in the garden, just to be near him, and endured the combination of agony and ecstasy. Instead, I watched him surreptitiously from behind the bedroom curtain, waiting for a glimpse of him walking to and from the walled garden. And then, the moment I had never imagined, when I saw him staring up at my window and dared to think that my feelings were reciprocated. I would never have acted on them, but I was flattered that he felt the same way about me as I felt about him.

Until I heard him having sex with Laure, and knew I'd been deluding myself. The humiliation of realizing that he hadn't been waiting for me each morning, and the injustice of it, tore me apart. After all I'd done for Laure, in becoming the object of Joseph's desire, she had betrayed me in the cruelest way possible.

Thoughts of them together tormented me. Memories of what I'd heard on the other side of the shed door plagued me. I began to hate Laure. I wanted her out of our lives, out of Joseph's life. And I had a new fear to contend with. I might have laid the seeds for her to be blamed for Pierre's murder, but what if she were able to prove that she hadn't killed him? What if his murder was eventually traced back to me?

I didn't kill her on purpose. The day after the storm, when I heard her and Joseph arguing, I decided to go after her. Gabriel had already mentioned that Joseph seemed to be tiring of Laure; he had seen him trying to disentangle himself from her embraces more than once, and I thought this might be my chance to get her to leave. Earlier that day, she had asked me to go for a run with her and I'd refused. But when I saw her leave, I hurried to the bedroom at the front of the house and called to her from the window.

"Laure!" I called. "I'll come with you. Wait for me at the stile."

She turned and gave me a thumbs-up.

It was then that I saw Joseph running toward the gate. At first, I thought he was going after Laure—but he turned left onto the road, not right, something I didn't mention to the police later, because by then, it suited me not to.

I was changing into my running gear when Gabriel called to check on me. I told him I was going to take a long bath. I'm not sure why I didn't tell him that I was going for a run with Laure, but maybe some instinct for self-preservation had subconsciously kicked in.

Five minutes later, I left the house and, as I approached the stile, Laure turned and smiled at me.

"Have you seen how muddy it is?" she asked pointing to the track over the fields. "There's no point in going for a run. Maybe we should go back to the house and wait until tomorrow."

"Why don't we go through the woods? It will be drier there. We could even run around the quarry," I suggested.

She raised her eyebrows in two perfect arches. "I thought we weren't allowed to go there."

"But people do, apparently. They go to pay their respects to Charlie. I've heard that some of them throw flowers down to where he fell."

"A shrine to him. That's lovely."

"Shall we go?"

She broke into a jog. "Why not?"

We ran through the woods to the quarry, then followed the path that took us up to the top. The grass was wet with rain and our ankles quickly became soaked. At one point, Laure slipped and almost fell.

"Let's stop for a moment," I said, panting after the upward climb. I pointed deep into the thicket of trees on our left. "I think this is where Charlie's bike must have left the path."

She peered into the woods, frowning. "Are you sure? Wouldn't his bike have hit at least one tree before he arrived at the edge?"

"Yes, I suppose. Maybe it was further on, then."

"Unless he meant to do it."

I stopped walking and turned to her. "What do you mean?"

"Just that maybe he rode over the edge on purpose. I don't know— maybe he had an argument with someone and it upset him."

I stared at her, my heart thumping so hard that I was sure she could hear it. I tried to push away the image of her tumbling over the edge of the quarry, but it remained lodged in my brain.

"So you mean he came in here, threaded his way through the trees, like this?" I plunged into the darkness, drops of rain falling on me as I brushed against branches, and traced a path to the edge of the quarry.

"Yes," she said, following behind me.

"By the way," I said, as we neared the edge. "I had a call from Samantha Everett this morning."

"Oh!" she squealed. "Did you get the contract?"

I turned and looked at her. "No, I didn't, because I didn't get back to her when she left a message asking me to contact her. And the reason I didn't get back to her was because you didn't give me the message."

She stared at me for a moment, then clapped a hand over her mouth, her eyes wide with horror. "Oh my God, Iris, I'm so sorry!" she said, removing her hand from her mouth and reaching out to me. "I completely forgot. I know that sounds awful but I—"

"Did you though?" I interrupted. "Completely forget? Or did you forget to tell me on purpose?"

"What? No, of course not! How could you even think that?" The reproach in her voice made me suddenly angry.

"Because you're selfish, Laure. Because you never think about anyone but yourself. It's time you left. Me, Gabriel, Joseph—we're all tired of you."

"Joseph? You know about me and Joseph?"

I laughed. "You're hardly discreet, Laure. I've known since the day I was meant to be going to London with Esme. You didn't want to come with me, remember? You said you were going to look for a divorce lawyer but what you really wanted was to be alone with Joseph. At the station I changed my mind, and came home. I went to look for you in the garden and I heard you and Joseph in the shed." She flushed. "When did it start? Before you went to Paris to see Pierre?"

She looked shocked. "No, of course not. But that day, I wanted to talk to Joseph about Pierre not turning up. I hadn't had a chance before as Gabriel was always around. So I went to see him in the shed. And it just happened."

"It just happened," I mimicked. "And now it's over. He doesn't want you anymore."

"No, you're wrong, he does want me. He wants me to move into his cottage with him."

"No," I said. "I heard you arguing."

"Yes, because he wanted me to tell you about us. He's been asking me to tell you from the beginning, he said I needed to be honest with you, but I didn't want to tell you because I knew you and Gabriel would be angry that I'd moved on so fast from Pierre. But I'll never be able to forgive Pierre for not turning up when he asked me to go to Paris. He's a coward, and I can't be with someone who's a coward." She paused. "There was something I thought of, a reason why, when it came down to it, he couldn't bring himself to tell me the truth. But I didn't want to believe it, so I pushed it from my mind. But now, I'm wondering—the day I spoke to Beth on FaceTime, a couple of days before I went to Paris, there was something about her that reminded me of Pierre. I might not have noticed it before, but because he was adamant that Claire wasn't the mother of his child and he wouldn't tell me who was, I've realized the truth. Is that what Pierre couldn't bear to tell me, Iris? Is Pierre Beth's father?"

My heart was thumping so loudly I was convinced she could hear it. "You're mad," I said. "Mad and delusional."

"No." She shook her head. "I don't think I am." Her eyes narrowed. "Maybe we should go and ask Gabriel what he thinks."

"No, no, you can't!" In my panic, I raised my arm and took a step toward her. Her eyes widened, she took a step back, and then another—and then she was falling, her arms flailing uselessly as she toppled backward over the edge of the quarry.

I can't remember if she screamed. I can't remember running back home, hoping desperately that I wouldn't meet anyone as I climbed over the stile and jogged the last thirty yards to the house, my mind already spinning the story I would tell Gabriel if he'd arrived home before me. I would tell him that I'd decided to go with Laure after all and that I'd taken the path over the fields, thinking that's where she'd gone. But I hadn't come across her, so had come home.

Fortunately, he wasn't there, so I hurried upstairs and ran a bath with lukewarm water. While it was filling, I shrugged on a bathrobe and went to the garden to see if Joseph had come back to work. If he had, he would think I'd just got out of the bath. But he was nowhere to be seen, so I went back to the house, up the stairs to the bathroom, took off my bathrobe, and got into the bath. Gabriel arrived less than ten minutes later, and during those ten minutes, I realized two things. The first was that once Laure's body had been found, with a carefully placed word or two, I could make Joseph look suspicious because suddenly, I wanted to hurt him. I wanted him to suffer, even if it was only for a while, because of what Laure had told me as we'd stood at the edge of the quarry, that he'd wanted her to move in with him.

The second thing I realized was that the one flaw in my plan to frame Laure for Pierre's death had now been erased. If Laure was dead, she had no voice, no way of defending herself.

It was easy to pretend to Gabriel that I'd been in my bath for so long that the water had got cold, and later that evening, to pretend I was annoyed with Laure for not turning up for dinner. It was easy to pretend that I was upset she might be having dinner with Esme and Hugh, and, as the night drew in and the next storm unleashed its winds and rain, it was easy to pretend concern at Laure being somewhere out there. When I went to look for her with Gabriel the next morning, I insisted on going to the quarry and made sure I wore exactly the same clothes and trainers I'd been wearing the previous day—which I'd dried overnight, in case I'd left any traces behind. And in the days that followed, I continued to pretend, to Gabriel, to the police, to Esme and Hugh. My finest hour was when PC Locke told me that Joseph had been taken in for questioning. But then Esme phoned to tell us that Hamish had been born, and when I heard that Joseph had been present at his birth and realized he had the perfect alibi, I quickly had to swallow my bitterness.

I also pretended to Gabriel that the reason I told the police he'd arrived home earlier than he actually had was so that I could be his alibi in case they started looking at him as a possible suspect. In reality, I was giving myself an alibi, because when the police questioned his whereabouts that afternoon, he had to say, because of my lie, that he'd arrived home at four fifteen and that I'd been in the bath.

My phone buzzes again. *It's over. Going for a drink with Hugh and Esme. I'll let you know when we leave Winchester.* The message, and the garden slowly coming into focus, startle me. Had I really been standing at the window that long, for the length of time it took to bury Joseph? Maybe his funeral hadn't lasted long, unlike Pierre's, which had seemed to go on forever.

I move to the bed and lie staring at the ceiling, my thoughts going back to the days after Laure died. The relief I felt was incredible.

Pierre and Laure were out of our lives, my secret was safe. Now I could concentrate on Gabriel and Beth. Joseph was out of our lives too. He hadn't been back to work since Laure's body was found in the quarry, and I didn't expect him to ever come back. I could put my humiliating encounter with him, when he'd found me in his bed, out of my mind. Yes, his bed. He had found me in his bed, not on the sofa.

The relief I felt was short-lived. Guilt over Pierre's murder and Laure's death consumed me. I was so scared of giving something away that I stopped talking to Gabriel altogether. I didn't know how I was going to get through the funerals of the two people I had killed. I managed to get out of going to Laure's on the grounds that she had killed Pierre. But I had no excuse for not going to his.

I don't know how I got through the service. The scene in the storeroom played over and over in my brain on a loop. I couldn't get the puzzled look on Pierre's face, when he realized that I'd stabbed him, out of my mind. And then, on the train on the way home, Gabriel dealt me another blow when he told me Joseph would be coming back to work in the walled garden.

For the next couple of weeks, I stayed out of his way and tried to put everything behind me. When Beth decided to defer her university place for a year, it felt like a reward for all I had done to protect her and Gabriel. With Beth around, Gabriel would snap out of his depression, and I would finally have the chance to bond with her. I began to relax.

The chance encounter in Markham with Hugh the week before the christening, when he mentioned how well Beth and Joseph were getting on, made me uneasy. But it was only when Beth told us she had decided to go traveling in Asia, and Gabriel told me why Joseph had been sacked from St. Cuthbert's, that a new fear gripped my heart. I tried not to reveal my anxiety to Gabriel, but the knowledge that Joseph might be a predator who had now turned his attention to Beth made me sick to my stomach.

There was another reason for the revulsion I felt. I might have despised Joseph by then, but not long before, I had dreamt about him, watched him, desired him. A burning humiliation flowed like lava through my veins. I couldn't let him get to Beth. I would have to go and see him, appeal to his better nature.

It was the Tuesday before the christening, a few days after Beth had told me and Gabriel of her plans. She was at Esme's, and Gabriel was out, so I went to the walled garden. I was shaking as I walked over to where Joseph was working, his anger at me still vivid in my mind.

"Can I talk to you a moment?" I asked.

He turned and looked at me, and in his eyes there was such contempt that my breath left my body.

"What do you want?"

My words came out in a rush. "Are you the reason why Beth is going to Bangkok? Is she meeting up with you there?"

He narrowed his eyes. "What business is it of yours?"

Fear made me careless. "Because she's my daughter and I don't want you anywhere near her!"

He gave a grim laugh. "Maybe she is your daughter. But she isn't Gabriel's, is she?"

I could only stare at him, the horror in my eyes giving him the answer he was looking for. "I-I don't know what you're talking about." It was a struggle to speak. "Of course she's Gabriel's daughter."

"Laure worked it out, but she convinced herself it couldn't be true," he said. "It was after she spoke to Beth on FaceTime the day Pierre asked her to go to Paris. She came to me in the garden after, and I could see she was upset. She said she'd just been speaking to Beth and that she had seen something of Pierre in her face, and in her mannerisms. 'But it can't be that, can it?' she said. 'Pierre said he wants to tell me everything, but it can't be that Beth is his daughter. How could she be? We would have been on our honeymoon.' Then she shook her head. 'No, it's not possible. I know Pierre, he wouldn't have been able to live a lie for twenty years. It must be something else.'" He paused. "I had never seen Beth or Pierre, and anyway it was none of my business."

"It's still none of your business," I spat.

"Oh, but it is, because Laure is dead, and not only is she dead, she's been accused of Pierre's murder. She would never have killed Pierre; if she had, she wouldn't have been able to hide it. She wasn't devious or spiteful. You, on the other hand, are." He took a step toward me. "You know what I think, Iris? I'm fairly certain you killed Pierre, and I'm fairly certain that you killed Laure, and if I thought I could prove either of those two things, I'd go straight to the police."

"You're mad," I said, backing away from him. "You didn't know Laure, you'd only just met her. You don't know what she was capable of. The fact that she thought Beth was Pierre's daughter only shows how deluded and unstable she was."

"You sound frightened, Iris."

"I am, of you! You're crazy."

And I fled from the garden.

Another WhatsApp message comes in. *Leaving Winchester now.* I screw my eyes shut, remembering the absolute terror I felt when Gabriel told me he'd arranged to see Joseph the night before the christening. I was afraid of what Joseph might tell him if Gabriel said anything about Beth going to Asia. But when I questioned Gabriel, he told me he wouldn't be mentionning Beth to Joseph at all. He had other things to discuss, he said. And in my relief, I didn't ask what that might be.

I already knew that I'd have to kill Joseph. Even if he didn't say anything to Gabriel then about Pierre being Beth's father, he could tell him, or Beth, at any time. I couldn't have that fear hanging over me, not when I had killed Pierre for that very reason. Remembering the story Esme had told me about him almost gassing himself to death, I decided to recreate the same scenario. The gas bottle would be my weapon, the day of the christening the time and place. First, though, I needed Beth out of the way because to have her at the christening would have only complicated matters.

The evening before the christening, I arranged for us to have a take-away and, while I was unpacking it in the kitchen, I added a good dose of a laxative to the prawn curries that Beth and I had chosen. I made sure I ate just enough for the laxative to have a mild effect on me. Beth ate far more, and although I hated that she was ill, it was a small price to pay for her not to be involved in what was to come.

It worked. Beth was too incapacitated to go to the christening, and stayed home. At the reception in the village hall, I went into the toilets with a bottle of water, emptied it into the sink and filled it with vodka from a bottle I'd hidden in my bag, then served it to Joseph. I can still see him raising his glass to me when I came back from the buffet table and saying, "You're not so bad after all, Goldilocks," a reference not only to the alcohol I had just supplied him with, but also to him finding me in his bed. The fact that he'd arrived at the church already inebriated facilitated the job I had to do. I didn't know then that I had Gabriel to thank for that. I only knew later that the previous evening, Joseph had tried to drink his guilt away because Gabriel had told him Charlie's real message.

I had already planned how, once Joseph was drunk enough, I would ask Hugh or Marcus to help me get him back to his cottage. Afterward, once Joseph was dead, we would be each other's alibis; we had taken him back to his cottage and had left him sitting at the table with a jug of water, and instructions to have something to eat. I made Hugh open the beans, tip them into the saucepan and put them on the stove so that it would be his fingerprints on the can. All I had to do, wrapping my fingers in a tea towel, was turn on the gas ring. And retrieve from my bag the bottle of whisky I'd taken from Esme and Hugh's drink cupboard a few days before and push it into Joseph's greedy hand.

I was counting on Joseph being gassed to death, and to avoid him being found too early, I invited Esme and Hugh back to ours straight from the christening. I thought that sometime in the evening, Esme and Hugh would go home and find Joseph dead in his cottage. The explosion came as a huge shock. But as I watched the smoke curl into the sky, I couldn't help thinking that it was a more precise ending than the one I had planned.

I raise a languid arm, reach for my phone and check the time. Gabriel and Beth will be home soon, I need to prepare something for dinner. I move from the bed, smooth my dress down. In the bathroom, I turn on the light and look at my reflection in the mirror. I let my eyes roam over my face, pleased with the new serenity I see there. I lost my way for a while, and no longer knew who I was. Now, I know who I am.

I am Iris Pelley, wife, mother, and murderer.

ACKNOWLEDGMENTS

As always, special thanks to my agent extraordinaire, Camilla Bolton. I'm forever grateful for your wisdom when it comes to all things writing, and for your ever precious friendship.

One of my favorite moments as an author is when I receive a foreign copy of one of my novels. It's such a thrill to hold it in my hands, and my heartfelt thanks go to the fantastic Rights team at Darley Anderson—Mary Darby, Georgia Fuller, Salma Zarugh, and Francesca Edwards—for making this possible so many times over. I would also like to thank Jade Kavanagh and Rosanna Bellingham. It's always a pleasure to hear from you.

Exciting things are beginning to happen to my books film-wise, and for that I have to thank the expertise and hard work of the brilliant Sheila David. Thank you so much, Sheila.

I am fortunate to have not one, but two amazing editors. In the UK, Jo Dickinson at Hodder & Stoughton, and in the US, Catherine Richards at St. Martin's Press. Thank you both for always being there for me and for taking *The Guest* so calmly and seamlessly from that very first draft to this final, more polished version. Your suggestions and advice are invaluable.

At Hodder, my thanks to Alainna Hadjigeorgiou, Alice Morley, Catherine Worsley, Sorcha Rose, and Phoebe Morgan. Also to my copyeditor, Charlotte Webb, and my proofreader, Helen Parham. It's reassuring to know I have such a great team doing everything they can for me and my books.

At St. Martin's, my thanks go to Jen Enderlin, Lisa Senz, Nettie Finn, Marissa Sangiacomo, Brant Janeway, Katie Bassel, Kelly Stone, John Morrone, Jeremy Haiting, and Lizz Blaise. Also to my proofreader Carla Benton, and to Danielle Christopher for designing such a beautiful cover. Some of you have been with me since the beginning of my journey as a writer. We're now on book seven and I'm humbly grateful for your continuing faith in me.

I'm lucky to have wonderful publishers abroad. Thank you for continuing to publish my books, and to the translators who bring them to life in forty-one other languages.

Authors are nothing without their readers. I can't thank you enough for reading my books, for taking them to your hearts, for talking about them, recommending them, and writing reviews. I am also greatly indebted to bloggers everywhere for the same reasons. Huge thanks to my author friends, with a special mention to Phaedra Patrick, Roz Watkins, and Annabel Kantaria, who have been with me since the beginning and are always up for a chat when things get tough—and when they're going well. And to my non-author friends, both in the UK and France, for buying my books and motivating me to carry on writing.

Last, but never least, my heartfelt thanks to my husband, Calum, and our daughters and their partners. I couldn't do this without your love and encouragement.